LOVE & WAR

SKY BLACK

D1521699

ISBN-13: 978-1-7966-6094-4 (Paperback Edition)

ABOUT THE AUTHOR

Sky Black aka Messiah Raye, is a collaborative pen-name from Stixxx, the CEO of Most Famous Entertainment and Shontaiye, from DreamHouse Publications. Shontaiye proudly admits that Stixxx is the creative force among the two, with him penning this novel from a jail cell with a notepad and an ink pen. Expect much more from him in all areas of entertainment.

PART I

INTRODUCTION

Present Day

The sound of the alarm system blaring through the house caused Pedro to jolt out of sleep. Snatching back the luxurious sheet set from his pajama clad body, he immediately went to reach over and grab his revolver from his nightstand. If he had to shoot, he wanted to be able to do so quickly. Before he could touch the Italian brass knob on his stand, he felt a gun firmly pressed to his forehead.

"Reach and I squeeze," Drew snarled, clutching his 9mm tightly. "Now we gon do this my way ... You're going to get up and deactivate that alarm — You do as I say, and no one gets hurt. Try some slick shit and I'll rock everybody in this bitch ... Get up," he demanded.

Drew wasn't new to home invasions. He knew he had about sixty-seconds to stop the alarm before police were notified. It still amazed him that as much money as Pedro was allegedly getting, his security system was bullshit. He was barely a step up from ADT. He didn't even have any of his henchmen hanging around.

Drew backed away slowly and cautiously, to make room and allow Pedro up. With his eyes struggling to adjust to the dark, Pedro led the way. Drew quickly followed him to the front door where he proceeded to deactivate the alarm. As Drew walked off, Spice and Tre hit the lights to find something to tie up Pedro's wife Anna.

Spice quickly tore through the closet and found a few long sleeve shirts. "Tie that bitch up. I'm about to search this mufucka."

As Tre did as he was told, Drew and Pedro walked back into the room. Pedro appeared deathly calm, however, no one could mistake the anger in his demeanor. Noticing the blatant hostility, Spice turned around and walked over to him. He withdrew his gun from his waistband, and violently smacked Pedro across the face with it. No attitudes were allowed. The fact he even had one, was an insult. He should have been grateful he was still breathing.

His knees buckled from the blow and pain shot through the top half of his body, but Pedro refused to cry out. Witnessing the assault, Anna, screamed out. "Please God! No, don't hurt him please!" she cried, in a fit of panic.

Tre immediately gripped her by the throat and squeezed. "Bitch, shut the fuck up with all that yelling!" he demanded harshly, before shoving her to the bed.

Taking control of the situation so they could hurry up and get out of there, Drew spoke. "I'm only gonna ask one time ... Where's the money and work? I'm not leaving without sumn. It's either gon be wit yo shit, or *wit yo life.* Starting with that loud ass bitch of yours," he said, using his gun to point to Anna, who was laid out on the bed tied up, and now gagged to silence her screams.

She appeared paralyzed with fear and her face was soaked from the constant flow of tears from her eyes. Drew didn't care. He didn't have time for games and theatrics.

Tre had told them that Pedro was a heavy hitter in the city, and that was who his father Antonio, got his product from. Tre's father ran the East Side and he knew that if he supplied Antonio, then he was definitely holding something heavy.

Still in pain and equally terrified, Pedro didn't hesitate to point to the closet. He lived and breathed for his family, and they were worth more to him than some dirty money. They could have the couple hundred-grand in his trunk. He'd have it back in no time.

"It's in the closet, underneath the shoes. The big green trunk. The keys in the top drawer over there," he stated quickly, while pointing to the dresser. He was still holding his face, blood oozing through the cracks of his fingers.

Pedro was clearly outnumbered, and he wasn't about to put up a fight. He just wanted them to take what they needed and get the fuck out. He figured they weren't there to kill him since they had on masks. He knew the saying all too well; *When they're masked up, they're coming for your ice. If they're bare faced, they're coming for your life.* He cursed himself for not having more security.

With dollar signs in his eyes, Drew waved for Spice to hit the closet and open the trunk. Pushing Pedro onto the bed beside his wife, he yanked the silk case off a pillow and shoved it into Pedro's mouth. Even though he was restrained, Pedro wasted no time trying to console Anna. He remained silent, as he rubbed his face against hers, silently ensuring that everything would be ok.

Spice snatched open the top drawer to the dresser Pedro had pointed to, and retrieved the simple, small, brown key to the trunk. They had been expecting a safe and were delighted by how easy the night was turning out to be.

"Yo, make sure that bitch tied up good, and then go search the rest of the crib. We got three minutes and then we out," he instructed Tre.

Tre grew irritated by Drew's requests, but once again, did as he was told. He wanted to be the one to hit the stash because it was his drop. Drew and Spice were his niggas, but he wanted to make sure they split the come-up evenly down the middle. He was younger than the both, and at times he felt like they tried to treat him like a sucka. Nevertheless, Tre made sure Anna was secure and began to head out of the room.

Over in the closet, Spice's eyes lit up like Christmas lights when he saw the old, green, trunk safely nestled underneath the dozen rows of designer shoes. With excitement fueling him, he inserted the key into the chamber.

Before he could push open the heavy top to the chest, the faint sound of a door swinging, along with subsequent running down the hall, stopped Spice in his tracks. The sound coming from the pitch-black hallway, also caused Tre to stop abruptly as he was walking out of the room to search the rest of the large house. Drew, who had been standing by the bed next to a restrained Pedro, also appeared stunned by the noise. As the sound neared, Anna and Pedro started to squirm, wiggle and shake to get out of their restraints. Their muffled attempts to yell caused Drew and Tre to grow alarmed. Someone else was in the house, but it was too dark to see who it was, and what they were carrying.

The rapid footsteps grew dangerously close and a Smoke appeared by the door. Fear gripped Tre and without thinking he frantically drew his gun. Before Drew could yell for him to wait, he fired through the door. The running immediately stopped and the sound of a body hitting the floor could be heard.

Tre lowered his gun and the image was clearer, the Smoke and person now visible.

"Shit," Tre cried out, with panic flooding him. They were fucked.

1

One month ago

"YOU CAN'T TELL ME WHO I CAN AND CAN'T HANG WITH. Those my niggas and besides, you act like you didn't grow up on the East. The same hood that made you who you are," Tre argued with his father, who was growing increasingly irritated with every word Tre uttered.

"That's some real live, hypocritical shit," Tre continued.

"Who the fuck you think you talking to? Don't get fucked up in here!" Antonio threatened angrily while rapidly approaching his son with clenched teeth and tight fists. He felt he was being challenged and he was about to give Tre something he wasn't quite ready for.

"As long as you live in my fuckin house you gon do what the fuck I tell you. You know, you really sound fuckin stupid. Yeah, those streets made me, but they didn't make *you*. You have no idea what I went through to get here. To give you and your sister a decent life. You're a fake ass thug and you're gonna wind up getting hurt. Although my name is strong on the streets, that alone don't mean shit to these other niggas out here trying to make a quick come up. You think Drew and Spice fucks with you on the strength of *you*?

If you do, you're dumber than I thought!" Antonio yelled to his son while trying to reason with him.

"Whatever, I'm not gon argue with you," Tre muttered angrily, before walking away and making his way to his room. He had pissed Antonio off big time, and he wasn't about to make him even angrier by continuing to argue with him. He was out.

Antonio shook his head in disgust as he watched his rebellious son walk off. He was sick and tired of Tre's shit and oftentimes blamed himself for spoiling him as a child.

Since the tender age of seventeen when he found out his girl Sheila was pregnant, Antonio Anderson had done his absolute best to ensure that his family would want for anything. Before the piss could dry on the pregnancy test, he started making moves. He hustled hard by pushing packs on the corner, to running his own blocks, to ultimately running nearly the entire East Side of the city. That alone was a milestone for someone like Antonio, who grew up poor with no decent role models and only the hustlers to look up to.

Landing on top didn't come without its fair share of bloodshed. Working for niggas was never a long-term option for him, so when he found out his only choices were to either push packs directly for the block runners, or pay them to hustle on the block, he chose the latter. To him it didn't matter, since within months he was running down on the runners and taking over the blocks. A lot of niggas had come up missing during his five-year rise, even a couple of his suppliers.

To him, only the strong survived and deserved to be on top. His takeover method worked in every aspect of his hustle, and now at the age of thirty-eight, most of the dope that was sold on the East Side came from him. It had been that way for nearly sixteen years.

With the lifestyle he led, he knew that his family would be most vulnerable. With his dedication to his family fueling him, he saved diligently and moved his children to the best area he could afford. While his daughter appreciated and embraced the life they lived, his son resented it because of its unglamorous boredom and normalcy. It didn't help that in his younger and more less intelligent days, he would often take a young and highly impressionable Tre with him during runs to the hood. Cash, fly cars, and pretty women were the norm to the boy. He admired his father's power and yearned to emulate his infamy on the streets of the small city.

As Antonio grew older, he grew wiser and purposely shielded his children away from the dangerous lifestyle. However, it was a little too late. It didn't matter to Tre that Antonio had established a legitimate family landscaping and property business, so that they could have something for themselves. It was very modest money compared to what he had seen in the drug world, but it was a lot more than what most people had. They literally wanted for nothing, and his kids even had trust funds tucked away and waiting for them when they reached twenty-five.

In his mind his children were above the cold streets he was bred in. He envisioned Tre as a future entrepreneur, not some fake ass wanna-be.

Tre was by no means a thug in any form. He would easily be considered a sheep in the street — food or prey; someone who was weak and vulnerable. To say he was privileged was an understatement. His typical attire included $100 button ups and $400 Giuseppe's. He was a suburban kid whose only ties to the hood was his father. Antonio knew that Tre name dropped every chance he got. His son was a follower who had been brainwashed by the false glamorization of the streets.

Antonio knew without a doubt, that if Tre were put in the wrong situation, the average cat would chew him up and spit him out. He would do everything in his power to prevent that from happening. He knew he wasn't going to always be around to save Tre, so he would do his best to keep him out of the hood, and away from the "wolves" he called his friends.

Hearing the commotion from the kitchen as she cleared the dishes out of the sink, Tiffany quickly dried her wet hands with the dish towel and went to calm her father down. A true daddy's girl, Tiffany knew exactly what to say to calm him. She was the lady of the house and had been so since her mother had been killed in an automobile accident ten years ago.

"You okay Daddy?" Tiffany asked softly, before giving him a kiss on the side of his face. She could tell he was still angry. His cheek was rock hard because his teeth were still clenched tightly together in anger. The deep crinkles in his forehead also solidified the fact that he was indeed still livid.

"Daddy you know how Tre gets," she said softly. "He's hardheaded. He doesn't think, and he really does believe that Drew and Spice are his friends," she said sadly. "I know it's frustrating he wants to be in the hood, but in reality, he's dying to be just like you."

She too agreed with her father, she just used a different approach to express her concerns and opinions to Tre. He was a lot like their father, and unfortunately, Antonio's delivery was what often caused their explosive disagreements.

Antonio went to reply in agreement, but quickly frowned in disapproval as soon as he heard a yellow cab honking out in front of the house, followed by Tre quickly taking off out the door before anyone could stop him.

"Tre!" Tiffany called out anyway, but to no avail.

"Don't worry about it Tiffany; I'll deal with his ass later," he said, before getting up to handle some business.

Tiffany sighed. They were always at it, and she was tired of being the peace-maker.

2

"TRE, WHY YOU ACTING STUPID? ARE YOU SERIOUSLY TRYING to piss Daddy off or something?" Tiffany asked as soon as Tre answered the phone. She was mad, and she hated to see her father so rattled over some stupid shit about Tre.

Rolling his eyes, Tre responded. "Damn. Hello to you too." He held his phone loosely to his ear as he prepared for the second bullshit lecture of the day.

"Cut the crap Tre. I heard you and Daddy arguing from the kitchen ... You know what he saying is true. Them wack niggas aint ya friends, and ya ass need to stay out of the hood. You gon end up getting in trouble, or worse: *hurt*."

"Yo, what the fuck you mean? We don't even be doing shit. Just chilling in the crib smoking and talking shit. That aint a fucking crime," he argued, growing irritated. He didn't even know why he was explaining himself to her — or anyone for that matter. He was grown.

He wanted to hang up, but decided to hear his little sister out. Both he and his father had a weak spot for her, and although she was the baby of the house, they admired her intelligence and outspoken attitude.

"Tre, you're hanging with those lames in a trap house. I ain't slow to nothing fast. I still fuck with bitches from the East and they tell me all the time that they be seeing you with Drew and Spice at Pat's house. Now, if I'm not mistaken, Pat is a certified fiend, and there's nothing good coming up out of her crib."

Tre didn't bother to respond. It was true, and he wasn't going to play on her intelligence by suggesting otherwise. Pat was certainly strung out and wouldn't hesitate to sell her children's soul to the devil if the price was right.

"Bottom line Tre, Daddy wants what's best for you. He's not your enemy, and he worked hard to get us out the hood and put us up in a gated community — for you to return to the East and sit in trap houses, that's like a slap in the face to him. He runs most of that shit, and people stay telling him they be seeing you out there. I mean ... he conducts business out there for God's sake. You're a target, *Einstein*. Do you know how easy you're making it for niggas to run down on you? You're the only idiot I know that would sit up in a dirty ass drug house when you don't have to. People do that when they have no choice. You're lucky and privileged as fuck Tre," she said, trying to reason with her brother. "You actually have a choice. And you're putting *everything* and *everyone* at risk. If some shit pops off and you get jammed up, Daddy's the first person you gon call. Why risk that? What chu think gon happen to us if something happens to Daddy behind ya dumb ass?" she asked.

"Ain't nothing gon happen," he said smacking his teeth.

"How the hell you know that?" she questioned. "People fucked up out here and you strolling through the hood with rent money on ya back. Driving a car worth two year's of the average persons salary — come on. Use ya head big bro," she pleaded.

At times, it was hard to tell they came from the same mother and father. While she soaked up all the knowledge her father bestowed upon them, Tre disregarded it. She was like a sponge, eagerly absorbing every drop of knowledge he had to offer. She admired, and literally adored her father. He had taken excellent care of them as a single parent and provided them with a life most kids would dream of. She didn't understand what the fuck Tre's problem was.

Tre sat quietly before pulling from his blunt and exhaling a thick stream of smoke. "I hear you Tiff," he replied nonchalantly, before plucking his ashes to the excessively stained carpet.

He had in fact heard her, but he wasn't listening. He wasn't worried about nobody trying to creep him since he stayed strapped. Besides, he was bored and tired of staying cooped up in the house all the time listening to his father rant and rave about him going to school or taking over his business. He knew he was destined for something else. *What* exactly, he wasn't sure. What he did know, was that he simply didn't have the patience to deal with that business shit like Tiffany did.

His father owned a landscaping business and about a dozen properties through the city. When Tiffany wasn't in class getting her degree in Business, she was helping her dad manage all his residential and commercial buildings. Non-stop phone calls, emails, and work orders consumed most of her day, in addition to her school work. She loved keeping busy, and for the life of him, Tre never could understand why. The shit was boring to him. He refused to work like a slave, while his father took the easy way out and sold dope.

He never understood why his father didn't take him under his wing and let him help him run the East Side; he instead tried to shield him from it. He didn't want to go to school with the square ass niggas. He wanted money, hoes, and fly ass whips. At twenty-one, he was still young and dumb, and angry that his father would not aid in his recklessness.

"Listen sis, I gotta go. I'm a chill for a quick minute and then I'm coming back in. You want anything while I'm out?" he asked, knowing full well he didn't have any money.

"No Tre. I don't want anything except for you to hurry up and get home," she sighed. He was so damn stubborn.

Everything she had said, had went in one ear and out the other.

"I will, alright. And tell Dad, I hear him and I'm sorry."

He did his best to sound sincere, but he wasn't. He just wasn't trying to come home and hear Antonio talk shit. He knew that if anyone could butter him up, it was Tiffany.

"I'll calm Daddy down, and *you*, text me when you leave. Love you."

"Alright, I will. Love you too sis. And don't worry."

Tre hung up the phone and continued to smoke his blunt. He didn't understand what the big deal was. Hanging with Drew and Spice was exciting. It sure as hell beat riding skateboards with the corny ass white kids in his neighborhood. Besides, he and his niggas had plans. Big plans.

3

SPICE SNICKERED AS TRE LOWERED HIS PHONE FROM HIS EAR to his lap. They had heard Tre's end of the conversation and had also heard Tiffany barking on him from where they were seated on the other side of the room.

"I see ya lil sister still got ya ass in check over their nigga," Spice cackled loudly.

Although Tiffany was three years younger than Tre, he and Drew both knew her fine ass was second in command in the Anderson household.

"Fuck you nigga. Ain't nobody got me in shit," Tre argued. He mashed his blunt out in a nearby ashtray that was already overflowing with cigarette butts and blunt roaches.

"Whatever nigga, you know Tiffany run shit ... When you gon put me on anyway?" he asked, trying to piss Tre off further, for his own amusement. He was well aware that his requests for Tiffany were never going to happen.

They constantly took shots at him about hooking up with his baby sister. At only eighteen, Tiffany was considered a bad bitch. 5'7 with creamy caramel skin, and a slim but curvy body she strongly resembled a young Vanessa Williams. Tiffany was stunningly beautiful and wore her naturally long hair, bone straight. Good looks ran in the

family, as Tre and his father both were considered "easy on
the eyes" to most women. Both men had caramel colored
skin, almond shaped brown eyes, and a perfect set of teeth.
Tiffany looked like her late mother, with a big innocent set
of hazel brown eyes.

Even though she was hands-down beautiful, she was by
no means self-centered and egotistical. She often helped her
father arrange fund-raisers and donations within the
community. She was an A student at the local university and
because of her intelligence her father's business had been
growing consistently since she began to oversee things at
the age of sixteen. Although sassy, once one knew her, she
was any man's dream come true.

Tre looked over at Spice and frowned his face up. "Stop
talking stupid nigga," he stated, his irritation on full display.

"Let's talk about those lame ass West side niggas talking
about running down on niggas when they see us. Little bitch
I met down at Starlite's last night put me on."

"Who she heard that from?" Drew asked, finally joining
the conversation. He had initially been too busy serving the
influx of fiends through the side door to participate in their
small talk.

"Shorty said her sister was just fucking with one of dem
niggas. I think his name was Dante or some shit like that,"
Tre added with a shrug.

"Well apparently she not feeling the nigga anymore
because he whopped her ass the other day. Blacked her eyes
and some mo shit. Now she ready to give up the nigga info
on some get-back — for the right price of course," he added.
"She also said the nigga we fucked up last night wasn't no
little nigga. That's why niggas came gunning quick after the
shit let out. Boy caked up and ready to war, *on sight*. I heard
they plan to squad up and creep through. I also got the drop
on where the lil young nigga Dante trapping out of," he
added sinisterly. They all knew what that meant — a
come up.

"Over on Westover," he continued. "A lil something we

can hop on for a quick come-up and show mufuckas we don't give a fuck about *none* of dem niggas," Tre stated proudly, hoping to gain his friends full acceptance and praise from the information he had obtained.

After listening intensely, Drew and Spice smiled. They were always interested in a come-up. They weren't too concerned with anyone looking for them or going to war. It was easy for them to lay low. They didn't fuck with many people, and mufucka's around the hood knew who they were, as well as what they stood for. If anyone gave up their location to allow anyone the opportunity to creep on them, they were dead. Not only were they dead, but so were their whole family if necessary. They had no problem proving their point. They would lay down a whole block if they had to — old ladies and babies. They gave no fucks and the hood knew it. That's what landed them in the rift with the West Side in the first place. It had just happened the previous night and was still fresh on their minds.

It was Thirsty Thursday at Starlite's, a hole in the wall club that purposely bordered the East and West. It was where all the hood niggas and ratchet bitches from both sides flocked to on the weekends.

The club was packed and as usual, the poor excuse for security would literally let in niggas with Uzi's and AK's for the right price. After sliding the security guard, a $50 bill, Tre, Drew, and Spice all entered the club armed. With no il intentions, Tre went in with the intent to have a good time. Drew on the other hand, had other plans.

Although densely packed and dark, blue club lights illuminated through the large room giving everyone a glow. Ignoring the party-goers around them, the trio made their way to the single crowded bar. After ordering multiple shots, they all seemed to be enjoying themselves. From their small dark booth in the corner, they hit on the small selection of pretty women and talked shit to one another over the loud music. As the unmistakable voice of Drake pounded through the speakers and shook the small club, Drew decided to proceed with his plans.

He scanned through the patrons in the club and quickly realized that it was literally filled with broke ass niggas. They were the majority. From the ran-down sneakers to the dingy, over-washed clothing he knew that it wasn't any hitters in the building. That was, until he peeped the young nigga in the far-right corner of the club. He'd quickly spotted a target. Drew smiled. The flashy nigga he'd just laid eyes on looked soft. What some would consider a "pretty boy." Light skinned with short curly hair, he rocked an old, but fly throwback Adidas short set. Drew could see the suits' designer emblem from across the room. He also couldn't help but stare at the trio of eye-catching Cuban link chains that he bore around his neck. It didn't stop there, as he also wore a thick gold bracelet, an iced-out watch, and a diamond encrusted pinkie ring. All of them sparkled brightly and arrogantly against its drab surroundings.

If "pretty boy" weren't so young looking, Drew would've sworn he was an 80's baby, as he looked like he was straight out of Paid in Full. Nevertheless, Drew didn't give a damn what era he was from, or what year he was born. His mind was focused solely on the stones he rocked. The jewels he wore would easily get him five-grand from the crooked jeweler he knew downtown.

He continued to watch his vic and his companion, a pretty big-butt light-skinned chick, with a silky weave that dangled to the tip of her ass. Both appeared to be slightly intoxicated and having a good time. It couldn't get any better for Drew. After several minutes of watching, the girl eventually got up, adjusted her skin tight bodycon dress, and started walking towards their side of the club. Her oversized faux-gold bamboo earrings bounced with her as she moved. Drew knew it was the perfect opportunity to put his plan in motion.

"Damn shorty bad," Drew said, pointing to the girl, while nudging both Spice and Tre who were at his side. She was quickly headed their way and he didn't want to miss his opportunity.

"She aight. A little too ghetto looking for my taste," Tre stated arrogantly in response to the pretty red-bone approaching.

"What?" Drew asked, smacking his teeth in disbelief. "That bitch bad. I bet *you* couldn't bag her. Matter of fact, I bet she wouldn't even give you her number nigga," Drew teased, hoping Tre would hop on the challenge.

"Yeah right nigga. I can bag any bitch in here," he argued. He was dressed to impress and always looked like money. He had no doubt he could pull the big butt, ghetto looking chick with ease.

Hopping up to quickly prove his point, Tre sauntered right over in her path with confidence. Grabbing her arm gently, Tre leaned over with a smile and whispered in her ear, "You coming home with me tonight?"

Immediately snatching her arm back with an attitude, she looked at Tre like he had lost his mind. She clearly wasn't impressed with his approach.

"Nigga you don't know me, so don't touch me. And furthermore, you can miss me with that lame ass approach," she said, surprising Tre.

Her pink glossed lips curled up intensely to express her distaste. She couldn't believe the nerve of the young boy. She only fucked with dope boys, and while the youngin in front of her was cute and well dressed, he looked a little square. He definitely wasn't in her lane.

With his ego immediately bruised, Tre grew instantly embarrassed, a feeling he didn't experience much. His embarrassment immediately caused him to grow angry. He had only been right about one thing. While he couldn't bag her, he was right that she was indeed ghetto. As loud as she was, everyone within ear shot had heard her play him like a game of hoops. Looking behind him, he grew even angrier at the sight of Drew and Spice stomping their feet and laughing hysterically at Tre's public rejection. It amused them that Tre always ended up looking like a fool while trying so hard to impress them.

"Bitch I didn't want ya raggedy ass anyway, wit that cheap ass dress. And do some fucking sit ups while you at it. Fucking stomach bulging out but thinking you tough!" he balked. He wasn't gon front though. She was cute ... but she wasn't that bad to be acting that stank.

"Nigga fuck you! Who the fuck you think you talking to? I'll get my nigga to fuck you up!" she yelled, causing a scene in the small establishment. She was known to go from zero to one hundred on anyone. She didn't care if it was male or female.

"I don't give a fuck. Get whoever you want," Tre argued back. He was tempted to hawk spit in her face.

Seeing the commotion from across the room, her companion "Rico" hopped up and quickly made his way over to her to see what was going on. Grabbing her by the arm, he pushed her behind him and stood in front of her to end whatever dispute she and the unknown man were having.

"No disrespect but wassup my nigga?" Rico quickly asked. He did a brief scan of the room for his squad. He was never alone when he was out partying, and he hoped that his niggas weren't far in case some shit popped off over his side piece. He wasn't really trying to war over her, but nevertheless, she had come with him and letting her be disrespected would've made him and his team appear soft.

Drew had already filled Spice in on the plan so they both hopped up from where they were seated as soon as Rico approached Tre.

Seeing his team out his peripheral view, Tre felt no need to filter his words. "Ain't shit popping nigga, but if she with you, you should tell that bitch watch her mouth," Tre said to Rico while pointing at the girl.

Rico sighed in disappointment. He was hoping they could talk it out like men, respectfully. The nigga in front of him, *had* to go left. With no tolerance for disrespect, Rico threw a hard right that met forcefully with Tre's jaw, sending him flailing backwards onto a table and directly on his ass. Surprised and now even more embarrassed, Tre ignored the pain shooting through his back and immediately hopped back up. His anger caused him to see nothing but red. Before he could swing back, Drew and Spice were already all over Rico, raining a barrage of brutal blows to his body. Rico did his best to defend himself, but was no match for the bigger, stronger men.

Rico's side piece yelled and swung to get the duo off him, causing Tre to knock her to the floor with a hard punch to her face. He felt no remorse as he watched blood instantly run from her nose, and she begin to scream out in pain and disbelief.

Bouncers from the club quickly rushed over, and after a quick struggle, managed to separate the men and throw them out of the club. Tre, Drew, and Spice through the front, and Rico through the back. While it seemed like their night had abruptly ended, it was actually just getting started.

"Yo we fucked that nigga up," Spice laughed hysterically as they all climbed in Tre's car.

"*And* we came up," Drew beamed proudly, while holding up Rico's stolen jewels so they could see. The gold pieces sparkled brightly in the dark car.

"Did you run his pockets too?" Spice asked Drew.

"Na, I didn't have time. Security was over there quick as shit."

Tre, oblivious to the plan, thought nothing of the conversation and figured Drew just grabbed his shit when the opportunity presented itself. It never dawned on him that he had been used as a pawn.

"Fuck that pussy," he spat. "He got what he deserved. Nigga hit me on some bitch ass shit. Over a wack ass thot bitch," Tre complained, before rubbing his aching jaw. He could already tell it had begun to swell.

"Aww stop crying nigga. You shoulda slid that nigga as soon as he came up trying to play tough," Spice said. "You standing there wanting to argue and shit. And can you slide over to 7-Eleven? Nigga hungry," he said to Tre as he drove down the dark city street. "Trying to get something to eat before I go fuck the shit out of Tracy ass," he laughed. Spice had a weakness for hood-rats and was a known trick around the way.

Tre merged onto Route 13 off Isabella Street in his new model Cadillac SRX, a late graduation gift from his father. Pulling into 7-Eleven, they weren't surprised to see the large crowds of people in the tight parking lot. They lived in a small city and there was only a handful of places to go to eat after the clubs let out. Tre pulled up to a parking space closest to the entrance, but furthest from the door. He hated crowds and wasn't trying to be stuck while trying to get out.

"Damn nigga. You parked far enough didn't you?" Spice complained.

"Nigga stop bitching. I ain't trying to be all day getting out this mufucka," Tre argued. Already irritated from being hit in the face, he was ready to head home. He felt at his jaw again and hoped it didn't get too big.

"Word," Drew agreed. "We in and out."

The trio made their way through the dense crowd to the entrance of the store, with Spice leading the way. Before he could touch the dirty metal handle of the door, shots immediately rang out. They immediately ducked for cover and quickly scanned the crowd to search for its origins. It didn't take long for Drew to recognize where the gunfire was coming from.

———

As soon as Drew spotted the short and stocky, dark skinned kid with a hoodie pulled tightly around his head, he already knew what time it was. He immediately recognized the face and build, as well as the reputation of Chubs. At twenty-two, he was known to the city as the "grim reaper." He was a shoot-out in broad daylight type of guy — A run in ya house and put the burner in ya bitch and kids mouth type of dude — He didn't care, and *that* was what made people fear him. He had numerous bodies under his belt, and not a single person willing to even so much as implicate him.

Chubs clearly was a force to be reckoned with in the streets, and he also happened to be one of Rico's right-hand men. Turmoil and chaos excited him, and he would gladly bust his gun whenever Rico gave him the word. This special night he was on a mission. He had been given the simple task of enforcing the teams, "*zero tolerance*" policy. He was to leave the three men before him lifeless, for their blatant, and outlandish act of disrespect. Chubs looked up to Rico and would make it rain bullets day and night through the city if necessary. The lesson for the night was simple; disrespect always ended in gunfire.

Chubs glossy eyes stayed glued on his target as he squeezed the trigger on his slate gray, Glock 19. He had only fifteen shots and he wanted to make each one of them count. This particular night, the three men he was gunning for had luck and coincidence on their side. Chubs was known for his accuracy; however, tonight he had been drinking heavily at the club and his aim would not be nearly as precise.

"*Pow, pow, pow!*" were the sounds that crackled through the air and sent everyone ducking for cover. People pushed frantically and nearly trampled one another, trying to escape an early death sentence.

After spotting Chubs twenty feet away, Spice too was quickly able to comprehend that the gunfire was a gift for them and was a direct result of the incident at the club.

"Shit!" Drew yelled, as he quickly released his grip from the door handle. There was no way in hell he was going to enter the closed-in store while Chubs still had rounds left in his gun. That would easily be a death wish. Not one of the three men were armed, as they had tucked their guns away after the club. The only thing left to do, was run like hell for cover. Clearly, they were no match for the ammo begging their bodies for penetration.

"Run! He from the club!" Drew commanded before taking off in full speed through the parking lot.

Tre, who had never been in a shoot-out, immediately took off behind his friends, desperately pushing past people to get back to his car. His feet slammed in rapid succession against the pavement as his heart thumped violently in his chest. As Tre ran, the unfamiliar feeling of fear plagued his body.

"*Pow! Pow! Pow! Pow!*" Bullets continued to rip through the air, while Chubs did his best to chase the trio through the hysterical crowd. They knew he was coming but they kept running. Fear wouldn't allow them to look back. They just prayed to God that they wouldn't get hit. Every one-second they ran, felt like ten, as they fled to the car in terror. As they ran, all three braced for the moment when one of the bullet's Chubs generously released from his gun, tore through their body. After what seemed like eternity, the three friends finally made it to the car, literally diving in for safety.

"Drive this shit nigga!" Spice yelled dramatically, as he crouched in the back seat. He quickly down and under the driver's seat, retrieving his .22 to return fire. He only brought the small gun for convenience reasons and now regretted it. He was flaming mad, and wish he had something stronger to let loose on Chubs bitch ass.

Drew too was furious, and quickly rolled down his window to expose his previously concealed pistol. The duo proceeded to exchange fire through the crowded parking lot, disregarding the innocent bystanders. The shots coming his way didn't stop Chubs who bit down on his lip in anger, and ran behind the now full-speed, moving Cadillac, still letting off shot after shot, until his gun was empty. *Lucky mufucka's,* Chubs thought to himself. The next time, he wouldn't miss.

———

"Ima body that pussy!" Spice screamed furiously in the car, spit flying from his mouth. He rocked back and forth dramatically with every word he spoke.

"Word — on everything I fucking love!" Drew agreed, as he tucked his gun back underneath his seat. "Anyone hit?" Drew asked, as he checked himself for wounds.

"Na, I'm good," Spice responded, his adrenaline running high, while his face remained contorted in a scowl.

He was going to murder Chubs the next time he saw him — and he *would* see him again. He didn't care where they were. He could be with his kids, his sister, or even his grandma — hell, they could be in church; Spice didn't care. He was going to empty his entire clip on him without hesitating.

Tre sat in the front seat and remained silent. His heart still pounded in his chest and his hands shook slightly as he gripped the steering wheel. He was trembling with fear but did his best to conceal it. Although exciting, he wasn't quite ready for the lifestyle that Drew and Spice had grown up in and ultimately become accustomed to. He also had no idea how the fuck he was going to explain the bullet riddled Cadillac to his father. His back window had been shot out and the rear of his car was now covered in holes from Chubs gun.

The beef wasn't over, not by a long shot. *This* was just the beginning.

4

"Yo, I almost had dem niggas," Chubs said excitedly, but at the same time, with disappointment. He was giving Rico an animated run-down of the shootout that had occurred the previous night.

"They was running like bitches," Chubs laughed, before pulling smoke into his lungs from the lit blunt he was holding.

Rico nodded with a smile. That's all he wanted to hear. He wasn't into spilling blood, but he wanted niggas to understand he didn't fuck around. He didn't personally know the niggas that had jumped on him, but he remembered faces. He probably would never even run into them again since they probably weren't on his level, but unfortunately for them, if they ran into any one of his niggas, they probably wouldn't be as lucky as the first time. He honestly didn't give a fuck about the jewels they had taken; he was a boss and the jewels meant nothing to him. However, his team didn't feel that way. It was the principle they said.

The streets always talked, and while no one really knew who Tre was, everyone knew who Drew and Spice were. It didn't take long before Rico knew exactly who they were and what they were about. He didn't really want to war personally, since he wasn't really into the drama, so he told his team to chill for the time being. The message had already been sent. If either Drew, Spice, *or* Tre, felt they wanted to continue the beef, then they would proceed with no mercy shown. However, Rico hoped they did the smart thing, and fell back. His team was strong *and* large. He ran the West Side of the city and could get either of the men toe tagged in 24-hours.

"I wish that shit had happened early though," Chubs exclaimed disappointedly. "I was lit, and my aim wasn't on point. It's all good though, I'll see dem nigga's again," Chubs reassured Rico.

Rico didn't doubt him one bit. Chubs had personally handled many niggas for Rico and he was very confident in his youngin.

"No doubt, my nigga, but I want you to hold off on that. Remember what I said right?" he asked Chubs. "Let em live for now. Let *them* decide if they ready to die."

Chubs frowned slightly, but eventually smiled. He admired his mentor, and although he didn't agree with all of Rico's decisions, he determined that the way he did things were usually for the best. Rico wanted the streets to remain as peaceful as possible. There was no time for war, as there was too much money to be made.

Rico stood up from the rickety oak table they were sitting at. It was mid-day and he had some business to handle. He made all his money out of the hood, but he didn't want to remain stuck there all day. The house he stood in was a stash house. It was on a quiet block with little activity; a place where they could meet, eat, and chill while they stashed the day's cash.

"Ay yo, I'm out. Bout to go handle some business and slide over my shorty crib," Rico said.

"Aight cool. Just hit me when you come back through," Chubs said, still seated.

Rico extended his hand and Chubs rose up and gladly grabbed it for their regular hood handshake.

"Aight my nigga, be safe," Rico said, before walking out the door.

They always departed that way. It was a jungle on the streets and only the strongest survived. Safety was the number one priority. The strength of his team ensured that they ate well, and there was no room *or* tolerance for weakness. That was exactly why he had no choice but to act fast after being disrespected at the club. That was how it had been, and that was how it always would be.

5

ANTONIO GLANCED DOWN AT HIS VERSACE WATCH. HE WAS early as usual but what puzzled him, was that Vince was also early. Vince was the client he was meeting. Out of all the years, Antonio had been meeting him, he was usually on time, sometimes running late, but never ever early.

Antonio often arrived at places early. He liked to beat others just to ensure they weren't being followed. He prided himself on being on point. Today he actually sensed he had reason to be.

Antonio looked around cautiously before exiting his new model BMW. Walking to the door he didn't notice anything unusual or suspicious, however he still proceeded into the building with caution.

"Hey Frank," Antonio yelled to the owner, who was behind the counter ringing up an unknown patron.

He had known Frank for years and had even helped him financially to expand the place years back. Because of this, Frank never questioned his meetings there, and would also let him know what was transpiring in the streets since his diner was smack dab in the middle of them. That was one of the main reasons, Antonio was a bit nervous by Vince's early arrival for lunch.

Just the day before, Frank had informed Antonio that

Vince had been busted by the authorities. His barbershop had been raided after someone ratted him out to the DEA. Those facts didn't sit well with Antonio, especially because Vince had never informed him of the incident. Vince had a lot to lose: three kids and a wife to care for. Under the right pressure, he had seen some of the toughest fold like bitches. Nevertheless, Antonio proceeded to the table cautiously, paired with the infamous smile he always wore.

"Wassup Vince? You're here early," he said, before sliding into the opposite booth. He grabbed the menu from the table and pretended to look over it.

"Yeah, I gotta hurry up. My girl wants me to pick up my boys from football practice. She tied up at the shop," he said, referring to the barbershop and hair salon that he and his wife owned, or more so, used as a front to hide his illegal activities.

"Oh ok, well I definitely understand that. How's business been?" Antonio asked, looking Vince directly in the eyes. The eyes always spoke the truth when the mouth did its best to deceive.

"Shit is good. Real good. Soon we'll probably open another location," he lied.

"Yeah?" Antonio asked. "Well that's definitely what it is. You know, I'm a firm believer in ownership. If you want to grow Vince, you have to be a boss. But listen. I know you came for what we had talked about, but things have changed. My people got jammed up and shit is dry. I don't have anything and probably won't for a while," Antonio said, being careful of his word selection.

He couldn't prove it, but Vince was working with law enforcement, and he wasn't going to be fucking around with no rats. His judgement had always been pretty good in the past, and his gut was telling him Vince was nothing more than a dirty rat.

"Damn Antonio, when you think you gon have something? I got hella people waiting on me," Vince complained.

Vince sounded genuine but Antonio knew that was a

front. His demeanor and movement spoke volumes. He was shifting around too much and every so often he would glance out the window. Antonio knew he had either been followed or was wearing a wire. Lucky for Vince, Antonio was years older and years smarter. Had he been in his early twenties, Vince would be dead by sundown.

"I can't say for sure. I'm just waiting on my folk's situation to change. When it does, I'll definitely call you," he assured him.

"Aight," he sighed. "I guess it is what it is," he sighed, before again, glancing around nervously.

"Well I'm gonna get moving man. Pick up my kids and shit before my girl start tripping."

"Oh no doubt. Be safe man," Antonio responded.

He had no intention of ever calling Vince again, or dealing with him for that matter. The couple grand a week he brought in wasn't worth the jail time. He would continue to keep his eyes and ears glued to the street. What he did know, had it not been for Frank, he would not have known not to trust Vince. He felt his time on the streets were numbered and he had to make some major moves soon, so he could get out of them.

6

ANTONIO HUNG UP HIS PHONE AND SIGHED DEEPLY. THE DAY wasn't even half over, and he had already been presented with more bullshit. Words couldn't describe how angry and disappointed he was in his first-born child.

He had just gotten a call from Tasteful Events Catering Services, a company he had a contract with, providing cleaning and landscaping services.

The owner had footage of one of his employees stealing the entire safe out of the executive office. The day in question, Antonio had some important business to tend to and had sent Tre and a small crew to deep clean the facility and provide landscaping service around the premises.

Although Tre had been in charge that day, he obviously wasn't supervising properly since he allowed someone access to the executive office. Usually, only the person supervising the crew would go into that room. Tre knew that is where most businesses kept their safes and petty cash boxes. How he could allow one of the employees to steal on his watch, baffled him. Tre always wanted to be in charge. He wanted to be a boss; however, he couldn't even handle the minor duties associated with that title.

Antonio quickly changed his route and made his way to meet the owner so that he could review the recording and repay whatever was taken. He couldn't believe that Tre would let this happen. He would get with him later, but for now, he would handle business and make sure he didn't lose one of his best clients behind nonsense.

An hour later, Antonio opened the door of his home and walked into the living room where Tre was lounging on the couch playing Hitman on his PlayStation. He took a deep breath. It was taking everything out of him, not to rip his only son off the couch.

"Tre, turn off the game, I need to talk to you," he demanded.

"Hold up Dad, I'm almost off this level," he responded, throwing up his index finger signaling for him to wait.

That did it for Antonio. He could no longer contain his anger. Now enraged, Antonio walked over to Tre, ripped the controller from his hands and hurled it at the TV. The blow shattered the screen and left Tre wide-eyed with confusion.

"I asked you to turn it the fuck off!" Antonio yelled.

"Yo, what the fuck is ya problem?" Tre asked with a bewildered look.

"You're my fucking problem," Antonio responded, before angrily snatching Tre by his shirt, and pulling him to his feet to face him. He'd had enough and was past fed up with his son's nonchalance and lack of respect.

"I send you to supervise my crew and you fucking steal!" he roared, before releasing him with a forceful shove onto the long sectional.

Antonio didn't wait for a response. He wasn't expecting one. He had seen it with his own eyes on camera. Tre had gone into the office and took the safe out of the drawer. Not one of his employees, but his own son. His own flesh and blood had caused him to nearly lose one of his largest contracts. If it wasn't for Antonio's history with the owner, his profuse apologies, and his immediate repayment, he would have surely lost a contract he'd held for five years.

He was ashamed and utterly embarrassed. He felt like a fool. Tre had no idea how it had hurt his pride to apologize over and over, while begging someone not to press theft charges on his son and allow him to keep his contract.

He shook his head in disgust. "You're a disgrace Tre. I pay you nearly double what I give to some of my best employees. Only because you are my son. And you do this shit. You're so fucking ungrateful," he argued as he continued to shake his head. Words couldn't describe the anger he felt. Nothing he did was good enough to make his son do right and appreciate everything he worked so hard to give him.

"You refuse to do the right thing. From stealing, to nearly getting yourself killed, to bringing your dumb ass in all hours of the night — I've had it Tre!"

Tre just stared at his father while he ranted. It wasn't nothing new. He fucked up, Antonio argued, and the process repeated itself.

"You no longer work for me. You have to find a job, or you're cut off and have to move out," he said with finality.

The comment didn't even faze Tre, who sat on the couch and did his best to appear remorseful. He knew his father wouldn't put him out on the streets and he wasn't going to find a job either. He wasn't working for peanuts.

Antonio shook his head and looked at his son in disgust. "You and Tiffany are like night and day."

The comment instantly angered Tre, but he remained quiet. He knew his father favored Tiffany to him, always had. To Antonio, she was his perfect child and Tre was the black sheep. Tiffany got a new BMW and condo while all he got was a factory model Cadillac. Tiffany received a salary as his "Administrative Assistant," while he got paid hourly for any work he did, and a measly allowance of $500 a month, barely enough to fill his gas tank up monthly and have enough left over to buy a sandwich. It was insulting, considering the fact, his dad had probably made millions in the drug game.

Antonio finally decided to make his way out of the room, but slowly turned around and stared his son in the eye.

"And one last thing ... If you do some underhanded shit like that again, I'm not just going to put you out ... I'm going to drag you by your fucking neck and *throw* you out."

He turned around and walked out of the room praying that his son didn't call his bluff. He meant every word he spoke and hoped that Tre didn't force his hand. Family or not, no one was going to tear down what he had worked so hard to build.

7

Tiffany quickly rose from her desk to answer her chiming doorbell. Her boyfriend was early. She hated unexpected guests. It was only 2:30pm and he wasn't supposed to arrive until 8:00pm. It was his way of popping up on her to make sure she was behaving herself. It wasn't the first time he'd done it, and it probably wouldn't be the last, despite her requests.

After checking the television-like camera screen mounted on her wall in her hallway, Tiffany proceeded to her front door. Before opening it, she placed her index finger on the touch screen keypad near the door.

She had only been in the condo for three months and her dad wouldn't even allow her to stay one night without the expensive state of the art security system. He was extremely protective and only allowed her to stay at her condo three days a week. The other days she stayed with her father and Tre at her childhood home. Antonio would have it no other way since her university was closer to his house. He also wanted to make sure she was going to class. It wasn't that he didn't trust her, he just liked to have control. Tiffany however, always obedient and eager to please her father, didn't mind the arrangement. She mostly stayed at her condo to relax and work on her school work as well as handle paperwork for his business.

Lately, she had been using it for "entertainment" purposes. Unbeknownst to her father, she had someone special in her life. She was trying to find a good time to introduce that special someone, but she had yet to determine when that would be. What she did know was that, she really liked him, and she would keep him a secret before she let her father scare him off.

"Hey babe," Tiffany beamed as she pulled open the door.

"Wassup," Rico said, smiling warmly at her. He was smitten with the young girl before him. She had her head firmly planted on her shoulders and she was about her business. He had never met anyone like her, and she was foreign-like compared to the females he had dealt with. Not only was she beautiful, she was also intelligent. He had met her months back at a party thrown at his uncle's house. Since most of the attendees there were older, it didn't take long before he spotted her and struck up a conversation with her. She was stunning and at that very instant, he knew he had to have her.

"You gon let me in?" he asked with a smile. "Or you got somebody up in there?" he questioned jokingly. He had been dating her for several months and he prayed she wasn't too good to be true. They usually were.

"Cut it out," Tiffany said with a smile before stepping back and letting Rico enter her small, but expensive and tastefully decorated home.

Rico stepped in and immediately wrapped his arms around Tiffany's small waist. Grabbing her ass, he pulled her into him and gave her a kiss. He inhaled her scent and felt himself stiffen. She smelled sweet. Tiffany kissed him back before pulling away with a smile. She could feel him getting excited. She didn't want to start something she wasn't ready to finish.

"I thought you were coming at eight?" she asked, while looking up into his eyes as he still held her.

"Yeah I was, but I was in the area and I figured I'd stop by early," he lied. He really *was* intentionally dropping in on her.

He was hoping she didn't mind. He wanted to spend the remainder of the day with her. Tiffany's expression changed slightly. She had plans that unfortunately, did not include him.

Sensing her hesitance, Rico let go of her waist, but took her hand to hold. "You busy or something? If so, I can come back babe. I don't mean to intrude."

"No ... I mean you're not intruding, but my brother was supposed to come through in an hour or so."

"Ohhh ok," he said with a smile, quickly catching on to her hesitance. "You don't want me to meet him yet?"

"Ummm. No, not really," she laughed nervously. "I mean." She paused. "I wanted you to meet my dad first, cuz Lord knows, he would have a fit if you met Tre before him."

"I can dig it, it's cool. I'll come back at eight," he said before glancing down at his oversized watch, mentally trying to figure out what he would do until then. He had no other plans and was in no hurry to go back to the hood. His side-piece Latisha, the red-bone he was with at the club, had been blowing him up all day. However, he wasn't interested in spending quality time with her.

"Thanks babe," Tiffany said, wrapping her arms around Rico's waist and leaning in for a soft kiss.

"No doubt," he said, his lips meeting hers. "I'll be back at eight."

He turned to walk towards the door, but Tiffany stopped him.

"What happened to your face?" she asked in concern. She trailed her soft, manicured hand along the fresh four-inch scratch that ran down his cheek. It was nasty, but it looked as if it would heal without leaving a noticeable scar.

"Oh that?" he asked, pulling back a little bit from her

touch. During the fight at the club, his stripped jewels had snagged, and cut into his face.

"I got in a little scuffle at the bar. It ain't about shit," he said.

"Mmmmm," she said with a frown, as she continued to carefully observe it. "Well you be careful babe. You too cute to be fighting. I'll clean it up some for you, when you get back."

She gave him another kiss on the lips before seeing him to the door.

"Watch my flowers," Tiffany complained, as her brother clumsily maneuvered his way through her condo. She frowned as he sat down on her cream colored, contemporary style sofa. She hoped they didn't leave a scent.

Tiffany was extremely annoyed, and she didn't try to conceal it one bit. Not only had Tre come reeking from the smell of weed, he also brought his friend Spice along. That hadn't been what they had agreed upon. She had asked Tre to stop by for dinner so they could have a heart-to-heart conversation over what was going on with him. He had been distant lately and over the past few weeks, had been hanging out more and more with Drew and Spice.

"Watch em for what? Them shits is fake as fuck. Can't kill em," Spice mumbled jokingly. Tiffany rolled her eyes and shot him a dirty look before redirecting her gaze back to her brother.

"Tre come to my office really quick. I want to go over something with you," she said, before walking off. It was more of a demand, than a request.

Getting up and following behind her, Tre's glazed eyes looked towards the kitchen. He was hella hungry and could smell the scent of the Baked Ziti Tiffany was cooking circulating through the air.

Tiffany stood on the side of her door until Tre came

behind her. She proceeded to close it, and once she heard the click, she went full in on her elder brother.

"Tre are you fucking crazy?" she asked, being careful to keep her tone and volume in check.

"What?" he asked, looking down at her with the same brown, baby face she had looked up to for so many years.

"Why would you bring that nigga to my fucking house? ... I don't want none of those low-life scumbags knowing where I live," she growled.

Tiffany couldn't stand either of the two cousins Tre hung out with. They were street dudes to the core and she felt her brother had no business associating with them on a regular basis, let alone traveling with them. They were the kind of guys that could get shot at the drop of a dime.

"Daddy would tie your ass in a knot if I told him."

"What the fuck ever," he groaned. "Damn Tiff. I needed a ride, and besides, the nigga is harmless. That's my man," he assured her.

"Stop being stupid Tre or you gonna wind up fucked over. Didn't you ever listen to Daddy when he said, *trust no broke ass nigga*." She looked at Tre in disgust.

"Then on top of that, you two come in here smelling like shit," she complained, referring to the smell of weed permeating off their persons.

"Tre, I love you, but you and ya so-called friend gotta roll. Take ya plate and skate," she said with finality.

"Alright, alright, damn. I'll leave," he huffed.

"Oh, and I almost forgot the reason I called you over here. What you did was foul. Daddy called me and told me about the stolen safe," she revealed, shaking her head in disgust and disappointment. She didn't wait for a response.

"He also told me that your car had to be towed to the body shop because the back was filled with bullet holes. You could've been killed Tre," she said, her voice trembling.

She knew she could never offer him any advice, as he would not accept it. Because of his naivety and senseless recklessness, she worried relentlessly about her only sibling.

"Get ya shit together Tre. Learn from your mistakes, or you gonna wind up left behind."

"Yeah, yeah whatever," he said in annoyance before heading out of his sister's office. He rolled his eyes, but he had heard her.

He knew what he had to do, and it wasn't sit around listening to his sister talk down on him just like his Dad had been doing. He was going to show them he was a man and could stand on his own. And he planned to do it, exactly how his Dad had.

8

"Antonio! Hola mi amigo. Como estas?" Pedro asked, while smiling brightly as he gave Antonio a strong handshake, before immediately inviting him into his home.

"I'm doing okay Pedro," Antonio responded with a smile. Pedro always greeted him with Spanish words in a jovial manner. Antonio suspected it had a lot to do with the amount of revenue he brought in for his Spanish elder.

"Just okay?" Pedro asked, exposing two rows of perfectly aligned, shiny white teeth, perfected by some orthodontist.

"As much money as you make, you should be doing great!" he said, in a hearty laugh and thick accent.

"Come!" he gestured with his hands.

Following Pedro through the palatial space, Antonio couldn't help but admire the intricate Spanish details of the lovely home he religiously visited twice a month.

The contemporary Mediterranean stucco style home, custom designed by Pedro's wife Anna, was a staple in her country, solidifying one's wealthy status. Growing up poor in Guadalajara, Anna would often dream of living in one of the homes her mother used to clean tirelessly. She and Pedro had been together for over twenty years, and every chance he got, he strived to make each, and every one of her dreams come true.

"Come sit down," Pedro said, ushering Antonio into his lavish office at the back of his home.

Antonio took a seat onto the leather couch across from Pedro's large, executive style, cherry wood desk. He was nervous, but he did his best to make himself comfortable. Taking a seat, Pedro retrieved a Cuban cigar from his drawer, lit it, and took a long drag from it.

"Care for one?" he asked. He already knew the answer. Antonio took pride in his physique and refused to pollute his body with any kind of toxins such as alcohol, drugs or smoke.

"No thanks."

"Ok. Can I get you anything at all? Something to drink? I can have Anna make you a plate of Paella. She just cooked it. It's delicious," he bragged. Anna definitely knew her way around the kitchen and Antonio had tasted some of her delicious creations on multiple occasions.

"I'm good Pedro, but thank you."

Pedro shrugged and took another pull from his cigar. A thick stream of smoke escaped from his lips as he exhaled.

"So, what brings you here my friend?" Pedro asked. He was early for his shipment and he hoped his premature arrival was for positive reasons. However, he wasn't so sure. Antonio seemed distant, and it appeared something was bothering him.

"Well, I wanted to talk to you about something important," Antonio said with a sigh before pausing. It was now or never, and he wasn't quite sure how it was going to go.

"Speak my friend. What troubles you," he asked, leaning back in his desk chair. His eyes pierced deeply into Antonio's, and revealed his curiosity.

"I don't know how to say this Pedro. But I want out," he admitted, silently breathing a sigh of relief. It had come out easier than he thought it would.

"You want out?" Pedro asked, pausing. He was confused and Antonio now had his full attention "You mean you want out of the game ... This lifestyle?" he asked for clarification.

"Yeah," Antonio responded, making eye contact with his mentor.

"I don't know what to say. In my country there is no such thing as *out*. The only way *out*, is death there."

Antonio swallowed hard but stood his ground through eye contact.

"Hopefully that is not the case here. I've been in this game for nearly twenty years. I've made you a lot of money. Money that enabled you to provide a beautiful life for your family. Right now, my family needs my full attention. I have a daughter in college, a growing business, and a son that is going to either drive me out of business or wind up dead in six months if I don't step in. Earlier today, I met with a client. One I've known and done business with for over five years. One I considered my friend ... That same client is under secret surveillance and tried to set me up." Antonio sighed. "So, you see Pedro, my time is winding down. All the signs are there. My only choice now, is to bow out gracefully, or let the streets take me and my family under."

Pedro said nothing. He sat stone faced and quietly stared at Antonio. This wasn't the news he was expecting, and he was extremely disappointed in Antonio's revelations; nevertheless, he could tell he was sincere and was deeply troubled. Pedro looked away briefly as he took his cigar and put it out in a nearby glass ashtray.

Directing his icy gaze back to Antonio, he continued to sit quietly. Antonio appeared nervous. He wondered what Pedro was thinking. He hoped and prayed that their conversation wouldn't go left.

"Antonio you're one of my best clients. You make me a lot of money; however, you're not just my client. You are my friend. If you want out, then you have my blessing. Family is the most important thing in life; after all, we do this for them."

Pedro let out a hearty chuckle, and it instantly lightened the mood of the room. Antonio had him thinking that something larger was troubling him. He had groomed Antonio for many years, and while he hoped that he would one day rule the streets, he understood his desire to retreat. Besides, he still had his young and hungry nephew who was more than eager to someday fill his spot as the largest supplier in the city.

"Thanks Pedro. I definitely appreciate it. You've done a lot for me to even be able to get to this point, and for that, I thank you."

"Of course. Of course," Pedro responded modestly.

Pedro had taken Antonio under his wing at twenty-two when he was a gun-toting live-wire. He'd heard about the youngster, along with his ruthless reputation. Initially Pedro was hesitant, but after some time, Antonio grew on him. He was ambitious, honest, and loyal to a fault. Over the years he'd resolved many issues for Pedro, some peacefully, and some through gunfire. He was one of his best men, and while sad to see him depart, he was happy that he had found a legitimate path to embark upon.

"Do you still want the upcoming load?" Pedro asked.

"Yeah, that'll be my last one and then I'm done."

"Fair enough," Pedro stated before getting up from his desk. "Same time, same amount?" he asked.

"Cool," Antonio responded, before standing up and preparing to depart from the room.

9

"NOBODY FUCKIN MOVE!" DREW SCREAMED, AFTER KICKING IN the front door with his .45 drawn. Spice was right behind him while Tre served as the lookout from outside.

"Ahhhh!" screamed a brown-skinned girl that was crouched over the young man who now sat wide-eyed in fear.

Both had been caught off guard, and the girl now quickly scrambled across the ground, on her knees in terror. She disregarded the ring of saliva that had formed around her mouth and seeped onto her shirt from her oral escapade, that had been abruptly interrupted by the masked gunmen.

"Where's the money and work? I want everything, and I want it now," Drew demanded.

It was simple. He wasn't playing, and Dante could tell that judging by his demeanor. The only thing he could see in the dimly lit house was the homicidal scowl Drew wore on his semi-masked face, and the big black gun that was aimed at his head. He wasn't ready to die, and he grew angry that the dude Paulie he was working under, had him posted up in the stash spot with no muscle. To make matters worse, Paulie had picked up earlier than usual, and there was nothing in the house worth taking. He prayed the lack of come-up for the robbers didn't entice them to kill him.

"It's in the back bedroom," he replied calmly. "Open the air-conditioner and you'll find it."

Moving from behind Drew, Spice scurried to the back of the house to find the treasure they had come for. He tucked his gun against his waist. He knew there was no one else in the house but Dante and the jump-off. They had been watching the crib for several days and knew that Paulie often left him alone.

"That's what I'm talking about," Drew said, while keeping his gun aimed at Dante. He wasn't worried about the bitch. She was part of the set-up. She knew they were coming; she just wasn't sure what time they would be there. Tre knew her sister, who in turn had convinced her to get back with Dante after he had whooped her ass a few days ago. She would get her cut later.

After several tense minutes, Spice returned with a scowl on his face. Handing over the small stack of money to Drew, he turned to face Dante.

"What the fuck is this nigga?" Drew asked, disgusted. He didn't even bother to count it as he knew it couldn't have been more than $1,500. They had been expecting at least five-grand in the house.

"That's all that's there. The big homie picked up earlier," Dante responded, growing increasingly nervous. He was starting to sweat. He began to say a silent prayer asking the Lord for protection.

"I'm about to pop this nigga *and* that bitch," Spice stated angrily. He reached in his waist to retrieve his gun.

"Chill," Drew stated firmly before grabbing Spice's arm.

"Fuck that shit!" Spice argued. "I don't have time for fucking games!" He was angry. They had been expecting much more since the girl Tre was dealing with, had bragged that they kept racks in the house in plain view. $1500 was a far cry from what she had been promoting.

"Let the bitch and the little nigga be. No need to catch no homicide over the shit."

To Drew, it was still a come up. They were still leaving with more than they came with. Disappointed, Spice smacked his teeth but stuffed his gun back in his jeans. He was angry, but ultimately agreed with his cousin. It was Dante's lucky day.

"Tape them the fuck up though so we can get the fuck outta here," Drew demanded. He looked at Dante, and then over at the girl. There was no need to waste any more time.

Spice grabbed the duct tape out of his back pocket and did as told. Taping them up would give them time to flee the scene before anyone knew what happened. By the time someone found them, they would be long gone.

10

THE RIVER VIEW FROM THE WINDOW OF THE CHATEAU WAS nothing short of stunning. It was exactly what Antonio dreamt, and he had gone out of his way to make sure he got the perfect table for Tiffany's 19th birthday.

"Thank you so much Daddy, I really love it," Tiffany beamed, as she looked out of the window and admired the view. Their seats were right near the window so she could see the water. The lights illuminating from the tall buildings downtown, cast an exotic glow on the still, black-like water.

"Anytime," he smiled back. Money was no issue when it came to his baby girl. The three-month reservations had set him back a grand, but it was worth every penny.

"And thank you for the bracelet Tre; it's beautiful," she smiled before glancing down at her 14k gold euro coin bracelet.

Tre nodded. He was happy she liked it. He had just picked it up at the last minute, and it had cost him every cent of the $500 he had gotten off the last-minute West Side caper.

Antonio smiled before stuffing a forkful of seared Porter House steak into his mouth. He had another gift for Tiffany.

"Tiffany, so I wanted to talk to you both about something." He paused for emphasis. "Next week I'll be focusing on the business 100%."

Tiffany dropped her fork and smiled brightly. "Oh, Daddy that's great!" She had longed for the day to hear the words that he would be exiting the drug game.

The admission caught Tre's attention, causing him to sit straight up. If his father was moving to the side, then he knew he would be passing the throne down to him. He was sure that Antonio had intentions of teaching him the ins and outs of the game.

"So, remember the building we saw when we rode downtown. Right near the park?" Antonio asked the two.

"We rode by there the other day and it had the *For Lease* sign up," Antonio continued, trying to refresh their memory.

"Yeah," they replied in unison.

"Well I just signed a five-year lease today," he smiled.

"Daddy that's awesome!" Tiffany squealed while literally bouncing up and down. "So, does this mean I get a new office?" she asked.

"You not only get your own office, but you also get the new title of *Director* of Anderson Enterprises."

"Thank you, Daddy!" she gushed, as she scooted from her seat and gave him a big hug.

She was honored that her father felt she could run his company and had given her an actual title acknowledging that belief. She wanted nothing more than to make him proud of her.

"So, what about me?" Tre asked. :What's my title? Do I get an office too?" he asked sarcastically. The positive vibe surrounding their table quickly soured as soon as Tre spoke.

Antonio cleared his throat before answering. "You won't' have an office Tre, but you will have a corner desk in the common area while Tiffany and I will take the back offices. Your title will be Account Manager. You will help Tiffany. She will basically oversea the specifics of all contracts, and then pass the tasks to you and the other Account Manager."

"Hold up, watchu mean, the *other* Account Manager?" Tre asked, confused.

"I plan to hire another Account Manager. Business is doing great and it will take two of you to handle the load. You will oversee the landscaping and cleaning sector of the business, while the other Manager will oversee the property portion. They will handle the work orders, rent receipts and complaints. You will send our crew out to handle cleaning jobs and landscaping jobs. You two will also work together keeping the outside of the properties maintained. You'll also oversee move-ins and move-outs.

"What kind of shit is that?" Tre asked, surprising his father and sister.

Antonio quickly glared at his son silently. He was taken back by Tre's lack of appreciation. He was trying to give him a chance by even giving him a job. Not only was he not worthy of any position, Antonio wasn't even confident that Tre was capable of handling the duties that came with the title.

"Come again?" Antonio asked angrily. He did his best to contain his anger.

"What kind of shit is that?" he asked again.

"Tiffany gets an office in the back with you, while *as usual*, I barely get shit. On top of that, you have me handling some bullshit ass lawn jobs while you're going to hire someone from outside of our family to run your properties." Tre's voice wavered between anger and hurt.

"First thing's first. I suggest you watch how you talk to me. Any decision I make is for the best interest of *my* business . Second, you're a fucking thief Tre. Why would I allow you to handle my properties and important shit like rent?" Antonio asked, trying his best to remain calm while reasoning with his son.

"Man fuck this shit. I'm out. You can keep ya funky ass job," Tre argued. "I'll find my own way. I don't want shit to do with Anderson Enterprises," he continued.

Tre pushed back in his chair and stood up from the table.

"Tiff, I love you. Hope you enjoyed ya birthday. Ima hit you later," he said before walking off.

Antonio continued to glare at Tre as they both watched him walk away. Tiffany wanted to call out to him but knew that it would do no good. He was too stubborn. To make matters worse, he had been drinking. She wasn't even going to bother wasting her breath.

Tre got outside of the restaurant and quickly hailed a yellow cab. He whipped out his phone to call his niggas. He had a major proposition for them — one he knew there was no way, they could refuse.

11

TRE STOOD OUTSIDE OF PAT'S HOUSE AND TOOK A LONG SWIG of Hennessy straight from the top of the bottle. He swallowed the bitter liquid quickly then breathed deeply from his mouth to get rid of the foul taste stuck on his tongue.

Tre tightened the lid back on his bottle and shoved it in the pocket of his khaki shorts. He peered down the street for a few minutes before he spotted the swift moving vehicle headed towards the house. It was Drew and Spice. It was about time. After leaving The Chateau, he had headed right over and had been waiting on them over a half hour.

Drew and Spice pulled alongside of the curb in front of the house and waved for Tre to hop in. Tre complied. The cool air in the car was welcoming in comparison to the brutal July heat outside. Before Tre could get comfortable in the backseat, Drew came straight with it.

"What's up nigga?" he asked curiously. "You call us out here on some urgent shit talking about you had a major lick for us. Run it down."

"Damn," Tre exclaimed. "I just stepped foot in this bitch."

"Well we don't have time for the pleasantries nigga," Spice sarcastically added. "What the fuck is up. You said it was major, so spill," he added. "And it better be better than

that bullshit lick we did the other night," he argued, referring to the West side home invasion that only produced
them around $500 a piece.

Tre sighed. He knew he was selling his soul to the Devil
for this one.

"Well as both you niggas know. My Pops is a heavy hitter
out here."

"Yeah, and?" Drew asked.

"Well he's leaving the game. He focusing on building his
business and shit." He paused. "So, because of this he plan-
ning to cop his last load in a week," he said referring to the
Heroin his father distributed in the city. Although Antonio
had not stated that at dinner, Tre had overheard him already
making plans to pick up from Pedro the following week.

"Now, being as though him and his connect been doing
business since I was a fucking lil nigga in diapers, I know he
gon throw him sumn extra. This shipment is going to be
large."

"So, what the fuck that gotta do with us," Spice asked,
wondering where Tre was headed with this.

"We're going to take it," Tre stated calmly, surprising
everyone.

"Wait a minute nigga. How the fuck we gonna pull that
off?" Drew asked. If it sounded too good to be true, it usually
was.

"Trust me, we can pull it off, and we will. You see, these
niggas are old school. They have the same routine and think
shit is sweet cuz they got bread. Every two weeks my dad
picks up from the nigga — right from his crib. He keeps it
there because he don't gotta worry about police raiding his
spot because he got a handful of those crooked ass
mufuckas in his pocket. The shipment comes in a day before
my Pops goes and grabs it. We're going to intercept that shit
before he goes and picks up, that way, we take everything
that's there, and we redistribute it to niggas who copping
from someone else at a much lower price."

"How the fuck we gon get in the nigga crib if he moving

major weight like that? His shit probably tighter than Fort Knox."

"Not at all. I've been to his house numerous times. He has a bunch of niggas around during the day, but at night he relies on just his alarm system."

"That's fucking crazy?" Spice said, looking over to Drew. If what Tre was saying rang true, then their lives would change in a matter of weeks. There would be consequences behind their actions, but they weren't worried. They would handle anything that came their way, and ultimately rule the streets.

"Cool. I'm with it," Drew stated.

"Me too," Spice agreed.

"Bet. We on that shit asap. I'll show you niggas where he rests, and you two lay low on the spot to become familiar —"

"Nigga we live and breathe for this shit. Just text the address," Spice stated firmly, cutting Tre off. He wanted Tre to know, he wasn't calling any shots. Never had, and never would.

Drew on the other hand, sat quietly pondering in his thoughts. He wondered what made Tre come off that type of information. After all, in a way, he was crossing his father too. He knew Tre and his father had that "love hate" relationship, but he never would have thought it would come to this. He wanted to ask, but figured he would do it a different way, another time. In the meantime, he would keep an eye out on Tre. If he would cross his father, he would cross anyone.

———

The next day, Drew and Spice rode by the address Tre had provided them with to peep out the scene. Tre was right. It would be easier than taking candy from a baby. Pedro had very little security around his crib. They saw extraordinarily little movement around the large home at all. Tre told them

Pedro was very selective with his clients, but the activity around the home seemed uncharacteristically slow for a drug king-pin. They were expecting a scene more along the lines of Scar-Face.

"There he goes again," Spice said, as they watched Pedro come out of the home dressed in a black robe and slippers. He nor Drew could believe that a man of his status was so easily accessible. Money and arrogance could surely make some people stupid.

Taking the binoculars from Spice, Drew looked through them. He passed them back once he too saw Pedro.

"If what Tre really saying is true, then this could be the mother-load." Drew's excitement grew as he talked.

Spice nodded in agreement. "With the work and bread we snatch outta here, we on," he added. A well-known trick in the city, he thought about all the bitches he would fuck when he came through pushing some crazy shit. Perhaps a Lamborghini.

Drew on the other hand, had other plans. Since Antonio was stepping down, he knew they could easily take over the East, however, he had no desire to run half the city with his idiot, whore-chasing cousin.

"*On* ain't even the word," Drew agreed. "In a few months' time, we'll be kings." He was sure of it.

Laying down the binoculars, Spice asked, "You ready to roll? We been out here for hours and this nigga ain't doing shit but taking out trash and setting out fucking dog food."

Drew agreed, and they left, only to return every day for a week. For that week, nothing else mattered. Scheming on a man like Pedro, was like finding a gold-mine. Tre had really come through this time.

12

Present Day

Over in the closet, Spice's eyes lit up like Christmas lights when he saw the old, green trunk safely nestled underneath the dozen rows of designer shoes. With excitement fueling him, he inserted the key into the chamber.

Before he could push open the heavy top to the chest, the faint sound of a door swinging, along with subsequent running down the hall, stopped him in his tracks. The sound coming from the pitch-black hallway, caused Tre to also stop abruptly as he was walking out. Drew, who had been standing by the bed next to a restrained Pedro, also appeared stunned by the noise. As the sound neared, Anna and Pedro started to squirm, wiggle, and shake to get out of their restraints. Their muffled attempts to yell caused Drew and Tre to grow alarmed. Someone else was in the house, but it was too dark to see who it was, *and* what they were carrying.

The rapid footsteps grew dangerously close and a shadow appeared by the door. Fear gripped Tre and without thinking, he frantically drew his gun. Before Drew could yell for him to stop, he fired through the door. The running immediately stopped, and the sound of a body hitting the floor could be heard.

Tre lowered his gun and the image was clearer, the shadow and person now visible.

"Shit," Tre cried out, with panic immediately inflicting him. They were fucked.

"What happened," Spice yelled in a panic. He had run back from the closet after hearing the single gunshot.

"Fuck, fuck, fuck!" Tre cried, as he dropped the gun and crouched down next to the seemingly lifeless figure. It was Christopher, Pedro and Anna's seven-year-old son. Tears began running down Tre's face as he stared into Christopher's innocent, dark-brown eyes. He had been hit in the chest and a large pool of blood was forming on his shirt.

"Fuck,' Tre cried as he frantically looked at Drew and Spice in panic. He had no idea what to do. Christopher was still breathing, but barely.

"Get something to stop the bleeding," Spice yelled to Drew.

He quickly snatched down a shirt that was hanging in the closet nearby and rushed it over to Tre, who was still holding Christopher. Lifting his shirt to find the wound, Tre pressed it against the dime sized hole in Christopher's chest; however, the bleeding persisted. A minute passed, and his breathing stopped. His chest fell still and the three grew silent.

Drew glanced at Spice and then said to Tre, "We gotta go Tre. He's gone, and if we don't leave soon, we fucked."

Tre didn't bother to respond. Either way, they were still fucked —big time.

Drew tapped Spice to go round up the drugs and cash from the safe before looking over at Pedro and Anna. Tied to the bed and helpless, all they could do was look on to the floor at their slain son. There tears were unseen and their cries were hushed, masking an unbelievable pain so deep, that it would leave one breathless. The pain they felt was indescribable. Pedro closed his eyes. He wanted to die, for if he lived, he vowed vengeance on each person involved. His misery and agony would be shared all through the city. He didn't even have to say it; Drew, Spice and Tre already knew.

Pillow case in hand, Spice soon returned with the goods they had come for. The three wasted no time fleeing the house in attempts to stay one step ahead of the mess they created.

"Yo fam! What the fuck happened in there?" Spice asked Drew, once they were away from Pedro's house and somewhat safe on the expressway leading back to the hood. He never saw Tre shoot, he only heard the sounds and then the shot.

"I don't fuckin know," Drew exclaimed, still in disbelief over the scene that had just unfolded. "Lil nigga just came out of nowhere running down the hall." His voice trailed off.

"And I panicked," Tre admitted quietly from the backseat. "It was dark — I couldn't see shit. I didn't know who it was." Tre paused. "I forgot all about Christopher," he revealed.

Drew stared straight ahead and shook his head. That was a vital piece of information that Tre accidentally omitted. That error would surely cost them if anyone found out if it was them.

"How the fuck you forget some shit like that Tre?" Spice yelled out in disbelief. "If we had known that shit, we would've grabbed his ass soon as we ran in the crib. Fuck!" he yelled.

Every fiber of his being wanted to tell Drew to pull over, so he could Tre's stupid ass and leave him on the side of the highway. He was far from soft but he didn't have time to be going to war with a Mexican Kingpin like Pedro. He could have them touched from all angles with the amount of money he had. Dope-boys, stick up kids, and even crooked cops would bring him their heads if the price was right. The streets would no longer be safe.

"Spice just calm the fuck down," Drew added. "What's done is done and we just gon have to handle it, if and when the time comes. First off, he gotta figure out who took his shit. For all he knows, it could've been anybody. Right now, we chill, split up the bread and wait to move this work," he instructed.

He turned and looked over in his rearview mirror at Tre, who was visibly shaken. "Tre, now's not the time to bitch up. You made a mistake, shit happens. Don't say shit to anyone, especially not ya Pops. We gon chill for a while and see what this nigga Pedro finds out. We deal with the shit how it comes."

Everyone nodded in agreement as Drew continued down the highway to his and Spice's grandmother's house. That was the only place they felt safe enough to divide the cash they had took. The drugs would remain in the stash until it was safe enough to move. None of them sure of when that would be. For all they knew, they should prepare for war.

13

TRE PULLED UP TO THE PARKING LOT OF TIFFANY'S CONDO AND quickly turned off his borrowed car. He had gotten it about an hour ago from one of the several females he was seeing. He hadn't long left Drew and Spice and his nerves were still rattled. At this point, he knew no other person to turn to. He knew he wouldn't be able to face his father right away, so he didn't even bother to go home.

Sighing loudly, he wondered what he had gotten himself into this time. Images of Christopher's dead body flashed through his mind and he quickly took a deep breath and shook his head to rid himself of them. Although he felt guilt behind Christopher's death, he told himself he would not let his emotions consume him. He had to make sure he remained on point, just in case shit hit the fan.

He scooped his book bag off the passenger seat and clutched it tightly in his palm. It contained around $60,000 in newly acquired cash that he wanted to put to good use.

Hopping out of the car, he quickly peered around once more before making his way up the steps and through the corridor of the brightly lit hallway. He knew he would be safe at Tiffany's. It was in a gated community and one had to have a key code to enter just to be greeted by security.

As he approached Tiffany's unit, a brown-skin cat, with

low cut, curly hair walked out and was now facing the door. Tre stared him down but couldn't place his face. He however, did look familiar.

———

Rico kissed Tiffany on her cheek as he stood at her doorway preparing to leave. He had only stopped by for a few hours but had to leave since he had business to tend to. As he turned to walk off, he saw a familiar face — his adversary approaching. He froze in his tracks. He never forgot a face and it was definitely the kid that had started the shit in the club. How the fuck he found him was unknown.

One thing for sure — he was always ready and trained to go. Tiffany was right behind him preparing to see him off. His thoughts raced frantically, and he pushed her back slightly, with the intention of drawing his gun.

"Shit," Tiffany hissed after peering to the left of her door to see what had stopped Rico. She said it loud enough for him to hear her, but not Tre, who was still approaching.

"That's my brother ... I guess now is the time you two meet," she said with an apprehensive smile. She hoped Tre wasn't rude.

Rico was shocked. *Her brother*. He would have never thought that. Tiffany was in a class of her own, and so was the clown ass, tough guy wannabe that was approaching them. Rico didn't say another word. He wasn't sure how the situation was going to play out. He knew Tre would probably recognize him, but he hoped that on the strength of Tiffany, they could talk it out as men. The situation could turn ugly if Tre forced his hand.

"Wassup Tiff?" Tre asked, once he got to the door. He glanced at Rico. "Who dis?" he asked.

"Ummm, Rico this is Tre, and Tre, this is Rico. The guy I've been talking about for the past couple months," she said, introducing the pair.

Rico stood quietly in mental awe. He couldn't believe that Tre really didn't recognize him.

"Wassup fam?" Rico said. The moment was surreal to him.

"Wassup," Tre responded with a light nod, seemingly uninterested. He had a lot on his mind and was literally on the verge of a mental breakdown. Tiffany was surprised by Tre's lackluster mood and was eager to find out what was on his mind *and* what brought him to her place at such an unconventional hour.

"You look kind of familiar. We met before?" Tre asked, glancing back at Rico and trying to quickly place his face.

"Na, but if you're a brother of Tiffany's, then you're one of mine," Rico stated. He wanted to end the encounter on a good note. Now wasn't the time for Tre to come to his senses and realize where they had met.

"Listen bae, Ima hit you up when I get to the crib," Rico said to Tiffany. "Tre ... nice meeting you," he added before walking off down the hall. The whole time he walked, he discreetly glanced over his shoulder to make sure no one tried to creep him. He trusted Tiffany, but Tre — he didn't trust him no further than he could spit.

14

Tiffany took a seat on her couch. She was in shock over what Tre had just revealed to her. She couldn't believe what he had just said. It couldn't be true.

"Jesus Christ, Tre? Are you out of your mind?" she asked in disbelief.

Just when she thought Tre couldn't fuck up more than he already had, he proved her wrong. She rubbed her temples to ease the tension she felt forming in her head. She looked at Tre for an explanation.

"I fucked up. I know. But I need you to keep quiet about this. I need to lay low," he admitted desperately.

He had told her about robbing Pedro and that things had went haywire. He needed to stay there for the night, as well as hide his money until he found somewhere else to put it.

"Tonight Tre. That's it. And then you have to find a way to fix this shit. You can't bring that bullshit over here. You better hope — better yet, *pray*, that Pedro doesn't find out it was you. If he does, it's going to be a fuckin shit storm."

Tiffany got up from the couch and walked off. The drama never ended with Tre. As much as she loved her brother, her father was right; he was a fuck-up. She didn't even bother to get into a long conversation about why he did what he did, and why he chose to do it to Pedro. It was pointless.

Tre was selfish, and he was going to drag everyone down behind his bullshit. Some things, people just shouldn't do. There was no morale guiding Tre. That flaw, along with his greed was sure to ruin him — or worse, ruin their father.

———

Antonio sat quietly on the couch as he watched his two children enter the front door of their home. Although they were far from perfect, he thanked God for them. He was still stunned by what he had found out just moments earlier.

"You okay Daddy?" Tiffany asked, looking at Antonio strangely before placing her purse on the console table next to the entryway. Antonio was sitting on the couch quietly, staring off into space, with not a stitch of electricity on around him. She figured something had to be up.

"Remember Pedro?" he quietly asked them, finally making eye contact.

"Yeah of course," Tiffany answered. She already knew what he was about to say. She kicked off her shoes by the door and prepared to join her father on the couch.

"Well someone robbed him and murdered his son," he replied solemnly.

Tiffany instantly felt weak. "Oh my God," she exclaimed with a gasp before quickly covering her mouth with her hand. She didn't even bother to look at her brother. He had deliberately left out the most important piece of his sick ass puzzle — the fact that Pedro's son had been murdered in their botched robbery. This was bad. *Really fucking bad.*

"Damn," Tre exclaimed, growing uneasy. "Do they know who did it?" he asked, faking empathy. Tiffany shot her brother a look of death as her father turned to face him. Tre saw it, but he didn't care. He had to know exactly how much Pedro already knew.

"Not yet, but they will. They took a lot of drugs and they

will surface soon. The streets talk ... And when they do, they will also bleed."

Tre swallowed the hard lump that had formed in his throat. He had no idea what the fuck he had just got himself into. Mentally, he wasn't ready for it. He was quickly learning that with real shit, came real consequences.

"The funeral is in a few days. Viewing is tomorrow. Be prepared to go and pay your respects."

Both Tiffany and Tre nodded quietly. Tre didn't even bother to protest since he knew that his father would have it no other way. There was nothing more left to say. From that point forward, all everyone could do was wait and see how the chain of events unfolded.

"Tre if this shit gets out."

"Lower your fucking voice," Tre demanded, looking around nervously. Their father was right in the other room.

"Fuck you Tre," Tiffany growled, stepping into his face so he could hear her better. "If you think I'm lying to Daddy for you, then you're fucking retarded," she added.

"Tiff," Tre begged, as he looked into her eyes. Fear shown in them. She wasn't sure what he was actually afraid of; the pending consequences from Pedro, or their father.

"You can't say nothing to anyone about this — and I mean anyone. Not even Dad."

"I will not lie for you Tre." Tiffany took a seat on her bed. She felt ill and wanted to lie down. No good would come of what had transpired. She predicted chaos in the very near future.

"Please Tiffany. You don't have to lie. Just don't say nothing," he begged.

"Tre," Tiffany said slowly. She rubbed her forehead in frustration before looking at her brother.

"You have no idea what you have done do you?" she asked. "You murdered his *son*," she said angrily. "His *son*,

Tre. He will see to it that everyone involved will pay. And he will find out who did it. It's only a matter of time. And when he does," she paused. "It will probably be a fucking war — a war that you, not Drew, and not fucking Spice, are ready for. Pedro has ties to people you wouldn't believe. He's richer than you think and a lot more powerful than you think. You fucked up big time," she said solemnly. "Not even Daddy is going to be ready for this shit. And you want me to leave him blind to what's taking place around him. I won't do it Tre. You tell him. Or I will," she threatened. "He has to know."

Tre swallowed hard. "I'll tell him. Just give me a few days," he agreed.

15

ALTHOUGH THE VIEWING HAD ONLY LASTED AN HOUR, IT FELT like a century to Tre, who was dying to leave. It was one of the worst situations he had ever been in. The guilt was eating him alive. He couldn't take it when he witnessed Anna literally wail in her husbands' arms over their slain child.

For the first time since Christopher was killed, Tre finally felt true remorse. Even after accidentally gunning down a seven-year old child, he never truly saw the aftermath of his actions until he saw Christopher's grieving mother. Her sobs were so deep they shook the room. No one could truly understand the magnitude of her pain.

Tre had done everything he could think of to get out of coming, but his father wouldn't take no for answer. Now that it was over, his plan was to make a quiet dash to the car. He could not face either of the grieving parents. It was all too much.

Just as he murmured his 10th "excuse me" and squeezed through the cracks of dozens of people, Tre heard his father call his name.

"Tre," he waved. "Over here." After spotting him through the crowds of attendants, Antonio gestured for him to join him and Tiffany so they could offer their condolences and leave. As he approached, he saw Tiffany in a tight embrace with Anna, while Pedro gloomily stared into space.

Tre began to sweat profusely under his fitted shirt as he walked up and stood beside his father, who was now shaking Pedro's hand and telling him how sorry he was for his loss. When he was finished, he released his hand from Pedro's. It was Tre's turn. A nervous lump had formed in his throat, but he did his best to rid himself of it. He looked at Pedro. The side of his face was swollen and had turned black and purple from where he had been assaulted.

Tre went to speak. "I know words can't express how you must feel ..."

In one instant, Tre's voice, when he spoke, stopped Pedro dead in his track and brought him to life at the same time. The feeling he had at the time Christopher was shot, washed back over him. It was *his* voice. Tre had been one of the intruders in his home that night. It was all starting to become clear.

PART II

16

———

THE VOICE WAS UNFORGETTABLE, AND FOR A MOMENT, PEDRO felt as if he were reliving Christopher's last moments. It felt like a hazy case of déjà vu. With his thoughts racing wildly, Pedro peered into the eyes of the man with that unforgettable voice. His heart rate began to accelerate. He remembered those eyes ... *and that voice* ... He would never forget that voice. It was one of the same voices that spoke before his son was murdered. He had no doubt that he was standing before his son's killer.

Tears of anguish began to burn Pedro's eyes and quickly ran down his face. His expression changed from that of sadness and grief, to anger and pure hatred. Tre continued to stare blankly, oblivious to the fact that he had been discovered.

"I'm truly sorry for your loss. If there's anything I can do," he said, before extending his hand for a shake.

Slowly releasing his grip from his wife's arm, Pedro's chest began to heave while the tears continued to run. It was then that he saw red — then black.

Without warning, Pedro lunged at Tre with the viciousness of a rabid dog. He swung wildly, landing several blows against Tre's head and chest, before finally resting his hands tightly around his neck. Tre, who had been caught off guard, was no match for the older man who seemed to possess abnormal strength due to his rage. Gasping for breath, tears from pressure formed in Tre's eyes as Pedro tried to literally choke the life out of him.

Family and friends in attendance did their best to intervene between the two. It had caught everyone off guard. No one questioned his actions. They simply thought he was having a nervous breakdown from the traumatic ordeal of losing his son. It took three people to pull Pedro off Tre, who was now red and coughing profusely while leaning against a built-in bench at the funeral home.

"Fucks going on?" Antonio asked angrily. While Tre talked to Pedro, he had made brief conversation with a few people he had had met through his mentor. The small talk he had engaged in caused him and Tiffany to stray away from Tre. Antonio now wished he had kept his son by his side. He had saw the commotion and rushed over to see what was going on. From the looks of things, his son had been attacked.

Pedro was now on the floor being restrained by five people. He had given up on trying to fight his way back to Tre. He now just lay on the ground crying. His pain was raw and Antonio had never seen a man so strong, in such a weak mental state.

"Tre what happened? Are you ok?" Antonio asked, as he looked down at his son.

"I'm good," Tre responded, still hunched over and struggling to catch his breath. "He just jumped on me ... For no reason at all — shits crazy." He rubbed at his neck and stood up. He was ready to get the hell out of there.

Seeing Antonio over his son, Anna went over to try and smooth things over. She liked Antonio and didn't want any bad blood between him and her husband. For all she knew, Pedro had lost it and it was all just a big misunderstanding.

"Antonio honey, I'm so sorry," she said sadly, as she took his hand into hers. She looked weary and ten times older than the last time he had saw her. "Pedro is taking this so hard." She choked back tears. "We all are. But he, he's breaking down. He's going blank and lashing out as everyone ... I am so sorry." She reached up and hugged Antonio. He reciprocated.

"Please forgive him. Give him a few days and he will be back to his normal self. Expect him to call with an apology for Tre."

Antonio nodded. He was still angry, but he didn't allow Anna to see it. She too was broken, and he understood. He understood Pedro's anger. He knew he would feel the same way if it were one of his own kids. Antonio decided he would let it go. He had known Pedro for many years and loved his friend; however, that would be the first and the only time he lay a hand on his son, as no one came before his family. Bullets would fly first.

17

"THAT WAS FUCKING CRAZY. WHAT THE FUCK JUST happened?" Antonio asked aloud to no one in particular. They were now in his car and heading away from Christopher's viewing — turned circus. That was the only way to describe it.

"I don't know," Tre said in response, while ignoring the ugly look his sister was giving him. He knew she wanted to tell their father what was *really* going on. Tiffany felt like Tre was putting her in a very difficult position. While she longed to protect her brother, she hated that her father was blind to the events unfolding around him.

"Dude just lost it," Tre continued.

Loosening his silk tie from around his neck, Antonio sighed. "Yeah. I probably would have lost it too if something had happened to one of you two," he admitted.

"Word," Tre said. That was all he could think of. Although he felt sorry about what happened to Christopher, he wasn't going to comment much on it to avoid implicating himself.

Tre looked over to Tiffany. She looked worried. He was going to have a talk with her as soon as they got back to the house. Since finding out Christopher had been killed in the robbery, she had been pressuring him with ultimatums: tell their father, or she would. He had been keeping tabs on her to make sure her and their father weren't ever alone together long. Since the robbery, Antonio had been keeping them super close and hadn't even been allowing Tiffany to go back to her condo unaccompanied.

"This is exactly why I'm out," Antonio argued.

After Christopher's death, Pedro had stopped movement completely. The streets were dry, and Antonio figured that he would bow out graciously. He didn't even want a new shipment. He was done.

"The streets have love for no one," Antonio added. "I've seen some the realest nigga's die in them — a jealousy, a beef, a female. One of many reasons you can easily be killed. I'm done."

Antonio wasn't worried about money. He had lots of money tied up in the streets, and once he collected it and added it to what he already had tucked, he was good.

It was then and there that he decided, he was truly and officially done.

18

"Tre you've gotta tell Daddy about what happened. You no longer have a choice in the matter. You either tell him or *I* will," Tiffany threatened later that day after their father had dropped them off to his house. Antonio told them he had some things to handle so as soon as he left, Tiffany wasted no time confronting Tre about confessing his wrongs.

The scene from the viewing at the funeral home was like a stain in her mind that, as much as she tried to, she couldn't seem to erase. What made the situation worse was seeing her Dad looking like a deer caught in headlights, oblivious to what was taking place right in his own circle and city.

"Listen Tiff. Pedro just lost it. He couldn't have known it was me because it was three of us. We all had on masks. There's no way he knows. Besides, he had all his nigga's in the building. Don't you think that if he knew it was me, he would've had me touched right then and there?" he asked, trying to reason with his sister, and convince himself as well.

"Well obviously something was up since he choked the shit out of ya ass," she replied snidely. Tre wasn't fooling anybody. She knew Pedro just like he did, and judging by the way Pedro reacted, he had to suspect Tre in some way.

"Whatever," he said waving his sister off. Tre no longer wanted to discuss the matter. He was already embarrassed by the incident, and she wasn't making it any better throwing in his face the fact that he had been choked out by an old-head.

"I don't want to hear shit you gotta say Tre. You either tell him — or I will. I'm not going to sit around and let Daddy walk around blind —"

Tiffany's ringing cell phone in the next room interrupted the argument between her and her brother. Tre was glad. She was getting on his nerves with her constant pestering. He had enough on his mind, and she wasn't making it any better by putting more pressure on him.

Upset, Tiffany walked off to answer her phone and tell whoever it was she didn't feel like talking.

"Hello," she asked with an exaggerated huff, after snatching her phone off the kitchen counter.

"You have a collect call from — Rico Ortega, an inmate at Wilton County Detention Center."

Tiffany's heart pounded in her chest as she gripped the phone tightly to her ear and waited for the automated message to play out. She instantly began to worry and wonder what happened for Rico to be locked up. After letting the recording play out, she pressed zero and answered the phone.

"Rico baby what happened? Are you alright?" she asked as soon as the call connected.

"Hey babe, I'm good. I got bagged last night on a bullshit charge," he responded, glad to hear her voice and happy she had answered from the unknown number. He had been locked up since last night and although it was late in the afternoon, it was the first call he had been able to make.

"Damn Rico. Are you gonna get out?" she asked, not truly understanding what was going on.

"Yeah, I'll be out in a few hours. I'm just waiting to see the commissioner, so I can get a bail. Soon as I get that, I'll call my people and they'll come pay that shit.," he assured her.

"Ok good babe. Is there anything I can do? You want me to call anyone for you?" she asked, wanting to help out her man.

"Na. I'm good. I'll take care of everything. You just be ready to see me when I get out of here later."

He appreciated her desire to help, but he wanted her to stay far away from his world. A part of him wanted to build with Tiffany and grow old with her, but the other part of him knew he wasn't even close to being done with the streets. When he was ready to settle down, he knew he wanted it to be with Tiffany, and he also knew he wanted their life to be as normal and legit as possible.

"Ok Rico ... I love you," Tiffany said for the first time with sincerity. Just the thought of losing him had her emotional.

"I love you too bae," he responded. He had for a while, but never had the courage to say so. "I'll hit you up as soon as I get out of here."

"Okay," she said, before hanging up. She placed her phone back on her desk and sighed. If it wasn't one thing, it was another. She walked back into her living room and saw her brother sitting on the couch. She wasn't done with him.

"Who was that?" he asked. Tiffany looked around strangely.

"Umm, last time I checked, my phone rang, not yours. It was — none of your business," she said sarcastically.

"Whatever," he replied nonchalantly.

"And back to ya ass anyway. Like I said before. You either tell Daddy, or I will." Tre looked over at her with a blank stare.

"I mean it," she continued. "Tell him, or I will," she repeated with finality.

"I fucking heard you the first time. Damn," he snapped. "I'm gonna tell him. You just be quiet and don't say shit to him. I'll do it my way." She was getting on his nerves. She didn't have to keep saying the same shit over and over. He also didn't appreciate her threatening to rat him out.

"Yeah, whatever. You just do it soon," she replied before getting up and walking out of the room.

19

'PEDRO BABY, ARE YOU SURE?" ANNA ASKED WITH A SNIFFLE. She took a seat on the nearby leather couch and placed her hand against her chest to indicate her shock from the news. She was at a loss for words. Still stricken from grief, she didn't' know how much more she could take. Everything that was happening around her was beginning to make her weak: her sons' sudden death, her husband's erratic, and violent behavior, and now this.

"I'm positive Anna," he said. "It was his voice. I will never forget those voices ... And then I looked into his eyes. He was one of them. It was him. I know it," he said with finality. "Ellos pagarán!" he yelled out unexpectedly in Spanish. That meant, *"they would pay."* He would make sure of that.

He took a seat at his desk and sat quietly for a minute, pondering in his thoughts. He had to calm down and think things through before he started making phone calls. His main concern, which also happened to feel like a big, dark cloud looming over him, was the question of whether Antonio was involved. He didn't want to believe that he was. He had watched Antonio grow into the man he was today. The man that he knew was loyal and had integrity. He no longer knew what to believe. In this day and age, cash was king, and people were no longer who they proclaimed to be. Pedro wanted to pour himself a drink but decided against it. He wanted to have a clear head when he made his decisions.

"Call nuestro sobrino," he said, referring to their nephew. It was Anna's late sister's son, but Pedro had too, watched him grow up from birth. He also happened to be his top lieutenant. He trusted him with every detail of his business and knew that he would also be the one to quickly and quietly resolve this issue. He was literally Pedro's secret weapon. His nephew wasn't well known, and he was also very discreet and quiet when it came to handling business. His most important characteristic that made him invaluable was the fact that he was half-Spanish, born to a Mexican mother. He was also the African American offspring of a drug-dealing Navy Commander who got both of them killed in a drug ambush behind his shady dealings.

With his creamy light brown skin and his ability to past for a full-fledged black person, it made his nephew extremely versatile. He could speak fluent Spanish and arrange deals with high-ranking drug cartel, as well as run a strong team of blacks, who in this city, ruled the streets — or so they thought.

"He wasn't at the service and I want to know why," he stated before grabbing a Cuban cigar off his desk. He hadn't been in the house long and it was already his second one.

"I tried to call him earlier, but his phone was going to voicemail," she responded wearily.

Staring off into space, Pedro spoke slowly. "I am going to avenge Christopher's death. Everyone involved. Everyone who knew ... will die."

The coldness in his light brown eyes revealed to Anna that he meant every word he spoke. The Pedro she knew and loved, was normally sweet and jovial. The man in front of her now, was angry and vengeful. He had become the murderous Pedro that he did his best to shield her from. She had heard stories and she knew he had a dark side, but never had she witnessed it.

"Pedro please," Anna begged as she got up from where she was seated on the couch. She walked over to her husband, took his hand, and slightly knelt so she could look him into his eyes.

"There has been enough blood spilled. We have enough money to move back to Mexico and live like royalty for God's sake. I already lost my son ... I don't want to lose my husband too." She wiped away her tears and waited for him to respond.

"My mind is made up," he said before breaking away from her grip and getting up from his desk to make the call himself. A cloud of death would soon fall over the city. He would make sure of it.

———

Antonio had just dropped off his kids and was now pulling up to the parking lot of his new office building that was in the heart of downtown. He had recently signed the lease and was now working on furnishings, signs, and his new business logo.

Pulling into one of his three reserved parking spaces, Antonio wasted no time exiting his car and heading into the single story building. He had come for a very important reason and was eager to see if his hard work had paid off for him.

After locking the doors behind him and securing the alarm of his new building, Antonio headed to his office. It was situated in the far corner of the building. Tiffany's office would be in the opposite corner. She was like his second pair of eyes and the way they were situated, they would be able to see everything that was going on. Once he entered his office, he made sure to immediately lock the door behind him. Although his security company had already installed his state-of-the-art system, he had long ago formed a habit of locking the door behind him when he was engaged in business. He never wanted to give someone the opportunity to barge in on him.

Antonio walked over to the couch that lined half of his office wall. A few days ago, it sat in his home office, but today, it now aligned his wall and sat to the right of his desk of his new building. That same regular looking, blue couch also happened to have a built-in safe underneath the cushions. No one would ever suspect. His purpose for coming to his office tonight was so he could sit down and count the cash he had on hand. It had been a while.

Forty-five minutes later, after carefully counting stacks of $10,000, Antonio had about $85,000 in cash. He smiled. Although it wasn't a lot compared to how much work he had moved over the years, he was happy. He had property and businesses that continued to generate him income, as well as a vacation home, his private residence, and several cars. He had tons of assets that included an IRA , as well as stocks, bonds, and trust funds for his kids. He figured once he picked up all his cash tied up in the streets, he would have around $125,000. His intention was to tuck that into an offshore account and let it grow since his lifestyle was funded off the income generated by his business.

After securing his money back into his safe, Antonio headed home. As he drove, the scene at the funeral continued to play in his mind. Although he hadn't witnessed Pedro touch his son, it still disturbed him that it had even happened. He wanted to call Pedro and find out what was going on; however, he figured he would show his respect by giving him some more time to mourn is son. He knew at some point they would have to sit down like men and discuss what had occurred. Antonio was a man just like Pedro, so out of respect, some sort of explanation would have to be given for his sons' assault. It was only right.

20

As soon as Antonio returned from his office and got settled in, Tre took a quick shower and managed to slip out of the crib unnoticed. Although his father had eased up some, he still monitored both he and Tiffany's every move. Tre didn't have time to argue with his father and didn't feel like answering his questions about his whereabouts. He turned his phone on vibrate and hopped in his Cadillac SRX to head to the hood. He was happy; he had just gotten it back that day. The body shop had done a great job of repairing the car. He couldn't even tell that it had been before riddled with bullet holes.

Earlier, Drew had texted Tre and said they all needed to meet up for something important. That's exactly where he was on his way to. Tre knew it pertained to one of two things: money or drugs. The cousins were eager to flood the hood with the dope they had seized. Although Tre was also ready to make some real money, he wasn't too fond of the idea of moving stolen dope so early. Shit was still hot, and patience was a virtue in the matter. If they did move, they had to do so strategically and cautiously. The wrong move, and Pedro would be hip. While Drew and Spice didn't have shit to lose, he had a lot.

Picking up his phone he decided to call Drew to see

exactly where he was. He figured he had a minute or so to burn while he sat at a stale red light waiting for it to turn green.

"Yo, what's popping?" Tre asked, as soon as Drew answered.

"Aint shit, just waiting on you nigga," he said while he continued to serve the fiends hand to hand that were lined up. The increased activity on the block was crazy and he couldn't wait until Tre arrived, so he could see it first-hand.

"Well I'm on my way now. I just got my whip back. Yawl nigga's in the hood?" Tre asked, still waiting patiently for the blood red light to change.

"Like mailboxes and stop signs," Drew replied.

"Bet. I'm on my way. I be there in ten," Tre stated before hanging up.

When Tre got to the hood, the shit was booming. He had never saw that amount of activity on that block before. He knew something was up. Fiends were coming down the block left and right to cop from the back of Pat's house. They had actually formed a line; it was surreal.

Tre parked his red Cadillac on the side of the house before hopping out and heading over to where Drew and Spice were posted in the back. As soon as he walked up, both cousins smiled widely before hopping up to greet him. At this point, befriending Tre was the equivalent to a winning lottery ticket. He had come through. The block was pulling in thousands from the dope they snatched from Pedro. The quality was top-notch and dope fiends from the entire hood were finding their way to them to cop.

"Damn my nigga. You finally came out of hiding," Drew said to Tre jokingly. Although they had spoken to him, they hadn't seen him since the robbery took place.

"Fuck both of yawl," he replied. "I see yawl got shit clicking out here! What's good?" he asked while peering around at the scene.

"Fa sho," Drew responded. "Instead of sitting on that

work, we decided to break some of it down and see how it move on the block. As you can see, the shit speaks for itself."

"I see it's popping ... But don't you think it's a little too early to be moving that shit?" Tre asked wearily. He was all for making money, but he wasn't trying to write his own death wish. "What if Pedro or someone else finds out we moving his shit?" he asked.

"Fuck Pedro," Spice answered without hesitation. "Right now, we going hand in hand, so the only way he would know some shit is if one of these dope fiend mufucka's tell him — and that aint gonna happen. They too busy trying to get their next fix. We got the best shit out in these streets. The purest. And from what I heard, Pedro ain't delivering no work right now. The streets are dry as fuck."

They spoke freely and paid no attention to the fiends surrounding them. They were all either: high, sick or desperate, if not all three. They were only worried about one thing: getting their next fix.

"True story," Drew continued. "They coming back left and right — with any and everything. We got a new TV in the crib, a computer, air conditioner. Shit, one of them mufucka's even came with a fucking fish tank full of water — *and* the fish," he laughed. "You know I hopped on that shit. Put that shit right in Pat's crib. Try to spruce up that raggedy mufucka," he added with a chuckle.

"Yeah aight, whatever," Tre said, not particularly amused. "So, when you breaking down the bread?" he asked.

"Nigga. Chill the fuck out," Drew stated with a frown. "You gon get ya fucking cut. Soon as we off all this shit, we gon split it three ways."

He looked over at Tre and thought, *he should be lucky he was getting anything.* He wasn't a hustler and knew nothing about drugs despite the fact his dad had hustled for years. He wasn't doing shit but was still ready to hound them about some paper.

"Bet," Tre said finally cracking a satisfied smile. Money was his language.

"You know this the start of the takeover," Drew said with a sinister smile.

"What the fuck are you talking about?" Tre asked, looking to Spice who too, was smiling.

"Nigga we bout to take the city over," Spice said confidently.

"Yeah aight," he responded nonchalantly. Although they left out of Pedro's house with several bricks of Heroin, they didn't find the rest of the work. He must have had the rest of the shipment tucked somewhere. The way the night unfolded, they didn't have time to search for the remaining product. A couple bricks of dope and $100,000 in cash wasn't enough to take over the streets. Nigga's like Pedro, take shits on that.

"You'll see nigga. Wit ya pop gone, the East will soon be ours. Soon we'll be moving enough work to start supplying them niggas on the West too. We just gotta find a plug. For now though, I'm about to close shop," Drew said, as he served the last of customers. The others would just be without.

"Tomorrow, ima hand this block over to some lil niggas. Spice done already put a team of youngin's together who on board to get this money. And we already got some shit lined up with this nigga name Jimbo. A nigga I used to go to school with that got a trap house out here on the East. The spot he got won't interfere with our shit, plus he good peoples and right now the price and quality he getting isn't up to par. We can definitely give him a better deal once we move this shit and secure a plug. We out though. Bout to head to Starlite's. You wit it?" Drew asked Tre.

"Hell yeah," he said, not really feeling it.

Tre felt like they should be laying low since they had just done major dirt only a few days ago. From what he saw, the money and come-up was going to Drew and Spice heads; nevertheless, he half-heartedly went along with the plan. He hadn't yet told the two about his encounter with Pedro at the viewing. He knew they would clown him big time and he wasn't trying to hear the jokes about getting strolled on. He figured at some point soon, he would have to let them know that Pedro might know a little more than they thought.

———

The call from Rico finally came to Tiffany around eleven at night. After informing her he wasn't far and she would be the first stop he was making after leaving his home, she hurried to take a shower. She was glad he was safe and wanted to show him how much she missed him. Rico had also missed her and had temporarily ditched his plans he had made with a couple of his lieutenants and Latisha to meet up at Starlite's. They could wait; Tiffany came first.

About an hour had passed and Tiffany had stepped out of the shower and was now lotioning herself down with one of Victoria's Secret's signature scent's, Love Spell. Once done, she unwrapped her wavy hair and then proceeded to finger comb it to add volume. She slipped on a sexy black, La Perla lace teddy that hugged her small frame in all the right places. She looked down at her four-inch Jimmy Choo stiletto's and smiled. She went to the mirror and admired her attire, smiling in approval. She had to admit, she looked good enough to eat. It was all or nothing, and she hoped Rico liked it.

After dimming the lights, Tiffany rummaged through her linen closet to find some fragrance to add to the air and enhance the mood. After some extensive digging, she managed to find a few candle sets she had bought from Bed Bath and Beyond. Luckily, they were all the same color. After careful application, red and white candles adorned the coffee table and lined the floor from the entrance, all the way to the back where her room was. The smell of strawberries and vanilla wafted through the home, creating an exotic and pleasant scent.

While she waited for Rico to text his arrival, Tiffany went and set her music system to her favorite album by Trey Songz: Ready. While she let the veteran R&B crooner serenade through the house, she went and took out a glass bowl and cut up some fresh strawberries she had just bought. She looked around her refrigerator and spotted some whipped cream to top them with. After spreading a generous layer of cream across the berries, she placed the bowl by her bedside, along with the bottle of sweet, red wine she had already been drinking on, and two glasses. As soon as she sat down the glasses, she heard her phone ding lightly from the kitchen counter. She went to check it, and just as she suspected, it was Rico announcing he was heading into her building. She walked briskly to her room and grabbed her robe to throw on. She wanted to surprise him later.

When Rico finally arrived at the door and was let in, he was taken back by the sound of romantic R&B music filling the air, as well as the effort Tiffany had put into the night. He was surprised since he wasn't expecting anything from her out of the norm. They had never been fully intimate. Kissing, cuddling, and sexual frustration is what their relationship consisted of. Initially attracted by her beauty, he had grown to love her as a person. She was smart, caring, and everything he wanted in a woman. Tiffany didn't care about his money; she just wanted him for him. She encouraged him and did her best to uplift him despite knowing that he was in the streets. Their lack of intimacy hadn't run him off; he got sex on the regular, so he was cool. Nevertheless, he was becoming excited by the mere thought of being with her.

"Damn bae, all this for me," he said, as he looked around with an appreciative smile. He watched in awe as rows of candles flickered softly through the house.

"Yea. I missed you," she admitted, as she leaned up and gave him a long kiss, her arms wrapped tightly around his neck.

Rico smiled again. He knew this night would be different

for sure. The kiss she gave him spoke volumes. It was needy; it was desperate; it was passionate.

Breaking her tight embrace, Tiffany took Rico's hand and with a mischievous grin, led him to her room.

"I gotta surprise for you?" she said seductively. The wine was having its way with her mind-state and that is exactly what she had planned. She had already had two glasses and her confidence level was at an all-time high. She had some serious plans for Rico tonight.

"Oh yeah? What's that?" Rico asked. He certainly had some ideas.

"Go sit and wait for it," she said with a smile, ushering Rico to her bed. He wasted no time following her demands.

"I'll be right back," she said, as she walked off.

Rico kicked off his shoes and made himself comfortable on the large bed. His heart was beating in his chest and the felt the muscle in his pants begin to throb with it. He waited patiently, looking to the door for Tiffany to return. While he waited, he noticed the song abruptly change. He listened. It was still Trey Songz, but he was now singing about making love for the first time.

You looking to good. What 'chu standing over there by yourself for? Won't you come over here ...

A few seconds later, Tiffany appeared at the door. Rico looked at her and his jaw dropped. She was stunning. The lace piece she had on highlighted every curve that existed on her body. He could even see her nipples peeking through the stretchy fabric. He felt himself stiffen even more. He wanted her bad.

Tiffany's creamy skin glowed against the candle light, making her appear exotic. She looked like a princess. Rico looked down to her feet and felt himself become concrete from the sight of her perfectly polished white toes peeking through her strappy caged sandal booties. He looked back up at Tiffany and stared. Her soft, wavy, black curls dangling past her shoulders. Trey's melodies continued to wade through the house and it was like the lyrics were written especially for him. It was exactly how he was feeling.

Ya hair long. I just wanna pull it. Baby wait a minute. Don't be timid. Don't be shy. You so fly. I just wanna take you on a ride.

"Surprise," she mouthed, as the music continued to play. Rico didn't respond. He just motioned for her to come to him. She complied and sauntered sexily to him, being careful to take her time. She didn't want to rush the moment. Rico moved to the edge of the bed and gently wrapped his arms around her waist. She leaned down and kissed him, before gently pulling away. She smiled and poured him a glass of wine and then proceeded to dig out a few strawberries to feed him. He looked at his woman lovingly and knew he could get used to coming home to her every night. Without a doubt, he was in love with her. His mind briefly shifted back to her brother. *Her brother.* She alone was enough for him to squash the beef. If it meant a chance at a future with her, then he was willing to let it go.

After kissing on one another and continuing to hand feed each other strawberries, the two talked, laughed, and sipped on wine until they were feeling nice and well past tipsy. Tiffany flirted non-stop until Rico was fed-up and could no longer take the teasing. Feeling hot and like he was ready to explode, he leaned in and gave Tiffany another kiss, this one longer and more passionate. She didn't fight back her desires. She had been waiting for him to take charge. He reached under her and firmly cupped her soft behind to pull her closely to him. Her lips parted slightly, the excitement in her chest slowly seeping through them in short, hot breaths. She touched him. Her fingers digging desperately in his skin. Her body immediately began to ache in spots she never knew pain could exist in. Rico released her and climbed on top of her. His mouth grazed her neck and the sizzling heat he produced, along with his desperate pants, caused Tiffany's skin to tingle. She wanted him to conquer her, and she wanted it badly.

Tonight, was different. She was no longer in control. He was, and she loved it. She closed her eyes gently and imagined what it would be like for his lips and tongue to explore every inch of her. Just as she had become consumed in her thoughts, Rico wasted no time showing her. He gently pulled down the sides of her lingerie and teased her breasts with hungry sucks and long, wet licks. Her chest heaved as she tried to control herself. Her pussy ached almost painfully. It was begging to be touched, begging to be kissed, and begging to be penetrated.

Rico continued to kiss her sweetly from her forehead, to her chest, down to her toes. He paid special attention to every corner of her body, being fair and leaving nothing neglected. As he explored her, she had managed to free herself from the clothing holding her body captive. She was now naked, and Rico smiled. While he smiled in admiration at the beautiful sight before him, he also smiled that he could now fully have his way with her. He kissed her stomach ... Then her thighs ... And finally made his way to her center. When his warm, slippery mouth finally met Tiffany's love nest, she almost exploded. She felt like she had died and gone to heaven. She dug her fingers furiously into the sheets. She needed something to hold onto since her body was about to let go. The feeling was intense, and she soon felt her body give way, collapse, and cave into the bed.

Tiffany embraced the feeling that Rico provided and gave herself to him that night. It was magical. Fighting the dizziness and weakness her body now felt, Tiffany tried to get up so she could return the favor, but Rico would not let her. He used his body to keep her from moving. He had switched things around on her completely. She had started it off all about him,and he was going to finish it, focused completely on her. Rico undressed and took his time entering her. He wanted the night to last, for her sake, and his. Her tight, wet canal welcomed his manhood and there was a moment he almost gasped. Tiffany moaned softly. She had been waiting for this moment and he felt heavenly inside her. Rico looked down at her in awe. He loved her, and she felt so good to him — so warm. They were a perfect fit. Her sugary walls dripped nectar and gripped Rico tightly while he stroked in and out of her in pure bliss. She was everything he imagined. Everything he had hoped for. For him, that moment sealed the deal. When he came, he thought about marriage, children, and having Tiffany in his life forever.

Tiffany too, was overwhelmed by the feelings Rico created within her. When they were finished, Rico held her tightly, and without speaking it, the two vowed that they were one. She was all for him, and he was all for her. Rico was willing to cut off any female he dealt with to prove that. Tiffany didn't even have to ask. He loved her, and he was going to show her.

21

When Tre parked his Cadillac in the parking lot of Starlite's and stepped out with his team, he was happy that he had worn something presentable since he didn't know he would end up there. He looked down at his lay and brushed off some stray lint on his blue, denim Robin's jeans. He was simply dressed, with a plain black Polo shirt, and a pair of high-top all black Maison Margiela's. Even though he was plain, he still looked like money with a lone, large gold Herringbone chain resting in the middle of his chest. Of course, everything courtesy of Antonio. His father was the reason he shined and looked like he was winning.

Drew and Spice however, had went all out, buying brand new Polo gear to party at the shabby club. Not used to having access to large sums of cash, they were spending their recently acquired money like it grew on trees.

After paying the bouncer's $400 so all three could carry in their guns, Tre, Drew and Spice found themselves in the clubs' VIP section. Although it wasn't much in the small club, it still spoke volumes for the trio and solidified their newly acquired baller status. Lined off with velvet rope on the second floor, the VIP section was visible from the front entrance. Three sections of white u-shaped couches and coffee tables were the only thing that separated the private spaces in VIP but that didn't stop Tre, Drew, and Spice from having a good time.

Bottle after bottle, blunt after blunt, the three enjoyed the obvious perks of having money in the privacy of VIP. Across the room also in VIP, Latisha quietly tapped one of Rico's young boys on the arm. "Yo Boobie, those the nigga's that hopped on Rico a couple weeks ago," she said carefully eyeing the trio.

"Where?" he asked looking around.

"Right across from us. I remember the brown skinned dude. He was the one that tried to holla. The other two were the ones that jumped on him," she said still looking at them.

Latisha was ghetto fabulous. Off her looks alone, she had set many nigga's up and was as grimey as they came. After being hit in the face by Tre, she gave zero fucks about casually pointing him out to be murdered. After spotting the two, Boobie got up to discuss the move with his team. Latisha sat and waited. She knew as soon as the club let out, shit was going to get real. She couldn't wait.

"Yo Chubs," Boobie said, after walking over to him in the corner and tapping him on the arm. After Latisha pointed out Tre and his crew, he got up and went to see how Chubs wanted to proceed with the information.

"Hold up ma," he said to the shorty he was talking to.

"Wassup?" Chubs asked Boobie. He was about to slide out with the freak, so he wanted him to make it quick.

"Let me holla at you real quick," Boobie said, giving Chubs the eye. His face was serious, indicating something was up.

Without saying a word, Chubs walked away from the girl and stepped off to the side to rap to Boobie. Although Chubs was short, Boobie was shorter, so Chubs leaned down closely towards him, so he could hear whatever it was he needed to speak with him about. Boobie too, was one of Rico's right-hand men and already knew the situation with Drew, Spice and Tre.

"What's good?" Chubs asked. "Something happen?" he asked.

"Na, but you remember the nigga's that got at Rico a few weeks back. Well they over there," he said, before silently peering across the room so Chubs could spot them as well. He quickly spotted the trio enjoying the festivities of the night. Their guard was clearly down, and they seemed to have no cares at all. They looked the same as they did the night at the convenience store. That was until he released his clip on they asses.

"What chu trying do?" Boobie asked. He was always ready for wreck. They weren't super deep. It was only him, Chubs, and Paulie. Rico had invited just those three out and was supposed to show up later himself. Latisha had signed off for his bond earlier, so he could be released. He said he had some business to take care of but would meet up with them later that night. So far, he had been a no-show. Their numbers didn't matter to Boobie though; three cannons were better than three hundred bullets. They were little niggas, but they were thorough enough to wipe out a whole neighborhood.

"Right now, it's a no go. Rico said to wait. He not trying to war with them right now," Chubs said glancing over at the trio. Rico's demands went against everything Chubs believed in. He wanted so bad to bang on them then and there, but Rico was the boss.

"Aight," Boobie said, expressing his hesitance to proceed in that manner. Letting them rock out untouched just didn't sit well with him or the team, but what Rico said was law. Boobie went to walk off, but Chubs tapped him.

"I hear what Rico saying, but if dem nigga's show out, we gon give em dat act right," he said, before patting his waist to indicate he was strapped.

It was 3:40 am and Starlite's had just announced last call for alcohol when Tre, Drew and Spice decided they were ready to go. They had picked up three freaks and were about to head downtown to The La Quinta Hotel for a smut session. It was Spice's idea of a nightcap, with him even agreeing to foot the entire bill for everything.

"Yawl can follow us over the teley," Spice instructed the four girls as he palmed and squeezed at ones' wide, but plump ass." She was Spanish and had light brown eyes and wild, curly hair. She had been the life of the party and Spice knew she probably was the wildest, biggest freak of the bunch.

"Ok boo. The La Quinta right?" another of the three girls asked.

"Yeah," Drew replied for him with a grin. He didn't usually do freaks, but she was definitely the one he wanted. He had been on her top all night and wanted to make sure he was the one who ended up digging out her insides. Although skinny, she had big breasts and danced like she sure knew how to drop it down on not just a metal pole, but a real pole.

"That's $250, right? ... A piece?" the older girl of the trio confirmed. She was brown-skinned and was the prettiest of the bunch. She had that "money over everything" mentality. She wasn't really feeling the nigga's her and her crew were leaving with, so she wanted to make sure she was getting the promised amount. Her box, head, and tricks didn't come cheap.

"Yeah. You gon get ya money. Stop tripping. And for $250 you better be able to do something with that mouth you keep talking shit from," Spice stated. He wasn't playing either. He could go get a little dirty hood bitch to freak out for $50. The only reason he was paying the price they requested was because all four were pretty and said they were from out of town. They were in the VIP section, so he assumed they were about a dollar and weren't broke hoes. They certainly didn't look like it. And frankly, he was excited to be able to fuck on some badder hoes.

"You'll definitely get ya money's worth sweetheart. Soon as I get to the room and touch my paper," she said with an eye roll and a smirk. They weren't new to this.

"Well green means go," Tre stated. He wanted her sassy ass for sure. As much shit as she talked, she had better put on a show. He intended to fuck her so hard she begged for mercy. He loved making examples out of shit talkers. Ass smacking, choking, and hair pulling were all fair game. He was on his Future shit: *he ain't have no manners for no sluts. She was gon get two thumbs in her butt.* Tre laughed to himself at his own joke as he took his last shot of Hennessy. He put down his empty glass and they all made their way towards the entrance with the girls leading the way.

After the last call was announced, many of the patrons began gathering their things to depart. With only twenty minutes left before the lights came on, the party was essentially over. The path to the entrance was congested and with Spice being intoxicated, he began to rudely squeeze past people to hurry out.

"Yo watch where the fuck you going," a short, stocky guy demanded angrily after he was pushed to the side and bumped by Spice.

Out of reflex, Spice spun around to say something but was met with a familiar face. It was Chubs. Spice's eyes did a quick scan of Chubs surroundings. He had a couple of niggas with him and he was also with the light-skinned bitch that was at the club the night the brawl took place. Spice knew that it was the worse place to come face to face with Chubs, but he was always prepared for gun battle — crowded club and all.

Chubs didn't realize his enemies were headed out the same time he was and he was surprised when the person that bumped him turned around to respond to his statement. He usually wouldn't have given a fuck; however, tonight was different. Rico had said to fall back on murdering the three nigga's standing in front of him, and that would prove to be costly. He hadn't been paying attention to the location of his nemesis' since he figured he would be heading out before everyone with the freak bitch he had been talking to.

As soon as Spice looked back, he looked around and immediately drew his gun. Spice had already made a vow to himself that when he saw Chubs, it was on sight. He knew that Chubs would be on the same type time when the opportunity presented itself. In the ghetto world he lived in, it was *kill or be killed*, so he lived by the motto of *squeeze first* to avoid the latter.

Spice didn't have to say anything. As soon as he reached, he looked back at Tre and his cousin, who already knew what time it was after Chubs opened his fat ass mouth. All three of them had their guns out in a matter of seconds. It wouldn't be like the first time when they were caught off guard and unprepared. This time was different. They had the upper hand. With Spice pushing past everyone in a hurry to leave, he was in front of Chubs and his crew. Drew and Tre were right behind Spice, essentially on the side of Chubs and his team. They were literally, almost surrounded.

The first bullet squeezed from Spice's gun, ripped through the chamber and missed Chubs head by inches, shattering rows of bottles behind him at the bar. The second shot aimed at Chubs came from Drew, who managed to hit him underneath his armpit as he struggled to withdraw and lift his own weapon.

"POW! POW! POP! POP" were the sounds of gunfire erupting in the air from multiple guns as Chubs' team and Spice's team opened fire in the small club. With nowhere to run, frantic patrons hit the slippery club floor in sheer terror, while others screamed, ducked, and dived behind bar stools and under tables.

The dark club had become an instant war-zone and resembled a hood version of The Wild West. Chubs and Boobie had run and jumped over the bar for cover, while

Paulie lay crouched in a corner doing his best to hide behind a bar stool. He had been hit in his shoulder and could tell that his arm was also broken. He knew if he tried to fire back he would likely be unsuccessful and would also probably end up dead instead of just wounded. Being caught off guard had put the three of them at a huge disadvantage. If they managed to make it out of the club alive, Rico would not be *asked*, he would rather be *informed* of their intent to war with the East Side. There was no way they could let actions like this be ignored.

Paulie watched as Latisha lay on her stomach on the floor across from him. Both her legs were broken from where people trampled over them as they ran for safety. As soon as gunfire erupted, people began to push one another to get out of the way. Latisha had fallen during the panic and now lay curled up on the floor writhing in pain. She couldn't even move so she used a chair to cover her head. She had no idea the night would end up this way. Glass shattering, bottles dropping, bullets ripping through everything they came in contact with, and pounding feet were all she heard as she covered her ears and screamed, praying that the nightmare would soon be over.

As Spice, Drew, and Tre continued firing, they backed and stumbled their way towards the exit. Teeth clenched, and fingers on their triggers, they released every bullet loaded in their guns. Spice used his screaming Spanish companion as a human shield while he forced his way out of the club safely. All three men were in kill mode and continued to fire until their guns were empty. As soon as the hot July air could be felt on their backs and they could see the orange glow from the city street-lights, they then knew they were alive and safe. Thus, they went into flight mode.

Spice released the Spanish freak with a push causing her to fall over. At that point, she didn't even care. She was happy to be alive. The three men ran full speed back to Tre's car. They tore through the parking lot, engine full throttle, and tires screeching over the pavement.

22

"ARE YOU SURE?" PEDRO ASKED ANDREW, ONE OF THE FEW local dealers he supplied. He too had worked with Pedro for many years and was extremely loyal to him.

"Positive. The young nigga Jimbo has been buying from me for a minute. He came to me a few days ago and said there was some nigga's trying to move a couple," he said referring to kilos of Heroin. "Only a few nigga's around here can supply on that level. These niggas weren't from out of town; they were local. He said he went to school with one of them. While he couldn't recall his government name, he did know he goes by Drew in the streets. When I asked around, he's part of a little trio of nigga's that be on the East. Two of them are true street nigga's and the third is not from around there. I'm willing to bet money, that's Antonio's son," Andrew said, giving Pedro more than an earful.

Right after the robbery, Pedro called and asked his dealers to keep an eye out for anyone trying to unload bricks of Heroin in the immediate and surrounding areas. He knew whoever had robbed him would be trying to get rid of the drugs in exchange for cash. After recognizing Tre's voice, he began to inquire about his friend's son. Things were all starting to make sense and Pedro felt like Antonio either orchestrated the robbery or knew about it. If he did either, he damn sure put on a great show of pretending to be hurt and angry over the situation. One way or another, they were going to be the first to be dealt with.

"So, he copped from him?" Pedro asked, referring to Andrew's client, Jimbo.

"Yeah. Boy said it was good shit too. Just got it from him first thing this morning. I got up out of my own bed and went to look at the shit. It definitely looks like yours," he added.

That was all Pedro needed to hear. It had been signed, stamped, and sealed.

"Say no more. I'll handle everything from here."

Pedro took a small sip out of his glass before picking up his phone and checking the time on it. It was 10:00 am and he had called his nephew an hour ago. He had declared the matter to be of the utmost importance and had told him to drop whatever he was doing and get there.

Pedro had been up all-night replaying everything that had led up to this point. The one thing that stuck out the most to him and kept replaying in his head, was his last meeting with Antonio and how he stated he was done after the last package. As much as he wanted to believe that Antonio wasn't involved, he knew there was no way he couldn't be. It pained him that he had to take the route he was about to take. The sound of his doorbell chiming loudly throughout his home paused his thoughts.

"Pedro!" Anna yelled, as she ushered her nephew through the door with a warm hug and kiss on the cheek.

"Hey baby," Anna said with a smile, while still holding on to her nephew's arm so she could get a good luck at him.

She hadn't seen him in several weeks and had been worried about him. With the lifestyle they lived, anything could happen. He too, was also happy to see his aunt and noticed she looked frail and weary.

"Hey Auntie. I am so sorry I missed the viewing," he added sincerely.

There would be no funeral for Christopher in the states. His body was going to be flown back to Mexico where he would be buried amongst family. Pedro and Anna eventually planned to move back to their home country and would reunite with him in the future.

"It's okay baby. We were just worried is all. I was just glad that you were alright," she added. She led the way to Pedro's office in the back of the house. She made small talk as she walked through the spacious home barefoot.

"After what happened, there was no way we could go through with another service for Christopher here. It was hard enough to see my baby boy lying in a casket, and with Pedro taking it so hard ... It's just too much. The viewing ended up being a disaster. We just no longer know who to trust and your uncle just lost it in there."

"What happened?" he asked with concern.

Anna sighed. "I'll let your uncle tell you," she replied just as they arrived at the door.

"I'll be in the dining room," she said before walking off, so he and her husband could have some privacy. "Come see me before you leave. I'll wrap up some food for you to take with you."

"Thanks Auntie," he said with a smile before going into the room to speak with his uncle.

"Nephew," Pedro said solemnly as he entered the room. He could tell his uncle hadn't slept well lately. His appearance was disheveled and he had bags under his eyes. Judging by his somber expression and demeanor, he knew it was going to be a serious conversation. He closed the door behind him. He walked over to his uncle's desk and sat across from him. He could tell he was angry and wasn't sure if it was because he had missed the viewing, or because of something else.

"What's going on Unc?" he asked.

"I found out who's responsible," Pedro said. His nephew already knew the situation, so he didn't even need to elaborate further.

"Who?" he asked curiously. Whoever it was, was a dead man.

"Antonio and his son Tre," Pedro stated sternly revealing his anger.

With a look of disbelief, he asked, "Unc ... are you sure? He's been your friend for years. I mean, how do you know this?"

Slamming his fist down on his desk in anger, Pedro glared at his nephew. His tone was ice cold. "Are you questioning me now?" he asked.

Doing his best to ease the tension, he responded. "Unc I've never questioned you ... ever. And I won't start. I'm sorry. On my life, if that's what you want, then both of them are dead."

Pedro eased back in his seat and sighed before rubbing his temples in frustration.

"How did you find out?" his nephew asked, still in disbelief that Antonio had something to do with it. Antonio had always been a stand-up guy. He didn't know much about his son since they had only met once at a party when they were younger. With a little digging, it wouldn't take much to carry out the request his uncle had made.

"Don't ask any questions, just fucking listen. Those Punta's did it, and I know for sure. Now I need this done loud and messy to send a message that this type of shit won't happen again. Now you wanna be a boss and takeover, here's your chance. I'm going to fly your auntie away from all this for a couple weeks. When I come back, those motherfuckers better be dead. If they aren't, I'll bring in someone to take your place and let them takeover ... *while you watch*."

"Say no more. It's done," he agreed. He had worked hard for the spot he was in. It didn't come easy just because Pedro was his uncle. He had earned it. No one was going to take that from him. He got up and gave his uncle a hug before leaving.

As they embraced, Pedro quietly said, "Make sure it's a message that the streets won't forget."

23

TIFFANY MOANED SOFTLY AND ROLLED OVER SO SHE COULD wrap her arm around Rico. To her surprise, the space next to her was empty. Rico was gone; however his sweet, but masculine scent still lingered. Tiffany was on cloud nine as she thought back to the night they had just shared. Rico had been so gentle with her and it felt like more than just sex; this was love. She wished she could have woken up to him; however she knew he had business to take care of. She now remembered him whispering to her this morning that he had to leave for something important.

She smiled to herself before pushing her body up in the plush, king-size bed so she could get up and get herself together. She usually didn't sleep in this late. Her alarm clock read 10:30 a.m. The lively melody from her ringing phone cut her thoughts short. She picked it up; it was her father.

"Hi Daddy," Tiffany greeted her father.

"Hey sweetheart. I need you to come by the house. I need to talk to you," Antonio said seriously. Judging by his tone, Tiffany knew something was up.

"Is everything okay Daddy?" she asked, growing worried. "Is Tre alright?" she asked. Usually when Antonio was upset, it pertained to something with Tre.

"Yeah, his dumbass is alright. And we'll talk about everything once you get here," he stated.

"Okay. I'm going to take a shower and I'll be there shortly." Still on the phone, she immediately got out of bed and headed for the bathroom. Her father had her full attention and she was now curious as to what was going on.

Alright sweetheart. See you soon. Love you."

"Love you too Daddy," Tiffany responded.

———

Tiffany shut the door of her father's house and wasn't surprised to hear the loud, intense argument taking place in the living room. She sighed. It would never end. Throwing her keys down on the table next to the door she headed in to see what was going on now.

"What were we supposed to do? Let the nigga just dump on us like he did the last time! We didn't have a choice," Tre argued. He was doing his best to explain to his father why he had been at the scene of another shoot-out with his crash dummy friends.

"Every time you go out somewhere with them, it's always some shit Tre! When you gon learn?" Antonio asked angrily. "Dem nigga's is going to get you killed!" he yelled. "What if someone points the finger at you saying you were involved. Money don't always make shit go away Tre!"

"Man whatever. Fuck this," Tre muttered before storming off through the large home. He was done going back and forth. He didn't give a fuck what his father had to say anymore. He was a grown ass man and he was getting his own money now off the dope Spice and Drew were moving. His only path now, was up.

Tiffany watched as her brother stormed through the house towards his room. She shook her head but didn't even bother to call for him. She knew the robbery had gone to Tre and his friend's head's. Here he was with some stolen money and drugs, thinking he was Antonio Tough-Guy. She loved him without a doubt, but this situation was going to have to unfold in an ugly manner for him to see the light. Just as she was about to walk into the living room to talk to her father, her phone rang. She quickly pulled it out of her small Dior bag. It was Rico.

"Hey babe," she answered quickly.

"Wassup wit you? You busy?" he asked. He could sense she was tied up by the way she answered the phone.

"Yeah, I'm uh at my dad's. Him and my brother going at it," she said. She didn't go into detail. She would only share small details of her life with anyone, Rico included. She had grown up to never say much, especially about herself or family. She hoped that would one day change, as she saw a future with Rico.

"Ok. Well I'll make it quick then. I just wanted to see if you wanted to go out to eat tonight. Maybe see a movie," he suggested.

"Yeah sure. I'm wit it," she said with a smile.

"And maybe soon I can meet that dad of yours," he added.

"I think that can be arranged." She was ready just like he was. She wanted Rico in her life and figured it was now or never. "I'll let you know when he's free. You just be ready."

After disconnecting the call, Tiffany tucked her phone back in her purse and headed back towards the living room to speak with her father. Just as she went to sit down on the couch, Tre was walking out and heading towards the door.

"Where the fuck are you going?" Antonio asked angrily, standing up. He had a scowl on his face that suggested he was about two seconds off Tre's ass.

Smacking his teeth, Tre ignored his father, but still muttered under his breath, "I'm a grown ass man."

"What the fuck you say?" Antonio asked, running up on him. He grabbed him by his Polo t-shirt and spun him around so hard, Tre stumbled. Tre snatched back. He didn't say a word. He just gave his father a hard stare.

"Oh, you grown huh?" Antonio asked testing him. He

dared him to say it again. His fists were balled at his sides. If he uttered another word, Antonio intended to stretch him out. He was sick of his son's shit.

"Well since you're grown, get ya shit and get ya grown ass out my house," he demanded.

Tre shook his head from side to side and looked at his father in disgust. In his eyes, his father was overreacting and him being in a shoot-out was a necessity to survive. He did what he had to do.

"I don't need it," he said referring to his things. He turned around with an arrogant smug and walked out the door.

Antonio walked back into the living room and sat down. He breathed heavily, and his head was beginning to pound.

"Daddy," Tiffany called to him softly from the other couch, snapping him out of his angry trance. "What happened?"

Antonio took a deep breath. "Tre was in another shootout. This time at a club. From what I heard, the police have no suspects, but of course, the streets talk and I heard he was involved. A couple people were shot, several people were hurt, and the club was destroyed," he explained. "I've had it with Tre. I no longer know what to do ... If I do nothing, he will end up getting himself killed. If I continue this route of arguing back and forth with him, he's still going to end up killed because he doesn't listen. Either way, I'm going to be a stressed and nervous wreck. I sometimes dread answering my phone. I'm scared I'm going to get a call that Tre's been murdered. At this rate, it is not a matter of *if* it'll come, it's *when*. It's come to a point where I ask myself: do I wash my hands of my only son, or do I continue to try in vain?" Antonio stared off out the window. He truly didn't have the answer.

Tiffany sat solemnly and silent on the couch. She didn't know what to say. Tre was indeed hard-headed, and he was beyond helping. She did know that she was now scared and needed to talk to Tre. She wasn't sure if this shoot-out had

something to do with Pedro, but if it did, she needed to tell
her father what was going on. From the looks of things, Tre
hadn't yet.

———

Rico sat at the table of his stash house and absorbed all
the information he had been delivered in the last few
hours. He was fuming, and he partially blamed himself.
Both Paulie and Chubs had been shot, while Latisha was
in the hospital with two broken legs. While Paulie and
Chubs had been released from the hospital this morning,
Latisha would be in for about a week and would have to go
through extensive rehab. Rico sighed stressfully. He had
made the wrong call and his entire team had made him
aware of that. He was not only embarrassed, he also felt
guilt behind the injuries that resulted from his judgement.
He had arranged the night at the club, and then didn't
even show. He had been too caught up with Tiffany and
his uncle's affairs, that he let his team down. While he
didn't regret the night he spent with his love, he did regret
that he had ordered Chubs and his team to stand down.
He also didn't regret putting things on hold while he went
to his uncle. That was his family and that is where his
loyalty was trained to lay. What he did regret was the fact
that he hadn't responded to any phone calls and hadn't
even bothered to check the text messages niggas from his
team had sent all last night and this morning. If he had
checked, he would have been informed of what had taken
place way sooner. Here it was the afternoon, and he was
just hearing about what happened. He had clearly underestimated the three niggas from the East, but he damn sure
would not let that happen again. It pained him that he
would have to proceed with more violence. Just hours ago,
he had been seriously contemplating squashing the beef
with Tre.

"So, what's the game plan boss?" Boobie asked slightly

annoyed. He had been the only one uninjured in the shoot-out and had called Rico dozens of times after it happened.

"We go to war," Rico replied. "And we gon tear dem nigga's asses up."

"That's all I need to hear," Boobie said, glad that Rico was finally with the program. If they had got at them like everybody wanted to, the attack never would have happened. No one spoke it, but Rico was definitely to blame.

"Gather nigga's up and tell them to meet here for a meeting around midnight. That way, we can let everyone know what's going on and to be on point. Anybody that crosses paths with any three of them fuck nigga's — they body em. A few of us can ride down on their block tonight after the meeting. I'll let you know the details later," Rico stated. They were going to war and he had to prepare everyone properly.

"Why you just don't send the young boys to do it?" Boobie asked. He felt that Rico was bigger than the street beefs. They could leave that to their lil goons and youngins.

"Naaaa. It started with me so ima let them niggas know; there's no pussies over here. This shit is personal, and I'll never hide behind my men. They want Rico, they gon get Rico."

"You da boss," Boobie said with a smile. If Rico wanted to hold court in the streets, then so be it. Besides, he was always down for a 187.

Later that afternoon, Tre parked his car on the side of Pat's house and quickly hopped out. As usual, business was still booming and drug-addicts were scattered sporadically up and down the block. Their dirty, disheveled appearance would scare away the average person; however to any hustler, they were dollar signs.

"Yo Pee," Tre called to one of the young boys who was manning the block for them. He couldn't have been no more

than sixteen years old. He had a brown baby-face and probably only weighed about 140 pounds soaking wet. With his
nappy, gangster style cornrows, he resembled a young
Snoop Dog.

"Wassup?" Pee responded, only briefly taking his eye off
the feenin junkie bitch in front of him. Heroin addicts were
notorious for their sheisty and treacherous behavior when
dope was involved. Pee had already once been the victim of
a snatch and grab, and he wasn't about to let that shit
happen again.

"You see them nigga's Drew and Spice?" he asked, as he
greeted the young boy with a quick hand slap.

"Yeah they up the street with them freak ass sisters, Tina
and Tiffany."

He pointed up the street to a shabby, two story yellow
house; however, there was no need to point, Tre knew
exactly where they lived at. They were the neighborhood
freaks and he too had fucked both.

"Good looking," Tre said as he walked off, leaving Pee to
continue his tasks of serving doped out junkies and making
money for the team.

Tre didn't bother to knock when he entered the sisters'
house where Spice and Drew were chilling at. It was essentially their hang out spot. The girls were young and the trio
came and went as they pleased. When he entered, the girls
were on the couch half-naked in panties and tank tops,
while Drew and Spice were counting wrinkled and balled
up money at the hand-me-down, 80's style dining room
table.

"Wassup nigga?" Drew asked Tre as soon as he walked
through the door. Spice threw him a head nod and
continued to count.

"Aint shit. Had to jet from my Pops crib. That nigga
heard about the shit at Starlite's and he tripping. Told me I
had to get out and all that," he said, still in disbelief. "Prolly
wasn't nobody but that old ass, nosey ass Frank that told
him. His old ass always running his mouth," Tre

complained. Store-owner Frank knew everything that went on in the hood, and he was one of Antonio's main resources when it came to gathering his information. Antonio tried his best to keep his source a secret, but Tre knew.

"Damn," Drew responded.

"It aint' about shit. I'm just gon stay with my sis for a few days until he calms the fuck down.

"Man, why ya pops been on that soft shit lately?" Spice asked, finally finished counting the stacks that now lay neatly in front of him. He had lived on the East for years and had heard stories about how Antonio used to air blocks out and terrorize the hood. He guessed time and age had made him pussy.

"Man, that nigga washed up," Drew mumbled. He certainly wasn't on the same time from back in the day.

"I don't even know what's going on with my dad for real. He older now and I guess he on to better shit. He trying to run his business and he ain't hip to how shit goes down in the streets now," Tre shrugged.

"Yeah, well fuck all that nigga. We got some shit to handle tonight anyway," Spice argued. He looked over to the sisters who were still watching television on the couch. "Yo. Yawl get up and go upstairs real quick," he demanded. "We got some important shit to talk about that aint for yawl ears."

Like the hoodrats they were, they quickly got up and went upstairs. It didn't matter that it was there crib. They let Drew and Spice do whatever they wanted. They ran the spot. While they all spoke freely in front of junkies, they didn't do that with average females. Bitches were nosey, and they repeated everything.

"I found out where that fat ass nigga Chubs chill at. We gon air the block out. We hitting any fucking body that's out there. You wit it?" he asked Tre, quickly testing his gangster. Tre had truly come a long way. He went from being a soft ass square, to busting his gun in a crowded club with no hesitation.

"No doubt," Tre quickly agreed.

"Say no more. Meet us back here tonight around midnight. All black."

"Bet," he said, before heading out.

Tre figured he would ride over to Tiffany's to get some sleep since he hadn't managed to do so last night. As he walked down the street his phone rang. Digging it out of his pocket, he checked it and it just so happened to be Tiffany. He hit ignore. He didn't feel like hearing her shit, besides he would see her later at her crib. He had a mission to prepare for.

24

It was around midnight when Tre parked his car near a bush behind Pat's house. Dressed in all black, he crept silently down the block to meet up with his team. They told him they would be in a gray Impala. Tre spotted the newer model car quickly since Drew's arm was dangling from the window, waving for him to come over.

"Get in nigga," he said, once Tre got close on the car. The locks clicked and Tre hopped in quietly. He was a little nervous, but knew he couldn't bitch up or show any signs of weakness. Beef came with the life of the streets.

"Who car is this?" Tre asked out of curiosity.

Spice looked back with a grin and responded. "One of my bitches rented it from Enterprise for me."

"Here you want some of this shit?" Drew asked before passing back a half smoked blunt of gas. Tre quickly reached for it. He needed it for sure. Between dealing with the beef with Chubs crew, and his sister and dad bitching at him all day, he needed to relax his mental state.

The drive to the West didn't take long at all since it was late and there was no traffic. There would be no lingering around. They were going to ride down on the block and quickly air it out. It was that simple. Spice and Drew knew that it wouldn't be long before Chubs and Rico's team came gunning for them. They weren't going to even give them the chance.

As they crept down the dusty, dirty blocks of the West side of town, they soon approached the residence they were looking for. As they peeped the scene on the street, their adrenaline kicked in and they grew excited. The block was live. There were about six or seven nigga's standing around the house; in addition to Chubs and Boobie. There were also a bunch of addicts strewn up and down the block. If they knew what was best for them, they would run when they saw the car approaching. Once the shots started to ring out, any and everyone was a target. No mercy would be shown.

Drew crept down the block slowly and stopped right in the center of the street, midway through. Spice and Tre gathered their loaded automatic weapons and put them in the proper position. Spice had copped the guns earlier from a nigga he knew. With their new-found financial status, they were able to upgrade their weapons. Gone were the normal semi-automatic handguns. They would carry those for general purpose. For a street battle such as this, they were rolling with automatic pistols, such as the MAC-10 and TEC 9. Spice and Tre each held one respectively.

Drew slowly rolled down the window. They watched as Chubs pointed towards the car and the nigga's started to back up. Spice knew they were suspicious and would soon reach for their own gun's. Seizing the opportunity, he yelled.

"Now! Go!"

Drew sped down the block and towards the house with his wheels spinning, as Tre and Spice aimed their weapons out of the window and opened fire on everyone. They didn't care who they hit; if they were in the way of bullets, then luck just wasn't on their side. Drew slowed the Impala down right as they got close to the house. The panic that shown on everyone's face excited Spice. He laughed and yelled out undetectable words. His face was maniacal as he leveled and waved his gun from side to side, to hit everyone in his path.

Chaos erupted on the streets as people did their best to flee the flurry of bullets being released. Bodies began rapidly falling from gunshot wounds. Just as the carnage was unfolding, Rico happened to be turning down the block to attend the late-night meeting he had called. He literally had stumbled upon the drive-by. It was more like a massacre that was unfolding right in front of his eyes. Dread rushed over him as he watched members of his team run and scatter frantically, while others hit the ground wounded. He watched as orangish-yellow sparks flew from the gun barrels and shell casings rapidly ejected and hit the pavement. The occupants of the Impala continued to fire shots as they sped away from the scene and up the street.

Rico quickly retrieved his weapon from his console. He stepped on the gas and rolled down his window to return fire on the car that had just opened fire on his team. The bullets that flew from the barrel of his gun shattered the back window of the tinted car and produced multiple holes through its body and interior. Drew, Tre and Spice weren't prepared for the return of fire and were stunned when the bullets ripped through the vehicle.

"Aaaahhhh fuck! I'm hit," Tre yelled in agony, right after a bullet shattered the back window. The hot bullet hurt like hell and somehow managed to produce pain all over his body. He had no idea where he was hit, he just knew he had been.

"Fuck!" Spice yelled, looking back at Tre who was now curled up in pain and bleeding profusely in the backseat.

"You gotta get me to the hospital," Tre begged. He was beginning to panic. He'd never been shot before. He didn't want to die.

"We can't take him to no fucking hospital with all these guns and bullet holes in here. They'll call the police," Drew stated firmly while looking over at Spice. He was doing his best to stay calm and come up with a reasonable solution to their situation. He wasn't about to get booked just to get Tre medical attention.

Everyone was aware of the risks before they strapped up and went on the mission. He didn't want to say, "*fuck Tre and his bullet wound*," but at this point, he almost had no other choice.

"Take him to his sister's. She'll know what to do," Spice said. Drew quickly agreed to that. It was still risky, but it was a lot better than going to the hospital. Tre rambled off the address and they began the race to Tiffany's.

25

"This shit fucking hurts man," Tre moaned as he lay stretched out in the back seat, blood running down his arm and soaking into the tan cushions. Blood was also all over the front of his shirt, so Tre still had no idea where he had been hit. His shoulder hurt, *but* so did his chest and back.

"Just hold on nigga," Spice said as Drew raced downtown to Tiffany's condo. He made it there in record time and got through the gates after Tre rambled off the entrance code. Luckily security was making their rounds and didn't notice the bullet riddled vehicle enter the complex.

Hopping out the front passenger side door, Spice ran to the back of the car and snatched the door open to help get Tre out. Drew had also jumped out to help. He looked around nervously and paranoia plagued him. He had begun to sweat profusely, and his stomach was doing somersaults.

"My key's in my pocket," Tre said referring to the spare keys his sister had given him after Christopher had gotten shot. Tre was in pain and he was starting to feel dizzy.

"Shitttttt," he moaned as he tossed and turned his head against the seat in agony.

Spice and Drew quickly looked around once more before cursing out loud. Drew knew that they were taking a significant risk by dropping Tre off in the ritzy neighbor-hood, but at this point, they had no choice. Their focused shifted to moving quickly. They had to get rid of the guns and car. Seeing the coast was clear and no one was around, they pulled Tre out of the car and carried him as quickly as they could to Tiffany's front door. Drew carried his feet, while Spice carried his bleeding torso. Once they got to the door, they sat Tre down on the pavement against the wall and dug in his pocket for his key to Tiffany's condo. After retrieving it and opening the door, they carried Tre in and laid him on the couch.

"Tiffany!" Spice called.

As soon as they heard her office door creek open and her footsteps approaching, they took off through the front door and back to the car. They knew she would know what to do and help get her brother some medical attention. They had to get the bullet-riddled car away from the building before some nosey neighbors saw it and called the police.

Tiffany walked into her living room angrily. She had recognized Spice's voice and wanted to know why the hell he was in her house, let alone yelling. As soon as she saw her brother bleeding on the couch, her heart felt like it flew from her chest. The sight of so much blood on her only sibling was enough to send her in a panic.

"Oh my God!" she screamed, as she threw her hand to her mouth and gasped. Terror and dread consumed her at once, but the love she felt for Tre instantly overpowered those feelings. She immediately sprang into action to help him.

"Tre baby, what happened," she asked, her voice trem-bling and chills running through her. She prayed he responded.

"I got shot," he replied painfully. "Get a towel and help me take off my shirt. We gotta see where I was hit," he instructed.

Tiffany ran from the living room frantically before stum-bling into the bathroom and grabbing a towel from the linen closet. She returned sobbing, tears streaming from her face. She was doing her best to remain calm but the scene before her was overwhelming. Her phone was nearby on the coffee table, so she reached and grabbed it to call her dad. With her hands shaking, she voice-dialed him. As soon as the call connected, she sobbed into the phone. Antonio knew something was terribly wrong.

"Daddy, Tre's been shot!" she yelled before he could say anything. "He's here and he's bleeding everywhere! Please come Daddy!" she wailed into the receiver.

"I'm on my way!" Antonio responded quickly. Dread washed over him. He had no idea what was going on, but he would find out as soon as he arrived. He prayed the entire way there that his son was okay.

Antonio made it to Tiffany's in ten minutes flat since her condo wasn't far from his own home. He must have run every stop sign and stop light to get there. After running through the parking lot and into the building he was shocked to see his son lying on the couch with his chest covered in blood. Antonio immediately took over.

"Tre. Son. Where were you hit?" he asked sternly. He knew it was vital that he didn't panic. It wouldn't help the situation. He had to remain calm.

"My shoulder," Tre responded.

While Antonio was in route, he and Tiffany had taken off his shirt and found the spot on his body where he had been hit. Tiffany, who was returning from the bathroom with another towel, walked around the corner just in time to see her dad leaning over Tre.

"Daddy, here's another towel," she said sobbing, before handing the dark blue towel to him.

"Let me look at it," Antonio told Tre. He had to see how bad the bullet wound was.

Antonio lifted the blood-soaked towel from Tre's

shoulder and observed the wound. He carefully lifted Tre forward towards him to see where the bullet had exited. He didn't see anything. Antonio sighed in relief. It was just a graze. At around three inches long, the graze was deep and nasty. Luckily for Tre, the bullet had not fully entered his shoulder.

"It's just a graze," Antonio informed him. "You're gonna be fine ... But how did this happen Tre?" he demanded to know as he looked his son in his eye. He put the towel back over the wound and applied pressure to slow down the blood loss. Tiffany stood behind her father thinking the same thing her father had just asked; how did this happen? More than anything, she was happy Tre was okay.

"I told ya ass to stop fucking with those nigga's in the hood," Antonio argued.

Tre moaned in pain as well as irritation. Now was not the time. Here he was, bleeding profusely and his dad wanted to preach. He now wished he had been shot in his ears so he wouldn't have to hear shit his father had to say.

Tre went to respond with a stutter. He was about to lie, but Tiffany abruptly cut him off.

"Tre tell him or I'm going to tell him," she demanded. He already knew what she was about to do. Enough was enough. The lies would end today.

"Tiffany please, not now!" he yelled, becoming angry.

"Not now, my ass! What the fuck is going on?" Antonio demanded to know, looking back at Tiffany. He gave her the look of death. She now had no choice.

"Tre, Drew, and Spice robbed Pedro and killed his son, and now Pedro got nigga's trying to kill him," she blurted out. As awful as the revelation was, she felt like a weight had been immediately lifted off her chest.

Disregarding his injured state, Antonio hauled off and smacked the shit out of Tre. Tre winced in pain, while the sound caused Tiffany to jump.

"What the fuck is wrong with you Tre!" he yelled furiously. Antonio got up and began to pace the room in a panicked state.

"You dumb muthafucka — you about to get us all killed."

Antonio stared at Tre in disbelief. He couldn't believe what he had just heard. *His own son.* Right then, everything was starting to become clear to Antonio; Pedro's behavior at the funeral, the shootout in the club, the unanswered calls to Pedro, and now this shit. It was just too much to digest. Antonio sat down on the couch opposite of Tre. He had to collect his thoughts and think for a minute.

Antonio glared over at Tiffany. He couldn't believe she too was in on this. She had helped Tre conceal his wrong-doings instead of informing him.

"I can't believe you," he said in disappointment. Not his baby-girl too. "You knew about this?" he asked in disbelief.

"I'm so sorry Daddy," Tiffany cried. The look Antonio gave her broke her heart into a thousand pieces. She hated to disappoint her father. She was only trying to protect Tre.

"Tiffany Just don't say anything else," he demanded. He didn't want to hear shit either of them had to say at the moment. To leave him blind to what was going on around him was the worst thing they could have done. They obviously had no idea how much danger they all were in. Once Pedro gave the word, their deaths were imminent. Tre and his friends had literally went on a suicide mission.

Tiffany turned around and stumbled out of the living room towards her bedroom in tears. Before she could plop down on her bed and cry into her sheets, her phone rang from the bathroom where she had left it when she ran to get another towel for Tre. She was about to ignore it but went to retrieve it anyway. She planned to shut it off for the rest of the day. They had to get Tre over to the hospital and she didn't want to be bothered. She grabbed the ringing, vibrating phone off the sink and looked down to see it was Rico. Although she wanted to see him, now wasn't the time.

She answered it while she did her best to control her voice and hold back her sobs.

"Hey baby, I gotta call you back, it's a lot going on right now," she answered with a sniffle. She sat up in her bed and used the back of her hand to wipe at her running nose.

Rico could tell Tiffany had been crying and something was wrong. "What's wrong?" he asked. Although he wanted to express his concern for her, he too had a lot going on and was desperate for a safe place to rest his head for the night. He knew there was no better place than with her. Fleeing from a street that was now littered with dead and wounded bodies, he was paranoid and desperate. He was going through it. Everyone in front of the house he had just left, was probably dead. There had just been too many bullets, and so much blood. He did his best to remain positive, but he knew in his heart that most, if not all his men were gone. It pained him that he couldn't even stay, as he knew the street would soon be blocked off and swarming with police.

"My brother was shot and we're about to take him to the hospital," she sobbed.

"Listen bae, everything is going to be okay," he said while peering around nervously. He said it more for himself then anything, since he was also trying to convince himself that as well.

Rico knew he was playing with fire since he knew he was the one behind Tre being shot. He figured he was in the clear since Tre's stupid ass still hadn't connected the dots. Tre didn't remember Rico's face and still had no clue he was in a relationship with his sister. Stupid was the only way Rico could describe him. The only thing that Tre knew was that he and his crew were beefing with the West side. He was actually glad that one of the bullets he'd sent, had hit Tre's ass.

"I'm pulling up to ya house now. I'll see you in a minute," he said abruptly before hanging up. He didn't wait for her to respond. No matter what she said, they both needed each other and he refused to take *no* for answer.

"Who were you talking to?" Antonio asked Tiffany in his deep voice, startling her. She had no idea he had come behind her and had overheard her conversation.

"It was my boyfriend Rico. I was trying to tell you about him," she said, as her voice trailed off softly.

Lately their conversations had been about Tre and business. Tiffany and her life had been pushed to the back burner.

Antonio peered at Tiffany and walked off back in to the living room. "Whose Rico?" he asked Tre. Tre looked at him perplexed.

"I don't know," Tre responded quickly with an irritated look on his face. It seemed like a dumb ass question, especially since he was still waiting to be taken to the hospital for the stitches he so desperately needed in his shoulder.

"You dumb ass!" Antonio yelled out of nowhere. How the fuck don't you know who your sister is dating? — You're lucky I don't shoot you my fucking self," he continued to argue.

Tre wanted to ask him, how come he didn't know who the fuck Rico was? It was just as much his responsibility as her father to know who Tiffany was seeing. However, the way Antonio looked at it, Tiffany was going to be more open to discussing her private life with her big brother, rather than her father. Tre was too wrapped up in his own bullshit to worry about anyone but himself.

"What the fuck am I going to do about Pedro?" Antonio asked aloud to no one in particular. He sat back down on the couch with a look of defeat on his face. His son was going to be the death of him, literally.

Now in the bathroom, Tiffany did her best to clean herself up so she could go meet Rico outside. He had just texted his arrival a few seconds ago. As she walked out the door, Antonio started gathering up Tre so he could take him to a nearby hospital for stitches. He didn't give a damn what either of them said from that point on; all three of them were going to have to lay low. If Pedro was really the one responsible for Tre's attack, it was only a matter of time before he succeeded in killing him. He knew how Pedro moved, and if it was a hit out on Tre, there was also probably a hit out on him as well.

26

Rico quickly hopped out of his Mercedes and speed walked into Tiffany's building. As he made his way through the hall, he saw her heading out to greet him. She looked distraught and the sight of her made Rico's heart melt in his chest. He needed her just like she needed him. Without a doubt he loved her. He just wanted to hold her, hug her, and take away whatever pain she was feeling. The irony behind the situation was that, he also happened to be the one who was causing her pain.

"Rico," Tiffany cried. She walked slowly and weakly to him. Her tear stained face had streaks of blood across them and her clothes were soiled from trying to help her wounded brother. He felt a twinge of guilt, but then remembered that her brother was the reason behind his team being gunned down. He loved Tiffany but gave zero fucks about her brother. He genuinely wanted him dead.

"What happened?" he asked.

"I don't know. He won't really say. The bullet grazed his shoulder," she cried. "It's just too much. I was so scared that he was gonna die. There was so much blood." She buried her head briefly into Rico's chest. She finally looked up at Rico.

"I guess now's the time you can quickly meet my

dysfunctional ass family," she said with a sniffle before using the back of her hand to wipe at her wet face. "My dad's here. Come on," she said, leading the way into her condo. Rico immediately became alarmed. He hadn't expected anyone to be there.

As Antonio helped Tre up and they headed out the doorway, they came face to face with Rico and Tiffany. Tre stared at Rico and because his mind was in a chaotic state, he instantly remembered where he knew him from. The night they met, had been the same: chaotic. It was the lame ass nigga from the club. The same nigga that had just been the leader of the team that had just nearly killed him when they returned fire. The name finally sunk in. *Rico*. It was the same Rico he and his team were going to war with.

As Tre locked eyes with Rico; so did Antonio. Antonio too, instantly remembered Rico. It was little mixed Ric, Pedro's nephew. Tiffany couldn't have had a clue. Pedro surely had sent him to murder his son. He wasn't about to let that happen.

Rico didn't miss a beat as he saw Antonio come out of Tiffany's condo. Everything now made sense. Tre and Tiffany were Antonio's kids. He couldn't believe he didn't peep this sooner. When he had met Tiffany at his uncle's party, she said that she was there with her father. He never knew it was Antonio! Nor did he pay attention to the significance of the name of Antonio's son when his uncle ordered them to be murdered. He was just as clueless as Tre was!

He looked back to Tre, who was now ice grilling him. He had been recognized in two ways. Shit was getting worse by the minute. He had orders to kill Antonio and his son. He wanted Tre dead anyway. He had murdered most of his team. With the new-found revelations swirling their thoughts, all three men reached for their weapons.

PART III

27

"DADDY, THIS IS MY BOYFRIEND RICO," TIFFANY SAID BEFORE either of the men could withdraw their weapon. The tension in the air was thick and everyone felt it — everyone except Tiffany.

While Antonio and Rico's hands rested obliviously by the butt of their guns, Tre's hands landed against his useless leather belt. He had forgotten he had left his gun in the Impala for Drew and Spice to dispose of. He cursed himself for being unprepared.

Playing it cool, Rico quickly extended his hand to Antonio's. "Nice to meet you despite the circumstances," he said, quickly glancing at Tre. "Tiffany has told me a lot about you and has done nothing but speak highly of you," he added respectfully.

"Nice to meet you as well. Unfortunately, Tiffany hasn't done me the favor of mentioning much of you," Antonio responded, before glancing at his daughter.

Antonio did his best to maintain his composure. He was caught between a rock and a hard spot. He was quite acquainted with Pedro's nephew Rico and knew how he got down. He was certain that Rico knew about the robbery. However, he felt powerless and vulnerable. His son was wounded, and his daughter was defenseless. It didn't make sense to shoot it out then and there with Rico.

As Antonio spoke and analyzed the situation, Tre stared at Rico. He wondered if Rico knew who he was. He couldn't have. He had literally just laid down a block of his people and he was standing before him with a silly ass grin. No way. However, Antonio knew better. Although he was unaware of what happened to Rico's team, he knew that he was very much like his uncle. He played chess, not checkers. Everything he did was calculated and he was not the one to act off pure emotion.

"Help your brother to the car while I speak to Rico," Antonio told Tiffany, who was an obvious nervous wreck.

"Okay Daddy," Tiffany responded hesitantly before reaching out and taking her brothers arm. She helped him keep his balance as he walked weakly to Antonio's car. Once the two were distant and out of earshot, Antonio wasted no time cutting to the chase. He figured he would skip the small talk.

"I think I know why you're here Ric," he said referring to him by his nickname. He'd known the youngster since he was merely a young boy.

"It's been a long time since I saw you. How's Pedro? I'm sure you heard about what happened at the funeral?" Antonio asked, wondering how much Rico knew.

Rico knew exactly what Antonio was doing. After all, he had practically grown up around him. He knew it was all tactic. Rico knew that Pedro had stopped answering Antonio's calls. He had basically closed himself off from the outside world, other than family and a select few he dealt with for business purposes. Personally, Rico was still struggling with accepting the fact that Antonio was truly involved in Christopher's death. He just couldn't picture Antonio betraying his uncle like that. Antonio had been loyal for years — he had a business and he had money. It didn't make sense for him to rob Pedro. Tre on the other hand, was another story. The more he thought about it, the more he was convinced that Tre acted without Antonio's help.

With Pedro giving Rico no information, he didn't have anything to go off. All he could do was assume. Unfortunately, he had only been given the simple task to shoot first and ask questions later. The problem for Rico was there was a huge conflict of interest: his love for Tiffany.

Without a doubt, he planned to kill Tre. He was going to do it in a way that Tiffany would never find out. Now her father, that was a different story. He respected Antonio and he loved Tiffany. Killing her brother was one thing; killing her father as well, would be the ultimate betrayal. However, Christopher was his blood. Carlos was family — but he loved Tiffany. Things were getting complicated.

"Me and my uncle haven't spoken in a while. Let's just say, we had some disagreements over business. I heard about what happened with his son, but that's his problem. I sent my condolences, but I have my own life, and I refuse to get caught up in his affairs," Rico responded quickly.

Antonio studied his face and held eye contact to see if he was lying. Rico's expression never changed. Antonio on the other hand, didn't believe a word he'd just said. He finally responded.

"Understood. I thought you two were still on the same team."

"We are. We will always be family. We just don't do business together anymore. I'm trying to get my life right and do the right thing for me and Tiffany."

Before Antonio could ask him what he meant by that, their conversation was interrupted by Tiffany's return.

"I hope y'all weren't talking about me," Tiffany nervously said, as she walked towards the two men. She had intentionally helped her brother to the car very quickly. She didn't want to leave Rico alone long with her father.

"Nah sweetheart. We were just finishing our conversation ... and I was just leaving. I'm gonna go ahead and get Tre over to the hospital to get stitched up. I'll call you. And

Rico," he turned and extended his hand out for a hand-shake, "We'll finish up later."

"For sure," Rico said, after shaking and releasing his hand from Antonio's strong grip.

"Alright Daddy. Make sure you call me."

Tiffany leaned up and gave her father a quick kiss on the cheek before he turned and walked out of the building and back to his car.

———

"Your sister's new boyfriend is also Pedro's nephew," Antonio said to Tre, who was buckled up and leaning against the car door in pain.

"What?" Tre mumbled in disbelief. With everything that had happened, nothing made sense to him anymore.

"That's Pedro's nephew," Antonio repeated with a sigh. "You don't remember him?"

He looked over at his son, who of course was just as clueless as a blond, white hoe. "He's at every single event Pedro throws at his house — the Christmas party, New Year's." Antonio sighed in annoyance.

"Damnit Tre!" Antonio angrily spat in frustration. "You must always be aware of your surroundings. How you didn't recognize him fuckin amazes me. You two are nearly the same age and even played together as kids." Tre went to speak but Antonio cut him off.

"What's done is done so fuck all of that. We have a new problem. Tiffany's seeing him. And from the looks of things, she cares for him — That we can't allow. He's gotta go. Now, I don't know if Pedro sent him for you or if it's just a mere coincidence, but Tiffany could be at risk."

"I doubt it Dad. She's been mentioning this guy for months," Tre said quickly. He wanted his father to shut up. He was in an immense amount of pain and felt like the sermon could wait. The beef had nothing to do with Tiffany.

"So, fucking what! If Pedro knows you had something to

do with Christopher's murder and he tells Rico to handle it, what do you think he's going to do? He's going to shoot first and ask questions later. In their culture, blood and loyalty outweighs love on any day."

Antonio didn't feel like he was thinking prematurely. Pedro was a smart man, and they had to be prepared for any and everything. What better way than to seek vengeance.

"For now, I'm going to wait, but I won't let my guard down. But I will say this ... if anything, and I mean *anything* happens to your sister, I will kill both of your so-called friends, and *you* ... I'll beat you so close to death, you'll wish you were dead."

He stared his son directly in the eyes, so it was clear that he meant every word of what he said.

"Soon as you get better, you need to be on point. I don't know about you sometimes. What I do know is that I will lay down the entire city for my family. I suggest you get on the same shit. *We* are all we have. You, Tiffany and I. Understood?" he asked sternly. He hoped they were on the same page.

"Yeah," Tre replied with a nod, only half listening.

"Babe, why don't you relax?" Rico said to Tiffany who was walking through her house, cleaning up non-stop.

When Tre came in after being shot, things got chaotic and Tiffany's living space reflected that. Pillows that once aligned her sofa perfectly, had been strewn on the floor. Her once organized linen closet and kitchen had been torn apart while she looked for supplies to tend to Tre's wound.

"I just want to get everything back to how it was," she replied in frustration before abruptly taking a seat in a stool at her kitchen counter. She grabbed an open bottle of wine that was sitting on the counter and popped the top. Putting her lips to the top, she tilted back the bottle and let the room-temperature liquid flow down her throat. She hoped it eased her mind and helped settle her rattling nerves.

Rico got up off the couch from where he was seated and walked over to her. Wrapping his arms around her tense shoulders, he kissed her cheek softly.

"I know the day has been stressful for you. Why don't you get your things and I take you somewhere to relax?" he suggested.

"I'll be okay babe," she responded without giving the gesture any thought.

"I'm not taking no for an answer," he whispered before giving her another kiss.

The kiss caused her body to shudder; however, Tiffany's thoughts quickly raced to her father and Tre. What would she tell her dad if he called and asked where she was?

"I don't know Rico," she quietly replied. She turned in her stool to face Rico, who still held onto her, only letting go briefly to adjust his grip. "I just have a lot going on right now."

"I know that ... and that's why you need to relax some. Let's get away. We can go to this little spot I know of and then get a suite downtown."

"At this hour?" Tiffany asked. It was nearly two in the morning and there wasn't much open.

"You let me handle that. I know people and can pull some strings. If your pops ask where you are, you just tell him you needed to get away and relax. There's no harm in that. He will understand. If he asks who you're with, just tell him you're alone. If he wants to come by, I'll leave ... Ok?" he asked, hoping she agreed. He too needed to get away and lay low.

"Ok," she replied. He had it all figured out. "Just let me take a quick shower and grab a few things."

"Ok," he agreed, before releasing her.

Sighing, Rico went back to the couch. He too was a nervous wreck. As soon as he thought things were safe and he could break away from Tiffany, he needed to call and see what was up with his team. When he had left, the scene wasn't pretty. He hoped everyone was okay, but he was no fool and he knew better. The suite would be a haven for him as well, until things blew over with the police. Now that Tre knew who he was, he was hoping he let his guard down, and when he did ... he was going to kill him.

28

"THIS IS REALLY NICE RICO. THANKS BABE," TIFFANY SAID TO Rico, who was seated across the table from her. Tiffany was now on her third drink and was finally relaxed. Her eyes were low and her movement, slightly delayed.

"Of course," he replied modestly.

"How'd you find this place?" she asked looking around.

Instead of taking her to an after-hours restaurant, he called up Alonzo, a private chef he knew through his uncle and made last minute, private reservations. Although Alonzo worked at one of the finest restaurants downtown, he also catered and did private, intimate dinner experiences, personally hosted by him in settings like the one they were at. Tonight, they were at a private condo owned by Rico's uncle Pedro. The condo overlooked the waterfront. To Tiffany, it was ten times better than The Chateau.

"I've been to a few parties here and took his information. He's dope, right?"

"He is. The food is amazing," she added between small bites.

Tiffany had the mushroom crusted miso rack of lamb, while Rico had the Filet Mignon with pomegranate burgundy sauce. Their dishes were both paired with roasted red potatoes and sautéed green beans. Rico was glad she liked it. It had set him back over $500. Calling up a busy chef such as Alonzo at two in the morning didn't come cheap.

"You okay?" Tiffany asked looking to Rico. He looked worried and lately he hadn't been his normal chipper self. She hoped her problems weren't the reason for his lackluster mood.

"Yeah, I'm good. Why you ask?" Rico responded as he continued to eat his food.

"I don't know babe, you just seemed quiet. Are you okay? I don't want to be adding extra shit on you with my drama."

"You don't have any drama," he laughed. "That's your brother's bullshit. And I'm good. Just thinking about you is all."

"And what's that you're thinking about pertaining to me?" she questioned slyly with a grin.

"Our future."

"Our future?" she asked with a puzzled look. "Rico Ortega wants a future with lil ol me?" she joked, while batting her eyelashes and grinning from ear to ear. It was the first time she'd smiled the entire night.

"Stop playing. I'm dead ass," he admitted. "I fuck with you — hard. I could see myself waking up to you every morning ... having kids ... marrying you. Real shit. All I ask is you always keep it a bean and fuck with me like I fuck with you."

Tiffany smiled and gazed at Rico before responding. "Baby I do fuck with you ... but I don't know," she responded, which surprised Rico. He thought she would want the same thing.

"You don't know what?" He was confused.

"Your lifestyle babe. I know ya work isn't 100% legal and I can't embrace that ... My whole life my father bust his ass to give us the best he could and shield us from that world. I would never disrespect my father the way my brother does by going against everything he worked so hard for. He worked hard to raise us up right and in a good environment. He did his best to make me a good woman. I deserve a good man. Now I know you can be a good man; I can see it in you; however, before I commit to anyone, we gotta be on the same page. I can't have a future with someone in the streets. Now I'm going off pure assumptions. I stay in my lane, mind my business, and don't ask many questions, but I'm not a square Rico. People talk."

Rico didn't respond right away. He was at a loss for words. He had certainly underestimated the woman before him.

"I can respect that," he responded as he stared at her intently. "I have a little money from some investments I made," he replied modestly. "I know that you're a good business-minded woman ... and you're smart. For you Tiffany, I'm willing to walk away from the shit I got going on and build a life with you. As long as you're willing to help me be the man you need."

Rico hadn't been raised up to be selfish; instead, he was raised to be family-oriented. Watching his uncle sacrifice his freedom to take care of his family was what he had witnessed his entire life. Many times, Pedro had sat him down and told him that whenever he felt like he should walk away, do so. Greed is what often destroyed a man. He always wondered why Pedro never practiced what he preached, even after Christopher had been killed. He wasn't going to make the same mistakes. He knew he had something special and he wanted to keep it. He would leave the game for Tiffany. Not right away, but very soon. If that's what it took to be with her, then he would do it.

Tiffany looked at Rico and knew he was sincere. She could see it in his eyes. "I can do that," she said with a smile before setting down her fork and pushing away her plate. She was full and wanted to go wash her hands.

"Where's the bathroom?" she asked.

"Straight back," he pointed down the hall. "You ready to go?" he asked.

He too was done, and anxious to get back to the hotel room so he could call his team, shower and relax.

"Yeah, I'm ready. Let me use the bathroom and wash my hands really quick."

As Tiffany headed to the back, Rico took out his phone and saw he had dozens of missed calls from random people. Many of the calls were from Latisha, who had texted him to call her back.

Rico figured Tiffany would be a few minutes. He decided to use the opportunity to call his team. First, he dialed up his right-hand Chubs. The phone rang five times before going to voicemail. Rico's stomach formed a knot as terrible thoughts plagued his mind. He called his second-in-command, Paulie. His phone rang twice before he picked up.

"Rico," Paulie answered. He sounded like he was whispering.

"School me," Rico said. He needed to know what was going on.

"Man, them niggas damn near wiped out the whole block. Chubs, Boobie ... they gone," Paulie said choking up as he fought back tears. His dear friends were dead. They had been a team for years. It was about more than just money; they were like family.

Rico didn't respond. He sat on the phone quietly, too stunned to respond. He blamed himself. It all started with him.

"Rico ... man you hear me? Chubs and Boobie is dead. Chubs got hit in the head and Boobie was hit in his back. He died at the hospital. I called Latisha, so she could get information from some of the hoes in the hood. She said they still got Chubs laying out in the street ... You gotta come through. I'm at the stash house."

Rico snapped out of his trance and finally responded. "Na, right now we lay low. Shit is going to be dumb hot. We'll meet tomorrow, but not at the stash house. You get the fuck outta there. Go somewhere safe ... somewhere you can lay low and rest up. I'll hit you up with the details. Bruh be safe," Rico said before hanging up.

Just as he was stuffing his phone back into his jeans, Tiffany was coming out of the bathroom. He watched as she walked towards him with a drunk grin on her face. He didn't understand how someone so good could be associated with someone so bad. Had Antonio not been present with both his children, only a D.N.A. test would have convinced him Tre and Tiffany were related.

"You ready sir?" Tiffany said.

"Yeah, let's go," Rico responded with his stomach still feeling as if it was in knots. The feeling of dread and grief briefly washed over him. He knew it was going to take a while for his mind to actually register the loss and what was happening. He also knew that he still wasn't safe and that the cops, as well as his enemies, could still very well be looking for him. He shook off thoughts of his fallen soldiers and got up to leave.

Rico lay face-down on the king-size hotel bed and stared into space while Tiffany gave him a back massage. After checking into a suite downtown, he took a shower and did his best to relax. Tiffany could tell he was bothered and did her best to comfort him. He had done an excellent job making her feel at ease after she'd had such a rough night. It was now her turn to return the favor. She had heard him on the phone and from what she'd gathered, something was wrong, however, she didn't like to pry so she didn't ask him any questions.

"You okay babe?" Tiffany asked again for what seemed like the hundredth time.

Rico had been aloof and unknowingly staring off into space. Tiffany's voice quickly brought him out of his trance. He flipped over unexpectedly and pulled her off him. She now lay underneath of his body. He stared at her, his mind randomly swirling with curiosity.

"I'm good," Rico finally responded. "Can I ask you a question though?" he asked unexpectedly.

"Of course," she replied curiously.

"Why do you care so much? About me?" He had to know.

The question was simple, and for Tiffany, the answer was even simpler.

"I see good in you," she replied without thought. "Your heart seems pure, and besides, I never judge a book by its cover, nor do I judge its contents by the opinions of others. I read it myself and form my own."

Rico couldn't do anything but smile. She was special. He had one more question. "Can I ask you one more question? But you gotta promise me you won't take offense."

"Sure," she responded.

"Do you see good in your father and brother? Just like you said before ... you heard rumors about me. Well, I've heard rumors about your family."

Tiffany sighed, then smiled and replied. "I'm sure I've heard them all as well. However, I never gossip. I observe ... My father is reformed. He did what he had to do to take care of his family. He is not perfect, and nor does he portray himself to be. The same man they may speak ill of, has also created jobs, and only hires people from poor neighborhoods. He's also the same man who makes his properties affordable and works with people who are experiencing financial difficulties, so they won't be out on the streets. So yes, I see much good in him. My brother on the other hand is a different story ... he is spoiled and feels entitled. I love him dearly and would shed blood for him. Does that answer your question?" she smiled again.

It did, but Rico didn't bother responding. To him, Tiffany was honest and extremely intelligent. He just hoped she wasn't intelligent enough to see his true feelings about her brother. If he were any other street nigga, she would be in danger. What better way than to avenge his team and issue vengeance against Tre. He had the ultimate pawn: his sister. Unfortunately, his heart said otherwise, and he loved Tiffany with his whole being. No harm would come to her.

"I respect your loyalty to your family," he said.

Rico silently wished there was another way he and Tre could resolve their issues. Tiffany wrapped her arms around Rico's neck as he leaned in to give her a passionate kiss. Even during what he was going through, her presence brought him comfort. He loved her something fierce. Their chemistry was undeniable, and their bodies needed one another. Rico grabbed Tiffany and hoisted her behind up in the air. His manhood pulsated through his jeans from anticipation. He leaned down and kissed her passionately. He aggressively ripped her panties apart on one side and pushed himself between her legs. She gasped slightly. His presence alone gave her body life and hers restored his. She needed him. They needed each other.

Antonio did his best to make himself comfortable in the hospital waiting room. He sighed when he realized it just wasn't going to happen. The building was cold, and the waiting room's basic chairs lacked the necessary comfort his tired body craved. He was ready to go home and relax. Relaxing his body would be easy; it was his mind that would need assistance.

Antonio looked over to the double doors again. The doors led back to the emergency care area. Tre had been in the room for hours and was scheduled to be released soon. He would be glad when that happened. His mind was racing because he had no idea what his next move would be. Pedro had been his plug for years and not only that; they were what one would consider good friends.

A part of him wanted to reach out to Pedro and try to resolve the issue, but that would be absurd. How could something like that be resolved? His son had been murdered in a botched robbery. How could one make that right? Had it been his own child, there would be no way. Only death would do.

Tre had really put him in a tough spot where he was without choices. It angered him that he was being involuntarily dragged in what could possibly be a street war. Knowing Pedro, it would be more of a hit. It seemed the more he tried to get out, the deeper he was being pulled in.

There was no question that his son would take precedence. It was settled. He was going to find out what Pedro knew, and then prepare for war. Family over everything. There was nothing left to discuss.

Tre moaned as the Hispanic nurse in front of him changed the dressing on his wound. It hurt; however, he considered himself lucky. Although superficial, the graze was still two inches deep. Had it gone further, he would be dealing with a real gunshot wound that could have done some considerable damage.

"Ok sweetie. It's important that you keep the area around the stitches clean. You can clean it with peroxide and alcohol. You'll also need to change the dressing twice a day. Do you have someone that can help you with this? That shoulder is going to be a few weeks healing. After that, you should have most of your strength back."

"Yeah, my sister will take care of it," Tre responded as she finished securing the gauze and bandages.

"Good. I'm going to print off your care papers and I'll be back with them, along with your discharge papers. You just hang tight," she replied with a warm smile, before walking out the room.

"Aight."

Tre sighed as soon as the nurse exited the room. He was irritated and ready to leave. He had shit to take care of with his team and still had to deal with his dad and sister. Truthfully, he felt like they were blowing everything out of proportion. Rico had no idea who the fuck he was, and neither did Pedro. Rico probably hadn't even put everything together yet. He couldn't have known that the same person he was warring with in the street had something to do with his own uncle's home invasion. During the robbery they had on masks, while the shootout that occurred was directly related to a club brawl, not drugs or Christopher's murder.

As much as Tre wanted to continue believing Pedro and Rico were blind to reality, he had to be prepared just in case that wasn't the actual case. Maybe Pedro did know; maybe Rico knew as well. Tiffany could be in trouble. He hated to admit, but if the latter were true, he would need his father. Tre made up his mind that he would confess to his father everything that had happened. If he needed him, he wanted him to be well-informed and thoroughly prepared. Although concerned about Tiffany, he didn't think that Rico was around her specifically for revenge. She had been talking about Rico long before he'd robbed Pedro. Besides, she had nothing to do with what was going on. The problem was, there was no telling how one's feelings could change when money, loyalty, and revenge were a factor.

29

PEDRO TOOK A HEARTY SIP FROM HIS WINE GLASS WHILE THE early morning moonlight cast a glow down on the private yacht he and his wife occupied. He loved to sit out, day and night and admire the beauty of the sea. Although they didn't own it, Pedro personally knew the captain and used the luxurious boat as often as he liked. Unfortunately, it wasn't often enough. He and Anna had left the States for a few days, only to bury their child and take a quick, but much needed vacation. However, when their vacation ended, he was headed back to take care of some unfinished business.

Ever since Christopher had been murdered, his mind was stuck on revenge. He wanted Antonio and his bastard kid dead. He didn't understand what was taking Rico so long to complete such a simple task. Pedro had done an excellent job maintaining his composure and concealing his feelings; however, he needed some reassurance that Antonio and his son Tre were going to be dealt with — soon.

Since Christopher's funeral, Antonio had contacted him numerous times offering a listening ear and his condolences. Unfortunately, to Pedro it was nothing more than an additional insult to him and his family. He would not be fooled by him a second time. He wanted justice for Christopher, and he wanted it sooner rather than later. He wondered why he hadn't heard from Rico. He tried dialing his number. After ringing five times with no answer, Pedro hung up.

For some reason, he felt some hesitance from his nephew. He wasn't sure why, and he really didn't care; he just knew that he wanted the job done. He decided then that he would need to bring in a for sure answer for his problem. Rico had until the end of the day to return his call and confirm that his problem had been resolved. In the meantime, he would call up Smoke; a hitman that never missed a target. He'd known Smoke since they were both boys in the slums of Guadalajara. Daily sights of murder and mayhem had made Smoke a stone-cold killer with no remorse or conscience. Some would even go as far as labeling him a serial killer. One thing that was certain, once your name was on his list, no one could save you; not even God himself.

Pedro took another sip from his glass while he waited for Smoke to answer his ringing phone.

"Hey old friend," Pedro greeted his friend in a jovial manner.

"Hey stranger," Smoke replied. He already knew who it was.

"Listen ... I got two tickets around my way." He wanted to cut to the chase. The less time on the phone, the better.

"Ok. That's two Curtis Jackson CD's," Smoke replied, not missing a beat. Even though they were considered older in the drug world, they were still hip to coding the term for murder. For every Curtis Jackson CD, it would cost $50,000.

"Done," Pedro responded before disconnecting the call.

Smoke was all about his money. He didn't ask questions and he got the job done quickly. As soon as Pedro put down his phone, he picked up his nearby laptop and proceeded to arrange a $100,000 transfer from his offshore account to Smoke's. Once he texted confirmation the money had come through, Smoke would call back from an untraceable, throw-away phone so he could acquire the details about his tickets.

Pedro looked out to the Punta Mita waters while he waited. Christopher had loved the water. He had been such a vivacious child, always wanting to explore. He was the reason they had purchased the million-dollar beach house a few hours from their home of Guadalajara.

Pedro quickly shifted his thoughts back to revenge. Once he got it, then he would be able to peacefully reminisce about the brief time he had with his only child.

30

TRE TOOK A GULP FROM THE GLASS OF WATER HE HAD POURED
after arriving in the house with his father. The cool water
eased his dry throat but did nothing to help with the task
that stood before him. He had to come clean and tell his
father what was going on completely with both Rico and
Pedro. He knew that Antonio wasn't going to be happy, if
not, borderline furious.

"Dad, I need to talk to you," Tre said nervously as he
walked into his father's room.

"What is it Tre? What else could you possibly want to
talk to me about?" he grumbled sarcastically.

Antonio stared at his son while he stood in his closet
and began removing his shoes. Despite the circumstances,
he was about to try and relax the best he could. As soon as
he walked into the house, Antonio went straight to his
liquor cabinet and poured himself a shot of Cognac. He
followed that up immediately with another.

"I know you're angry about everything that's going on
but —"

"Angry," Antonio smirked, cutting his son off. Tre
couldn't possibly understand the magnitude of the situation. He was clueless. Antonio unfortunately, knew what

Pedro stood for and he knew that his son had crossed over into the big leagues and had absolutely no fucking clue.

"Angry doesn't describe my feelings. If Pedro knows what really happened, our days are numbered. The only way we'll survive is if we become fucking animals ... and *you* son are no animal. There's going to be a war ... but you probably won't even realize it, because by the time it starts, you'll be dead before you can fuckin blink."

"I know shit is real," Tre responded with aggravation. He was sick and tired of being underestimated. "That's why I wanted to talk to you. With everything that's going on I know it's important that you know what shit is. I understand that things may get crazy. That's why I wanted to hip you to all the details ... some important one's that I left out." Tre looked to his father nervously.

Antonio looked up angrily and glared at his son. What could Tre have possibly left out. Shit was bad enough. He prayed it didn't get any worse; however, he knew that was like asking for a miracle.

"The situation with Pedro is bad ... I know," he admitted reluctantly. "But I wanted to also talk to you about the shootout. The shootout was between my crew and Rico's crew."

"What?" Antonio asked puzzled. He didn't understand.

"The shootout at the club was something separate from the shit with Pedro. It had nothing to do with the robbery at Pedro's house. Rico and I had an argument at the club over a female. We got into a scuffle and he sent niggas blazing at us afterwards. I never knew who he was ... or that he was related to Pedro... or that he was the same guy Tiffany had been dating."

Antonio sat down on his bed solemnly and sighed. Tre had been busy. Things were becoming more complicated by the minute.

"So, this," he said, pointing at Tre's wounded shoulder. "This wasn't from Pedro? This was behind the shit with Rico?"

"Yeah," he said swallowing the new lump that had formed in his throat. "Me and my crew ran down on the block they be on and let loose. They fired back, and I got hit."

Antonio just glared at his son. Tre continued. "It gets worse ... When we ran down on the block ... we fucked it up. People got killed. I haven't watched the news yet or heard anything. But, I'm pretty sure we left some bodies out there."

"So, now you're not only worried about Pedro retaliating. You're also worried about Rico retaliating. *And* you need to now worry about the two of them teaming up to retaliate. So not only one war ... two wars. One stupid ass street war over a bitch, and one war fueled by revenge. A war that's probably gonna end with a fucking hitman climbing through the windows and killing us all."

He buried his head in his hands and massaged his temples. They were fucked. Actually, they were beyond fucked. They would probably need to skip town. Antonio was by no means soft. However, he didn't have enough energy or manpower to deal with the danger Tre had put them in.

Tre didn't bother to respond. There was nothing he could say to make the situation sound any better. His nervousness grew while he waited for his father to respond to his silence. Antonio finally picked his head up.

"What do you plan to do Tre?" Antonio asked.

"I'm gunnin," he responded nonchalantly.

Antonio nodded in response. As much as he wanted to have confidence in Tre, he couldn't help but shake the feeling that he would soon have to bury his son.

"Where are you?" Antonio asked Tiffany without bothering to say hello.

Immediately recognizing the voice of her father, Tiffany jolted out of her sleep.

"I'm just waking up," she replied groggily. "I stayed in a hotel last night." She sat up immediately and wiped the crust out of her eyes. She glanced at the clock. *5 am.* They must have been in the hospital for hours.

"Well listen, I need to sit down and talk with both you and Tre. It's important. Is Rico with you?" Antonio asked abruptly. Tiffany hesitated, but before she could bother to respond, Antonio cut her off.

"Listen, I don't care if you two stayed the night together. You're an adult. But I do want you to answer me honestly, because what I have to say is important. Just answer me yes, or no. Is he with you?"

"Yes," she responded quietly, while glancing over at Rico, who was sleeping peacefully underneath the thick, hotel sheets with the comforter tangled up at his feet.

"It's important that you *do not* discuss any of our family business with him. Nothing at all. At nine o'clock you need to be here, so we can talk about important matters. Understood?" he asked.

"Understood," she quickly responded. She knew it had to be something important. His tone was serious, and it almost scared her. She wondered what he had to talk to them about that was so important. She got up and went to shower. She had too many thoughts that were now racing through her head. She knew she would never get back to sleep.

31

"WHAT SHORTY SAY ABOUT THE CAR?" DREW ASKED SPICE, after he walked through the door of their trap house holding a crumpled McDonald's bag.

"Fuck that bitch. I told her to make up a story," Spice replied, while pulling out a double cheeseburger wrapped in greasy white paper with orange lettering.

Drew laughed. "A story to who?"

"I don't know. A story to whoever gives a fuck."

He laughed but he was serious. The female who had gotten the car for him had already been told that if she implicated his name in anything, she would pay dear consequences. She wasn't stupid, so he wasn't worried.

"But anyway, what's up with ya man Tre?" Spice continued.

"Nigga, that's ya man," Drew teased.

"Na. That's your clown ass homeboy crying and carrying on about a lil pussy ass wound on his shoulder," he said, referring to the graze Tre had suffered from. As soon as Tre had left the hospital and got to his phone, he had sent Drew a text informing him of his condition.

"You want one of these jawns?" Spice finally offered as he chewed relentlessly from the bite of burger he had just taken.

"Lil bitch stopped me to Mickey's before we got here. I didn't have time to call you. Shorty was bugging; rushing me and shit, talking bout she was gon be late to work."

"Na I'm good. I don't want none of that shit. Nasty ass McDonald's be fucking with my stomach. Thanks though," Drew replied.

"Fuck outta here," Spice mumbled as he took another bite of his sandwich. "On some gee shit, we need to find out where Tre's pops got that money and work at," he suggested between bites.

"True indeed," Drew replied. His eyes lit up at the mere thought of coming across more money. "I know that nigga got a nice stash."

"Hell yeah. I'm sure he's sitting on something husky," Spice cosigned.

We bout to get on top of that asap," Drew added with seriousness and finality.

32

ANTONIO SAT STIFF AND UPRIGHT IN HIS RECLINER, STARING towards the front door waiting for Tiffany. It was 8:45. He was expecting her to walk in any minute. She was an early riser unlike her brother, who was still sleep in his room. For the life of him, Antonio couldn't understand how Tre seemed to sleep so soundly with all that was going on around him.

Despite Tre's recent revelations, Antonio felt like a small weight had been lifted off his shoulders. He had asked Tre for the details of the home invasion. Even after he had explained it, Antonio made him repeat the story several times over so he could visualize the events in his head, as well as make sure he wasn't being lied to. As much as Tre hated to divulge the details of his dirty deeds to his father, he did so honestly. Based off that information, Antonio concluded that there was no way Pedro actually knew who the masked men were that entered his home the dreadful night he was robbed. Even if he suspected Tre, he was sure he didn't have any actual proof. Antonio was now hopeful. He felt that with a proper plan and strategy, he could possibly fix the mess his son had created. The first thing he had to do was fill Tiffany in on what was going on.

As soon as the thoughts entered his head, he heard

Tiffany's jingling keys tapping lightly against the door. After slipping her key into the lock, she let herself into the home. She deactivated the state-of-the-art security system, sat her bag on the table and walked into the living room. She knew her father would be there waiting for her.

"Hey Daddy," she said awkwardly. Still slightly embarrassed from just admitting to staying the night with a man, she struggled to maintain eye contact with her father. "What's going on now," she huffed while plopping down on the large sectional across the room.

Antonio felt no need to beat around the bush due to the severity of the situation. He had to let her know what they were up against. He quickly and thoroughly told Tiffany the story that Tre had given to him. When he was finished Tiffany sat on the couch fuming. Not only was she upset, she was in shock that all this had been taking place right under nose.

As much as she didn't want it to, it all made perfect sense. She remembered Rico telling her about getting jumped at Starlite's, but he never mentioned who the perpetrators were. She distinctly remembered the nasty, now almost-healed scar on his face. Tre also never disclosed to her who he was beefing with. She felt betrayed on both ends. Tre and Rico had come face to face several times in front of her, and neither of them had been man enough to inform her of what was going on. Her brother had been shot behind the nonsense. He could have died.

She loved Rico, but she had been raised with the beliefs that family took precedence over everything. She was confused and was livid that she was in such a difficult position to have to choose. Her hands were tied. Because of her stupid brother, she would have to cut ties with the man she loved. She was sick and tired of her life being dramatically affected by her rebellious sibling.

With all the details laid out in front of her, Tiffany felt a cloud of emotions envelop her. Tears stung her eyes. She placed her face into her palms and began to weep softly.

"Please don't cry Tiffany," Antonio said. He knew she was frustrated and just as fed up with Tre's bullshit.

"I think I can fix this. If Rico genuinely loves you, I'm sure we can fix this. If I bring them together with you there, I'm sure they would agree to squash the beef and end the drama they have going on in the street. Underneath of Pedro, Rico is still a leader. If he says the war stops with his team, then the war stops. Tre and I can talk to Drew and Spice and put an end to this." It made sense; he was hopeful. However, he wasn't sure if his plan would work the way he wanted it to.

"What about Pedro," Tiffany asked with a sniffle, while briefly looking up at her father.

Antonio sighed deeply. "I don't know. The first step is to end the issues between Tre and Rico. If I can convince Rico that Tre was not involved, I'm sure he could act as a mediator between Tre and Pedro. It's far-fetched and I know I would have to speak for Tre, but it's the only shot we have." Antonio paused. "Because if that doesn't work, Pedro is going to try to kill Tre ... and he's also going to try and kill me because he knows that he will see me in rare form to protect my own. I've laid down blocks for that man. For my family, I'll lay down this city," he said with finality.

When Tre woke, he heard his sister crying in the living room. Although faint, he still could detect the sniffles she did her best to conceal. His initial reaction was to go comfort her; however, he hesitated. With all that was going on he figured she had called it quits with Rico. Their father had mentioned he would be informing her of what exactly was going on. He knew when it was all said and done, Tiffany was going to be beyond pissed with him. Tre figured he would shower and get dressed. He had to get up with his crew and fill them in on what had transpired. He figured they would be waiting for him.

After taking a hot shower, Tre proceeded to get dressed. He pulled out a plain, white Polo tee and a pair of pressed Polo jeans that were hanging up in his designer clad closet. He didn't feel like being dapper today. His shoulder hurt like hell and he couldn't wait to pop one of the Tylenol 3's the hospital had prescribed. Since it was well after 10am, he figured his father had already filled his prescription. He headed to the kitchen to see if he had left it on the counter.

As Tre made his way to the kitchen, Tiffany spotted him. Seeing her brother since her father had told her what he'd had been up, further upset her already fragile emotional state. Without saying a word, Tiffany jumped off the couch and lunged at her brother, her arms flailing.

"This is all your fault!" she sobbed while swinging wildly, missing Tre's face but still landing a few harmless blows to his body.

"Yo, chill the fuck out Tiff," Tre responded in shock, as well as pain. He expected her to be mad, but not this mad.

He weakly grabbed her arms and held them to end the assault. He knew she was upset because she'd struck him. Tiffany was not a physical person. Additionally, she knew he had just gotten out of the hospital and was in a great deal of pain. Tiffany, however, had seemingly forgotten that. The way Tre saw it, his sister was acting way out of her character, all because of bitch ass Rico. That didn't sit well with Tre. It actually angered him.

"I don't give a fuck what you gotta do or what happens to them niggas in that hood, but you're squashing the beef between you and Rico," she demanded between clenched teeth.

"I ain't squashing shit," he responded angrily before releasing her. "And I'm riding with my niggas," he said while looking her directly in her eyes.

"You gonna do what the fuck I tell you to do!"

Antonio's booming voice surprised them and seemed to shake the house. Through the commotion they never heard Antonio enter the home with Tre's prescription in hand. Tre rolled his eyes angrily and headed towards his room. Of course, Antonio would take Tiffany's side. He was sick and tired of everyone trying to tell him what to do. He didn't have to put up with the bullshit.

Antonio stormed behind him. He'd had enough of Tre's shit. He didn't want anyone telling him what to do, yet everyone was being affected by his reckless and irresponsible actions. Not only that, but he was also calling on everyone for help when things proved to be more than he could handle. Antonio had long ago seen things for what they were. His son was a selfish, weak-minded follower.

"Them niggas don't give two shits about you!" Antonio yelled once he arrived at the entrance of Tre's room.

He watched as Tre moved around hastily and angrily, searching for his keys and a pair of shoes so he could leave. The pain from his shoulder slowed him down, further annoying him.

"These the same niggas that left you bleeding and never once called to check to see if you were ok."

Tre didn't respond because he knew his father was right. There were no missed calls or text messages from his so-called friends. Neither Drew nor Spice had reached out to his family inquiring about him. Neither of the cousins had even bother to respond, even after he sent Drew a text letting him know he was okay.

Antonio continued. "You started this bullshit and now you have the nerve to tell your sister what you *will* and *won't* do. And sit the fuck down!" he demanded. "You're not going anywhere."

Tre smacked his teeth and sat down at the foot of his king-size bed. He figured it was best if he calmed down. Based on his father's demeanor, he wasn't for the bullshit. Besides, he was in enough pain. Tiffany walked into the Tre's room, running her hand through her disheveled hair in frustration.

"Daddy tell him he's going to squash the beef. He doesn't have a choice."

"You will end this Tre," Antonio said. "Your sister is going to talk to Rico and see what he says first."

He looked to Tiffany. "Whatever you do, do not mention the robbery of Pedro's home. You understand?" he asked sternly. "We don't know what Pedro really knows. The way shit looks, he may believe that Tre did have a role in the robbery. If that is the case, then they're going off pure speculation. We're not going to confirm their suspicions. Understood?" he asked firmly.

"Yes. I understand," she murmured. Frustrated, Tiffany proceeded to head out. She had to get ready to do damage control.

33

"Wassup?" Tre greeted Drew as soon as he picked up the phone. "Y'all in the hood?" he asked nervously. He looked around and made sure no one could overhear his conversation; namely Antonio and Tiffany.

"Yeah, we at the trap house," Drew responded.

"Good. I'm about to come through. I have some important shit we need to discuss."

"Bet. See you when you get here," he said before hanging up.

While Tre called a taxi, and made his way out to the hood, Drew wondered what could be so important. An hour later, he walked into the trap house and approached Drew and Spice while they sat at the kitchen table conducting their routine tasks.

"You want some of this shit?" Spice asked. He extended his arm out to Tre with a lit blunt dangling between his index and middle finger. Tre declined and figured he'd get right down to business.

"Listen, I didn't come to smoke and shit. The nigga that we been going at it with for weeks ... Rico—"

"What about him?" Drew asked, now curious.

"That pussy is Tiffany's fucking boyfriend," he said angrily. "Now my Pops is on some, "*let's make peace* shit.""

But that's not it. This nigga Rico ... is also Pedro's nephew."

Drew sat down the money he was counting, while Spice immediately smashed out the blunt he was smoking.

"What do they know?" Drew asked.

"We're not sure what either of them know. What I do know, is that Rico knows who the fuck I am. That's for sure. He came to the house right after the shooting. We stood face to face. His expression said it all. He even reached for his gun. And my dumb ass wasn't even strapped. The only reason that nigga didn't buck is because my Pops was there. But he definitely knows."

"What about Pedro?" Spice asked. "Does he know it was us?"

"That's the fucking problem. We don't know if Pedro suspects us or not. If he does, then Rico is in on that suspicion. He's one of Pedro's top lieutenants."

"What the fuck that gotta do with us though Tre?" Drew eyed Tre.

"My Dad wants us to squash the beef and maybe use Rico as a middleman to clear our names with Pedro."

"Fuck that," Spice said firmly. "Fuck Rico and fuck that old bitch Pedro."

"That's a no-go Tre. I don't trust them Spanish motherfuckers. Rico's loyalty is going to his family. Now, you may be an exception because of the history between your father and Pedro. It also helps that Rico is fucking Tiffany. But not us. We are not an exception. And on some gee shit ... I really don't think you would be either. Especially if they really think you killed the nigga son."

Tre listened intently. What Drew was saying made sense.

"I say you meet that nigga Rico. Let ya Pops arrange that. You find out what that nigga knows. Put him at ease and let him think shit is sweet. Then, when we creep up on him and lay his ass down, he won't expect it," Spice said.

"Word. Tell him you speak on behalf of us all. Agree to squash shit and we kill that nigga later," Drew added. "Word on the street is that we done already took down most of Rico's team. He's weak right now. We lay him, and then we lay down the rest of his team. Shouldn't be hard. Then we take over the Westside."

"Shit don't stop just because we got a little beef Tre. This is the fucking takeover nigga. We deal with Pedro when the time comes," Spice cosigned.

Tre thought about it for a minute. He knew he was in way over his head, and it showed. He was a little reluctant about how to proceed. If they truly wanted to take over the streets then what Drew and Spice was saying, was right. However, he knew their actions would devastate his sister. It could also potentially make matters worse with Pedro.

"I'll handle it," Tre said.

"Good," Drew replied. "It's gonna work out Tre. I know you don't want to be at odds with ya Pops, but you gotta remember, that nigga done made his money. He's old and washed up. You're making the right choice if you really want to be a part of this takeover. We gon run this fucking city. We gon have more money than we've ever seen."

"No doubt," Tre replied.

34

RICO SAT IN HIS DARKLY TINTED MERCEDES AND LISTENED TO the rain tap repetitiously against the body. He stared at the blue, Tiffany Box he held in his hand and knew that he was about to do the right thing. The box held Tiffany's engagement ring. He was going to propose tonight. He had purchased it at the last minute a few days prior and promised himself he would give it to her when the time was right. With all that was going on and him not knowing how things would turn out, he decided not to wait any longer. He loved her with all his heart, and he wanted her to be a part of his life indefinitely.

Rico still had a problem. He had to figure out how to deal with Tiffany's father and brother. Pedro had ordered him to kill the two. He was now forced to choose between the love of his life, or the loyalty to his uncle and the crown to an empire. Truth of the matter was, he didn't have a problem with killing Tre, he just couldn't bring himself to off Antonio. He knew Tiffany would never forgive him if he killed either one. The longer he stalled on the matter, the more he lost control.

If Rico didn't get the hit done, he knew Pedro would delegate the responsibility to someone else. That someone else, wouldn't hesitate to get the job done. Pedro wasn't fond of waiting. Pedro wanted Antonio *and* Tre dead. Their deaths were imminent.

Tiffany sat on the edge of her bed and did her best to make sense of the situation she was faced with. She didn't understand why Rico would keep the issue with her brother away from her. Tre had gotten hurt behind it; better yet, he could have been killed. She knew Rico, and she knew that it had to be a good reason why he had hidden their beef from her. It had better be good, because if it wasn't, it was over between the two of them. The thought of losing Rico hurt. However, she had been raised with loyalty. She would side with no man over her family.

She concluded that if Rico really loved her, he would end whatever issues he had with Tre. She prayed he would. In the meantime, she decided to take a hot bath. She knew that would calm her. Before she went to bathe, she decided to make a call. She picked up her phone from the night stand near her bed. She tapped in the familiar numbers and waited.

After several rings, Rico picked up.

"Hey babe," he answered.

"Hi," she responded softly. Her jaws were tight from her clenched teeth, but she did her best to conceal her anger.

"I need to talk to you. It's important. When can you get here?" she asked.

"Actually, I was gonna slide through there in a few anyway. I wanna talk to you about something also."

Tiffany's forehead crinkled slightly. She wondered what he had to talk about. Maybe he planned to come clean about everything that had been going on.

"Okay. I'm all ears. So, when can you get here?" she asked.

Rico brought his wrist up to eyesight to look at the time

on his watch. "I gotta make a run really quick, but I can probably get there in about an hour."

"Ok. I'll see you then."

Tiffany hung up the phone abruptly, surprising Rico. Something was wrong. He could sense it. He looked down at his phone and was tempted to call her back. He quickly decided against it. He would find out what was up when he got there.

Rico pulled his car into the parking lot of Tiffany's building and stared out the window. His stomach was doing somersaults and his feet felt heavy, delaying his exit from the vehicle. After several deep breaths, he opened the door to get out. Before his first Givenchy clad foot could touch the pavement, his phone rang. He sighed deeply. It was his uncle.

35

ANTONIO SAT SILENTLY IN HIS OFFICE. HIS ARMS WERE RESTED on his desk, while his fingers were locked together. He stared straight ahead, deep in thought. He contemplated his next move. He still had a large number of drugs left, but lately hadn't been able to focus on getting rid of it. The situation with Tre had been occupying most of his time. Keeping his family safe was his priority; however, he had to get rid of the drugs he was sitting on. He was determined to reach his goal so he could fully walk away from the drug trade.

Antonio picked up his cell phone from his desk and made a few calls. Most were to his high-end clients. The rest were made to a few dealers he knew that were trying to purchase wholesale. After notating the deals, he grabbed his things to leave. He retrieved his money from the couch and pulled his gym bag full of work from the closet. He usually didn't keep work in the office; however, he had tucked it there a few days ago for safekeeping.

This was his last package, so he was trying to move it quickly. He was cutting all kinds of deals to rid himself of the drugs. His plan was to drop his money off to his house and later distribute all the drugs. Once he was done, he was getting his kids out of the city for a while. At least until things died down.

Gathering up his bag of cash and bag of dope, Antonio headed to his office door to leave. Before he could touch the handle, his phone rang. He dropped his bags to the floor and fished his phone from his pocket. It was Tiffany.

"What's up Unc, how's Auntie?" Rico asked, doing his best to sound normal.

He knew Pedro was pissed. The job hadn't been done and Rico had missed several of his calls.

"Everything is good Sobrino," Pedro responded. "Why haven't I heard from you?"

"I've been busy trying to handle that problem."

"Yeah? Well looks to me like you can't handle this one. Doesn't seem like you're ready for this empire. Am I right?" Pedro asked.

"Na Unc I got it. I just want to make sure I handle it right," he responded, doing his best to sound convincing.

"Silence," Pedro sharply stated. "I'm tired of waiting. I contacted Smoke. You stand down. He will handle it."

Rico forced down the knot in his throat. "Ok." He knew there was nothing left for him to say. Pedro had spoken.

"We will talk when I get back."

Rico looked down at the phone. Pedro had hung up.

"Fuck," he muttered through clenched teeth.

Jamming his phone back into his pocket he glanced in the direction of Tiffany's condo. She had no idea. Rico knew exactly who Smoke was, as well as what he was capable of. Without a doubt, he knew that Antonio and Tre would both be dead soon. He decided he would keep Tiffany close over the next twenty-four hours. That's usually all the time Smoke needed. Rico knew that Smoke left no witnesses. If Tiffany happened to be with either of his targets when

Smoke decided to carry out his hit, Rico knew that she would wind up just as dead as they were.

———

Tiffany opened the door solemnly and allowed Rico inside of her home. She didn't bother to greet him. She walked over to the couch and sat down. She picked up her wine glass from the coffee table and took a drink.

"What's up with you babe? Everything okay?" he asked with a frown. He could sense something was wrong.

"You tell me Rico," she said sternly, finally allowing her anger to show. "Why the fuck didn't you tell me about what has been going on between you and my brother?"

Rico looked away and bit his bit down on his lip. He was caught off guard. He wondered how she found out.

"Look baby, I didn't know how to tell you," he stammered. "How do you tell someone you love some shit like that?"

"Don't give me that bullshit Rico," she argued, slamming down her glass, and jumping up from the couch. "You and your fucking homeboys are beefing with my brother and he got shot behind it," she growled through clenched teeth.

"Fuck," he mumbled. He didn't realize she knew that too. She probably knew everything.

"You've been fucking lying and hiding shit from me this whole time," she cried. "I can't believe I didn't see this shit."

Rico didn't respond. He just stared at her. It hurt to see her hurting. He had fucked up.

Tiffany shook her head from side to side in disgust. "Tre told me about the club shooting."

"Tiffany, I didn't know he was your brother," he admitted sincerely.

"You still could have told me Rico!" she yelled. "You could have come to me."

"Look babe, I'm sorry. I try to leave that street shit in the street. I didn't come to you because that's not a part of my life that I want to share with you. That's because I want to keep you safe." He walked towards her and stopped when he stood in front of her.

"Look. If you want the truth, your brother started the shit. Him and his homeboys jumped me at the club. I didn't know any of them. I left right after. My team reacted the way they did and retaliated. I never pulled a single trigger that night," he explained.

"Okay. But what about last night?" Tiffany asked, referring to the latest shooting involving Tre.

"I did participate in that shooting. *But* that's only because Tre and his crew came through the block and shot it up. We acted in self-defense. Two of my friends died that night Tiffany," he said angrily. "Nigga's I've known for years. They're fucking dead. I'm no fucking angel, but neither the fuck is Tre!" he replied angrily.

Tiffany stood in front of Rico and stared quietly into his eyes. His tone had startled her and caused her to stare him down with anger. The look in his eyes didn't lie. He was hurt; he was angry, and he was tired. She believed him.

"I'm sorry Rico but I need you to end this, or end us."

"It's over. If he stops, we'll stop. I'll end my beef with Tre," he agreed almost immediately with sincerity. He wasn't losing her.

Rico wrapped his arms around Tiffany and hugged her.

"I love you babe, and I don't want to lose you. You mean everything to me," he admitted. He meant every word. "Just give me a time and place and it's done."

"Right now. Right here." Surprised, Rico pulled away from her. He hadn't been expecting her to say that.

"Okay," he replied nervously.

He would go ahead and appease her by making amends. He knew it wasn't going to be much longer before Smoke killed Antonio and Tre anyway. At least when they died, Tiffany wouldn't think that he had a hand in it.

"Good. I'm gonna go ahead and call my dad. He'll bring Tre."

She ran to the kitchen to grab her phone while Rico took a seat on the couch and prepared to make amends with his foes.

"Hey Daddy," Tiffany said to Antonio as soon as he answered his phone.

"Hey baby. You caught me at a busy time," he stated, glancing down at his bags on the floor. "I was just on my way home. Getting ready to handle a few things."

"I'm sorry to bother you but I got Rico here at my house. If you can get here with Tre, we can go ahead and settle this foolishness between them."

"Okay. I'll get up with Tre and we'll get there soon," Antonio agreed.

"Thank you, Daddy. He means a lot to me, and so do you and Tre. I just want everyone to get along."

"I know Tiffany. Everything will work out. We'll settle it soon. I'll be there shortly ok."

"Alright Daddy. Love you."

"Love you too. We'll be there soon."

As soon as he hung up, he called Tre and told him to meet him at Tiffany's house in thirty minutes. He quickly filled Tre in on what was going to happen there. Although hesitant, Tre agreed. He knew it was for the best.

After hanging up from Tre, Antonio scooped his bags back up from the floor. He figured he could handle business later. For now, he would drop off the work and money to the house and head out to Tiffany. When he was done, he'd swing back through, grab his work, and distribute it. He knew that it was still premature and only at the beginning stages, but he truly believed that things were going to work out just fine.

TRE STUFFED HIS PHONE INTO HIS POCKET AND WALKED INTO the kitchen. Drew and Spice were still seated at the table from earlier.

"Ayo, I gotta roll. My sister got this bitch nigga Rico at her crib. Bout to go dead this shit with him. For now, anyway," he said with a smirk.

"Cool. Go ahead and take care of that shit," Drew added.

"Bet, I be back soon," Tre responded slowly with lazy eyes.

"Nigga you better focus up and shake that loud the fuck off," Drew stated firmly, referring to the high-grade weed they had been smoking for the past few hours. The same loud that Tre initially said he didn't come for.

"True. I'm good though," Tre replied, wiping his eyes as if that would do any good.

Spice shook his head from side to side and glanced at Tre. "That nigga stupid," he mumbled.

For all they knew, Tre could be walking into an ambush. It wouldn't be much he could do about it since he was flying high off loud.

"Whatever," Tre replied before walking out the door and stumbling to his car. He had shit to take care of.

RICO SAT ON THE COUCH AND WATCHED AS TIFFANY SHUFFLED around in the kitchen. He couldn't stop thinking about how hurt she was going to be when Smoke caught up with her father and brother. It wasn't a matter of if. it was a matter of when. Rico loved Tiffany and didn't want to see her hurt; however, there was nothing he could do to prevent it.

"Babe, my dad just texted me. He's pulling up. You ready?" Tiffany yelled from the kitchen. She came into the living room and smiled warmly at Rico.

"Yeah. I'm ready," he replied nervously.

He contemplated telling Antonio that he and Tre should leave town. For Tiffany's sake, he wanted to give them a warning that Pedro knew Tre was behind the robbery and death of his son. Antonio was a smart man. Once given that information, he would know that there had been a hit put out on him. Anyone that dealt with Pedro knew how he operated. Rico quickly decided against telling Antonio anything. He still had to exhibit a certain level of loyalty to his uncle.

"Listen babe. You hang out here. I'm going to go talk to your father outside," Rico stated. He got up from the couch and headed to the door to leave.

"You think that's a good idea?" she asked reluctantly, still standing in the living room.

Rico shrugged. "Yeah. I don't see why not. Besides, I don't want you in the mix of that kind of shit. Some things aren't for you to hear," he added, with his hand now resting on the door handle.

"Yeah, I bet. Some things you just don't want me to know," Tiffany replied sharply in frustration. "Like the night you and Tre got into it, you were fighting over a bitch."

She stared him down. The look in her eyes dared him to lie to her face. Rico turned around to face her. Tiffany's face was now contorted into a frown. She was angry.

"Babe it wasn't even like that," he said with a sigh.

Tiffany stepped back. "Wel,l what's it like then?" she asked. She stood and waited for him to respond.

"Shorty came with me to the club that night. Tre disrespected her and I went to intervene and ya brother got real fly with me. I reacted. It wasn't about no bitch. It was about the disrespect he showed. If I had let Tre disrespect her while she was with me, my whole team would have seemed soft. I couldn't let that happen … Listen, I don't give a fuck about that girl. I didn't then, and I don't now. I love you, Tiffany. You know that."

Tiffany looked down to the floor. She couldn't help but feel jealousy; however, she believed him. She quickly shook off the feelings and refocused on what mattered.

"It's all good. But don't let that shit happen again," she said with a smirk. "But go ahead. Daddy's waiting. You'll want to catch him before he heads in."

Rico smiled and headed out the door. He couldn't wait to present her with the ring he had bought. He was about to make her his forever.

38

THE MAN WATCHED RICO AND ANTONIO QUIETLY FROM THE driver's seat of his parked Dodge Caravan. The two had been immersed in conversation several minutes and never noticed they were being observed. It was now or never. He got out of the car, being careful not to shut the door fully. He didn't want the sound to alert them.

Rico was standing in front of Antonio, while Antonio's back was to the man as he quickly approached. The clunk his combat boots made against the pavement caused Rico to glance in his direction. Rico's heart began to race. He knew the man. His eyes widened, but he said nothing. There was no time.

In one swift motion, Smoke snatched his gun from his waistband and squeezed down on the trigger. The silencer on the gun muffled the sound of the shot, but the forceful impact from the bullet caused Antonio's body to hit the ground with a thud. The quarter sized hole in Antonio's head produced a pool of blood and left Rico standing in shock, coated in a red mist.

"Ric go. Get the fuck out of here," Smoke said before turning around and heading back to his van. One down, one more to go.

39

TRE DROVE THROUGH THE GATES OF HIS SISTER'S COMPLEX AND immediately began searching for a parking spot close to her building. He didn't want to be there long. He had shit to handle. He spotted a gray van leaving and pulled directly into the spot they had just left from.

Tre saw his father's car parked a few cars down. Realizing he was probably the last to arrive to Tiffany's, he quickly parked his car and stepped out. As he made his way through the parking lot, he spotted Rico standing near the sidewalk in a daze. As he neared, Tre noticed Rico was covered in blood. He stopped abruptly when he realized Rico was standing over top of a body; a dead body, that happened to be his father.

Tre's heart felt as if someone had taken it and squeezed down on it. His breath seemed to leave him as he struggled for air. Tears of rage flooded his vision. He couldn't think. He couldn't speak. All he could do was respond. Armed, Tre pulled his gun out of his waist and fired on Rico. In a blind rage, he kept his finger on the trigger, squeezing long after his clip was empty.

When Tiffany heard the gun shots, she knew something was wrong. Barefoot, she raced out of her condo and into the parking lot. The sight in front of her stopped her in her tracks. She clutched her chest and went to cry out; however, no sound came from her mouth. She looked around wildly and tried to make sense of what she was seeing. Her father was lying on the ground in a pool of blood ... and so was Rico. However, Rico was still alive. His body twitched, and his hands were balled up in tight fists as he fought for his life. She ran to him and grabbed his upper body to try and sit him up. Still in a daze, Tre stood over top of Rico and watched his sister cradle Rico into her arms.

"What did you do?" she tried to yell. It came out in a whisper. Her energy and strength seemed to be dying right along with the men she loved.

"What happened?" she yelled. Tre still didn't respond.

"Ti- Tiff," Rico tried to speak but couldn't finish his words because of the blood forming in his mouth. He stared into Tiffany's eyes while he felt the life began to seep from his body. He wanted to give her something before it was too late.

With his final bit of strength, he reached into his pocket and tried to pull out her engagement ring. It fell to the ground. She picked up the blue box and opened it. It was beautiful. Tiffany's lips quivered, while tears and snot began to work their way down her face when she realized Rico had taken his last breath.

"No, no, no!" she cried. She tapped the sides of his face repeatedly to wake him. He was gone, and so was her father.

Tiffany buried her head into Rico's shoulder while she clutched his body tightly and wailed uncontrollably. Coming out of his daze, Tre realized he had to get away from there. He knew that the scene would soon be crawling with cops. He looked down to his hand that held his still smoking gun. He tucked it back into his pants and then reached down to try to pull Tiffany away from Rico. She angrily snatched away.

"Get the fuck off me!" she cried out. "I'm not leaving them," she sobbed, referring to Rico and her father.

Tre didn't bother to respond. He looked around and saw Tiffany's neighbors starting to come out and peek from their doorways. That was his cue to leave. Instead of running, he walked quietly to his car and drove off. He had to get out of town. He would send for his sister later.

40

TRE SLAMMED THE FRONT DOOR OF HIS HOME AND RAN TO HIS room to quickly pack a few bags to leave town. He could barely think, as things just seemed so surreal to him. He wasn't sure what he was going to do. He didn't have much cash and the credit card his father had given him for emergencies, only had a $5,000 limit. That wouldn't carry him long. He ran into Antonio's room to search for cash. As soon as he pushed open the door to his father's room, he nearly tripped over two large duffel bags. He reached down and unzipped one. He couldn't believe his eyes. It was full of cash. He unzipped the other. He stared down in amazement. It was full of neatly wrapped bricks of Heroin. From the looks of things, Antonio was planning to make a move and get the fuck out of dodge.

Tre reached down into his jean pockets and grabbed his phone. He called Spice. After a few rings, he picked up.

"Wassup?" Spice asked.

"Listen. I gotta make this quick," Tre panted. "Some shit popped off at my sis crib. Nigga killed my pops so I murked him," he explained.

"Who?" Spice asked, not completely following Tre.

"The nigga Rico. We were supposed to meet up at Tiffany's. I get there and my Pops is dead on the ground and he was standing over top of him. I shot him. But listen, I gotta get low for a while. My pops left a bag of weight. I need one of y'all niggas to come through and grab it to move while I'm gone."

"How much weight we talking about?" Spice asked.

"I don't fucking know. It's like three. Some leftover shit he had. But fuck all that. I don't have much time. Come grab this shit," Tre demanded.

"We'll be there," Spice replied before hanging up.

Drew and Spice had raced over to Tre's house as quickly as they could without getting pulled over. Not even thirty minutes had passed since they hung up from him. They parked near the entrance of the garage, where Tre usually kept his car. Exiting their car, they saw Tre carrying bags to his Cadillac.

"Tre," Drew called.

"Bout fucking time," Tre said in frustration. He was drenched in sweat and his eyes were darting around wildly from the earlier events that had taken place.

"Where the bag at? We gotta grab that shit and get the fuck away from here," Spice said to Tre.

"Come on. They right on the kitchen counter," Tre replied.

Tre turned around to head back into the house. He never saw Drew pull out his gun and fire once. The bullet from Drew's gun, pierced Tre's skull and killed him instantly. He fell into the house in a heap.

Spice stepped over him and headed into the kitchen. He grabbed the bag containing the bricks and passed it to Drew.

"Ayo. It's another bag on the floor just like it."

"Probably more bricks, But, check anyway real quick and see what's in it," Drew said. "Hurry up though. We gotta get the fuck outta here."

Spice scooped the bag up and sat it on the counter. He quickly unzipped it and looked inside. The neatly wrapped stacks of money caused his eyes to light up.

"Bingo!" he yelled out. "It's cash."

"Grab it and let's go!" Drew yelled.

Spice grabbed the handles of the duffle bag and the two of them fled back to their car and drove off, never looking back.

———

Smoke watched quietly as two unidentified men drove away from Antonio's home. He had sat across the street in his van and watched the scene quickly unfold in the garage. They had finished the job for him. His work in the States was done for now. He took out his cell phone and made a call. He waited a few rings and then the phone was answered.

"It's done. Two tickets," Smoke stated without saying hello.

"Good," Pedro responded before hanging up. He could now rest.

PART IV

41

A week later

"DAMN MY NIGGA, WE ALMOST OUT ALREADY," SPICE SAID TO Drew. He had a huge smile on his face as he walked into the kitchen to the table where Drew was sitting at. They were in their stash house, and judging by the looks of things, they would soon need another one … or two.

Drew blew out a thick cloud of smoke and replied, "Word. That shit Tre's pops was holding was a missile."

The three bricks they had taken from Tre had literally moved overnight. Drew picked up a pile of money that was lying on the kitchen table amongst several other large stacks. He began counting it with a smile.

"Shit. We did numbers nigga. On some Frank Lucas, Blue Magic numbers shit," he boasted while referring to the notorious New York drug king-pin.

Spice nodded his head with a smile in agreement. Drew took a quick pull and then passed Spice a blunt filled with loud. He happily accepted it, but also reached over and grabbed one of the uncounted piles of cash on the table. He wanted to help speed up the process of getting all the money tallied up. He had plans with one of his hoes tonight and wasn't trying to be tied up with Drew's ass.

"So, what's popping, we gon fuck with Tony or what?" Spice asked, his voice distorted from a mouth full of smoke. While waiting for a response, he continued to count. His eyes never left the money.

"I don't know. I'm a holla at him."

Tony was one of the plugs Drew and Spice worked with. He always had decent work and his prices weren't bad. The problem the cousins were faced with, was that they had never bought a large quantity of weight off of him. That alone had Drew a little hesitant to deal with him at their newly acquired drug level.

Drew and Spice had really moved up the ladder. They were moving a lot of work through the neighborhood and their names were starting to ring bells. Before the robbery, they had been buying twenty to one hundred grams together. Now they were trying to buy four bricks.

"How much work you got left?" Drew asked Spice thirty-minutes later, after the last of the money was counted.

"A little under ten grams," Spice responded. "The way shit moving, we'll probably be out by the morning."

"Aight. Well check this out, we got close to $270,000. I'm a call Tony and go holla at him to see what he can handle."

"Cool. Just hit me after you rap to him," Spice said.

Drew agreed, and they began stuffing their money in the safe that they had bolted down inside the refrigerator. While they did that, both of their cell phones rang continuously. Spice was steadily lining up sales with clientele who he was instructing to meet at their trap house in the hood. Drew was doing the same; however, he was directing everyone to meet Spice. After loading up the cash, the two parted ways. Drew went to call Tony, while Spice was off to meet clients.

———

Drew sat in his car and waited patiently for Tony to answer the phone. He couldn't help but think about how he and

Spice had really taken over the East. The joy and happiness he felt was indescribable. The mere thought of what they had sitting in the safe, along with what they were trying to buy, gave him immense pleasure.

After several rings, Tony finally answered the phone with excitement in his voice. A mid-level Spanish dealer, he was always happy and at times, animated.

"D, my man what's up? How you?"

"I'm good T! Sup with you? Hope you're well?" Drew replied in code.

"I am. All is well," giving off the code to imply that he had work.

"Good. Good. Well, I need to holla at you."

"Ok. Come through."

Drew already knew where Tony wanted him to come to, so he replied simply. "Bet. I'm on my way."

As soon as he hung up Drew called Spice to let him know where he was headed. Anytime they were out handling business they always informed one another of their locations. This was in case anything happened.

He finished his phone calls and began the short journey to Tony's. Drew smoked his fifth blunt of the day while maneuvering through the streets like he owned the city. When he pulled up on Tony's block, his first impression was that Tony probably had some bullshit work. His block was dead. No fiends lined the streets and there was hardly any activity bringing the block to life. However, Drew was firmly aware, that looks were sometimes deceiving.

Tony only sold weight and niggas couldn't come through to cop unless they were buying ten grams or better. Drew and Spice on the other hand, sold anything. Tony wasn't dumb by a long shot. He had his game tight with niggas posted on the top and bottom of the block with walkie talks. This allowed him to be notified when anyone was coming down. In addition to his look-outs, he had shooters posted up on the porch and across the street from him. His "eyes" kept him informed and his muscle surrounding him, kept him safe. Anyone thinking they were going to come on that block and make a quick come-up off Tony, was on a suicide mission.

Drew pulled up in front of the house where Tony was sitting on the porch waiting for him. Drew knew Tony was a stand-up guy, but he also knew how money would make the smartest man do the dumbest shit. He knew that if Tony really wanted to take him off, it wasn't much he could have done since he was out-gunned, as well as out-manned. If Tony was truly able to cover the order, then they would have to meet somewhere mutual because there was no way in hell he was going to bring that much money to the block.

Tony walked onto the porch as soon as he saw Drew pull in front of the house and park. He had been inside, sitting at the round table with a small team of his young boys. Drew got out and the two met at the steps. They greeted one another with a quick hand-shake. Tony wasted no time cutting to the chase.

"Damn, D. I've been hearing a lot of good things about you and your team."

Drew wasn't new to the life. He knew the streets talked. He smiled sinisterly and replied. "Yeah we stepped our game up a lil bit."

Tony liked the sound of that and wanted to hear more. "Good. So, what can I do for you, my friend?"

Drew immediately became serious. The pleasantries were over. He didn't play when it came down to business. "I'm trying to buy four whole ones."

Tony stared at him blankly. He had been caught off guard. He sold weight, but Drew was trying to get a lot more than what he expected. He had heard about Drew and Spice making noise, but he didn't think they had stepped their game up that much. The most they had ever bought from him was 100 grams.

"Damn. You really moved up huh?" Tony said with a smile.

Drew's look and tone remained serious. He didn't have

time to play around with Tony. Either he could supply him, or he couldn't. "Yea we did. Times have changed. But I really need to know if you can cover the order. I only need four. Wassup?"

"That's a heavy order my friend. I don't know if I can cover it." Tony pursed his lips together and thought for a minute. "This is what I can do ..."

Drew listened intently. He was interested in what Tony could possibly do for him, since he couldn't supply him with the work he needed.

"Give me 24-hours and I will talk to my friend. He only handles major things. Sort of what you're asking for. I'll see if I can set up a place to meet and discuss things. Maybe he can do something for you. How does that sound?"

Drew knew Tony was a standup guy and he had never heard anything bad about him or his dealings. This was just what he and Spice needed. They needed the head honcho; the big guy. Drew's hopes immediately went up. He could soon be staring right in the face of a new, direct connect.

"Sounds good Tony. I appreciate it, and for this, I owe you a favor."

Tony smiled. "My friend, I'm gonna hold you to that favor," he said, followed by a hearty chuckle. The two shook hands and prepared to go their separate way.

"No doubt. And I will be waiting to hear from you."

"Ok my friend. I'll see what I can do for you. Take care."

42

———

SPICE PULLED IN FRONT OF HIS TRAP HOUSE AND WAS AMAZED at how much traffic had begun to accumulate in front. It was like a soup kitchen where they served free meals. He smiled. The booming trap house was a blessing to he and Drew.

After sitting in his car for a few minutes taking in the scene, Spice finally got out. Before the car door could slam, several of the dope fiends tried to run up to him to buy a quick fix. Spice quickly denied them by waving them off with his hand. He had his big hat on and didn't mind flexing his power. As he approached the house he yelled out, "You bitches better get in line before I get some crowd control out this muthafucka."

Spice was naturally aggressive, and he stayed on his best bullshit. He didn't play any games with the dope fiend's that frequented his locations. Truthfully, he had an extremely low tolerance when it came them. Dope fiends were extremely disloyal and known to do the grimiest things to get high. For that reason, he watched them carefully and wouldn't hesitate to put one of them down.

As soon as Spice walked through the door, one unruly female addict ran up to him. "Spice baby do me a solid til later. You know I'm good for it."

She looked at Spice crazily with desperation in her dark,

black eyes. The dope had sucked the color and life right out of them. Her mouth was twisted up and her eyes were buck. She was dope sick. He could tell by the way she was twitching and constantly scratching. Spice looked down on her as if she disgusted him. If looks could kill, she would have been dead within seconds.

"Bitch what I look like, a fucking credit union?" Spice asked with ice in his voice. "Get the fuck outta my face!"

He tried to walk off, but she grabbed his arm to stop him. She knew she was out of order for grabbing him, but the lack of drugs had a strong hold on her and there was no limit to what she would do to chase her next high. Spice on the other hand wasn't about to go back and forth with her. When she touched him, he felt violated. One would've though her hand was a dirty diaper because of the way he quickly snatched away from her touch.

Fire formed in his eyes while he bit down on his lip in anger. Before she could utter another word, Spice cocked back and slapped her with all his might. His hand landed against her face forcefully and violently, sending her fragile frame to the floor with a thud. The sound of the smack echoed through the house. Spice said nothing before casually turning around and walking away like nothing had just happened. He could now continue uninterrupted.

Spice's mind was on money. He knew his two young boys Cam and Will were done with the bundles of dope he and Drew had left for them to move. As he entered the kitchen, he smiled to himself. The thought of smacking the junkie chick to the floor amused him. Spice got a serious rush before, during, and after committing any acts of violence. Truthfully, Spice wasn't a good hustler. That was the main reason Cam and Will were posted up going hand to hand in the trap. Spice knew drug money was good, but there was no money like free money. He would rather rob and kill for his funds. Trapping was Drew's thing.

"What y'all got? And that shit betta not be short," Spice said loudly, surprising Cam and Will with his presence. The duo knew first-hand how Spice got down, so they wasted no time handing over the three grand they had for him.

Cam and Will were both fifteen going on thirty. The two were way ahead of their time. Drew and Spice had practically raised them. They both came from drug riddled households and were true examples of products of their environments. After accepting the $3,000, Spice counted the bills to ensure accuracy. As usual, everything was on point.

"That's why I fuck wit you niggas," Spice said with praise. He smiled at them the way a proud father would smile at his two young sons.

From his pocket, Spice pulled out a brown paper bag and sat it down on the round oak table Cam and Will were seated at. "This is the last of eight grams, so y'all niggas better take this shit to the max. We want back $150 off each gram, but y'all should at least double up from them."

Cam and Will accepted the package and nodded in agreement with Spice. He told them to get at him later and walked out. He was confident they would take care of things. He admired how they always handled business. They were loyal soldiers.

As Spice exited the house, he noticed the same dope head chick he had just slapped, sitting on the living room couch shooting up. He laughed and shook his head. *"Mufucka's do anything to feed that monkey on their back,"* were the thoughts that came to his mind. He walked out of the house and as soon he stepped on the front porch he nearly lost his composure. He couldn't believe his eyes. He whipped out his compact Glock 30 and cocked it, loading a bullet in the chamber.

"Shawty like the way that I ball out. I be getting money till I fall out."

Drew rapped along with Bobby Shmurda's *Hot Nigga*. The song blasted through his car speakers as he made his way to the house to meet Spice as planned. Drew couldn't wait to tell him about the meeting with Tony. Things were really starting to fall in place. Drew was excited.

The only issue standing in their way was that they had yet to establish a legitimate plug. Securing one would keep them in motion and not stuck sitting without product. If things went well with Tony, their problem would be fixed. A small piece of Drew felt bad. What Tony didn't know was that, as soon as he and Spice got the opportunity, they were going to take his ass out. It would be "lights out" for his ass. If things went well and Tony got them lined up with his connect, they were going to figure out a way to snatch him up and make a little change off him. Maybe they would grab him for ransom. Drew wasn't sure yet, but he knew Tony should be worth something nice.

Drew was a grimey nigga, and the only person he was loyal to was his cousin Spice. He didn't care about nothing or no one else. Tre had learned that the hard way. They did whatever it took to get to the top. His motto was "*by any means.*" Pulling his phone out, he called Spice. The phone rang five times before the voicemail picked up. He hung the phone up in frustration.

"What the fuck is this nigga doing," he muttered aloud in aggravation. He couldn't stand when he wanted to talk business and Spice was unresponsive. He decided he wouldn't call him back. He wasn't that far from the house and he knew Spice was out there.

Before Drew could turn his music all the way back up, he heard his phone ring. He figured it was Spice calling back, so he didn't bother to look at the caller id.

"Yo, what up?" he asked, expecting to hear the voice of his cousin.

"Hey Daddy," a female voice purred seductively into the phone.

Surprised, Drew quickly looked down to his phone, so he could match the face with the voice. It was Sabrina. Her pretty, caramel colored head shot had been saved in his phone months ago. He was usually busy making money, so he didn't have much time to entertain, nor put her number to use.

"Hey sexy, what's shaking?" He waited for her to respond, while he lowered his speed until he was at a standstill in front of a bright red light.

"What's up with you? I'm trying to see you tonight."

"Yeah? That's what it is. I'll see what I can do. You know a nigga be busy and shit."

Although Drew liked pussy just like the next nigga, he wasn't pressed for it. Money motivated him, not women. As far as looks, Sabrina would certainly be considered a bad-bitch; however, she was still your average sack-chasing hood-rat. Drew knew her kind all too well and he did his best to stay on point with those types of females. While they were trying to get a dollar out of him, he was trying to get information out of them. The city they lived in was small, and there were only a handful of bad-bitches that knew all the power players in the game. Sabrina was his favorite. She knew everybody and usually after a few drinks, got diarrhea of the mouth. Lately, he hadn't needed her. Tre had replaced her in male form.

"If I do come through, it's gon be kinda late. I got some shit to take care of. I'll let you know," Drew continued.

"Okay, Daddy, let me know," she said before hanging up.

Before Drew could respond, his phone chirped, alerting him to a new caller on the other line. It was Cam.

"Cool. I'll hit you later though. My lil man on the other line." He disconnected the call.

"Yo, what's popping?" he asked Cam, as he continued his way to the house.

"Yo, you close to the hood?" he stammered. He sounded nervous, like something was wrong.

"Yeah I'm around the corner. Wassup?"

Tony sat in the back room of his stash house and replayed the conversation he had just had with Drew. He couldn't believe that Drew, who was at the most, just buying one hundred grams, was now trying to buy four keys. His curiosity was killing him. He now wanted to know, who did they rob to inherit their new fortune?

In all honesty, Tony didn't care who it was, as long as it wasn't someone from his circle. However, he knew it couldn't be. None of his crew were moving any dope on that scale. He made a mental note to investigate the matter and do a little research. His goal now was to profit off the two cousins. He knew his plug could cover the order ten times over. He just had to convince him to meet the two. Although U.S. born, Tony was full blood Mexican; so was his connect. They did business with one another with no problem but were hesitant when it came to blacks. The younger generation of black guys had no respect; they had no loyalty.

Keys of top-grade dope were going for about sixty-five. He was getting them for fifty. He figured if he could convince his plug to keep the price the same but let him conduct the deal, he would make quite a bit off that one transaction. It would be sweet, easy money. He knew that his connect would want to meet and okay whoever he was supplying on that level. However, that would be the only time. Tony would act as middleman from there on out, charging them fifty-five firm, after the first purchase. That way he would make five grand off every kilo they bought. He figured he would go ahead and place the call now. He got up from the couch and stepped outside so no one would hear his conversation. After punching in the memorized number, he waited for an answer. After a few rings, his plug answered.

43

AFTER STEPPING ONTO THE PORCH, SPICE FLIPPED AT THE sight of Black Mike standing in front of *his* trap house, surrounded by a group of junkies. The same junkies that were at one point standing in *his* line waiting to be served.

With rage running through him, Spice ran off the porch with his gun in hand. He couldn't believe that Black Mike was bold enough to stand outside of their trap house selling his own work to their clients. It was completely disrespectful. Black Mike might as well have spat in Spice's face. It was the ultimate way for him to say, "*Fuck you and Drew.*"

Too busy serving the desperate fiend's, Black Mike never saw Spice fly off the porch like a bat out of hell. In the streets, one should always pay attention to their surroundings; it was a dire mistake that he would learn from. As Black Mike had his head down, thumbing through a bag of vials he held in his hand, Spice approached him violently. He never saw it coming. Before anyone could gasp or make a sound, Spice pushed the light-weight, drug-addicted male to the side who had been standing in front of his target. With one swift motion, Spice slammed the barrel of his gun downward onto the left side of Black Mike's face.

A deep bloody gash instantly opened on the side of Black Mike's face by the corner of his eye. The force from the gun caused him to fall to the ground in pain. The bag he was carrying fell out of his hands and spilled onto the ground. Like a pack of wild wolves attacking a piece of meat, the fiends raced to the ground to collect the scattered vials.

Black Mike yelled out in pain. He held the cut and struggled to see through his bloody and blurry eye. Before he could make out his attacker, Spice followed up with another blow from his gun. He grabbed hold of Black Mike's shirt with his free hand and shoved his gun in his face.

"Bitch, you must be crazy," Spice spat angrily, through clenched teeth.

As soon as he heard the voice, Black Mike knew who his attacker was. He had fucked up big time. He did his best to control the bleeding from the cut above his eye. He was leaking profusely.

"I'm sorry!" Black Mike pleaded, in attempt to beg his way out of the situation. He knew no one was coming to his aid. The fiends who had scooped up his vials had all vanished like roaches when the lights came on.

"Shut ya bitch ass up," Spice roared. He smacked him with the gun again, this time opening a cut down the middle of his forehead. The vicious blow caused Black Mike's body to shake. The pain nearly made him lose consciousness. Spice released the grip he had on Black Mike's shirt, causing him to fall flat on the ground. He was not only bloody but also weak from the assault.

"As a matter-of-fact bitch, kick that shit out," Spice demanded menacingly as he dug deeply and aggressively into Black Mike's pant pockets with his free hand. His Glock occupied his other hand. He held it steadily in Black Mike's trembling face, daring him to fight back.

Black Mike didn't reply. He just lay on the ground helplessly holding his bloody face. He knew he was down bad, and all he could do was hope that after Spice took his belongings, the ordeal would be over. Little did he know, Spice was just getting started. Spice was about to make a serious example out of Black Mike. He was going to send a message for anyone who tried to pull a stunt such as this again.

"Yo, this nigga Spice out her trippin," Cam said to Drew through his cellphone.

Drew shook his head and chuckled. Spice was always doing something stupid. "How? What my nigga done did?" he asked lightly. He was completely unaware that Spice had taken things to a new level.

"Man ... soon as this nigga get to the crib, he slaps the dog shit out dope head Gina. And now this nigga out front going ham on —" Drew cut him off before he could finish.

"Yo, I'm pulling up on the block now," he said before quickly hanging up. He shook his head in annoyance. They were supposed to be focused on money, not doing stupid shit. He couldn't help but chuckle lightly although it wasn't a laughing matter. He could only imagine how Gina looked after Spice slapped her. She would be talking shit in about a week, after Spice calmed down.

Pulling up to the house, he noticed someone naked in the middle of the street. As he got closer he noticed it was a man covered in blood. The man was standing with his hands in the air like they had been ordered there by the police. Once Drew parked, he saw Spice standing in front of the naked man. He couldn't recognize the man because his back was against him. He hopped out of the car and walked toward the altercation. He saw that it was Black Mike. He couldn't believe that Spice's dumb ass was making the block hot with his behavior. He also was completely unaware that for the past twenty-minutes, Spice had beat, robbed, and humiliated Black Mike for selling drugs in front of their trap house.

"Bitch say you sorry!" Spice yelled at Black Mike.

"Please Spice! I'm sorry," he sobbed uncontrollably with blood and snot running down his face. He had not only been stripped of his belongings; he'd also been stripped of his pride.

Drew shook his head in disbelief at the sight of a grown man begging and pleading. Even though Spice was clearly out of order, Drew couldn't help but smile. Spice was indeed, bat-shit crazy. That was what the two had most in common. They both thrived off violence. Drew knew there was no limit to how far Spice would go to get his point across, so he figured he would go ahead and put an end to Spice's theatrics.

"Yo Spice. Chill out. Let him go. We got shit to do," Drew stated loudly.

"Naw fuck that! This bitch ass nigga thought shit was sweet," Spice yelled in response, without taking his attention off Black Mike. His back was turned to Drew, and he refused to lower his gun away from Black Mike.

"Come on Spice, I'm sorry. It won't ever happen again ... Please," he begged. He was so scared, he felt his bladder weaken. Piss spewed from his exposed penis for all to see.

Spice erupted in a fit of laughter at the sight. "Shut the fuck up bitch! Ol' scared ass nigga," he replied as he taunted Black Mike by poking his gun in his face.

"Yo! Chill the fuck out. You making shit hot with this dumb ass shit!"

This time Drew said it with much more authority. He moved from behind Spice and was now standing in front of him near Black Mike. Spice looked to Drew angrily but slowly lowered his gun. He knew his cousin was right. A small crowd was already forming, so it was only a matter of time before the police showed up. Because of Spice's shenanigans, they would all have to close shop and leave the block for a few hours. Maybe even the rest of the night.

Rums' gun was now at his side, but he still wasn't done. Out of nowhere, he angrily grabbed Black Mike by his throat and started to choke him.

"Bitch, I better not catch you in the hood. I'm a kill you. You dead in this hood. You banned in these streets. You got

seconds to get the fuck away from here before I body ya
h ass," he snarled through clenched teeth. He released
with a shove.

Black Mike wasted no time fleeing the scene towards his
parked around the corner. He didn't even bother to grab
clothes that lay on the ground in a crumpled heap. He
naked from head to toe, but he figured, at least he was
e. He knew Spice meant every word he said. He made a
that he was going to get his revenge one way or another.
words that Spice spoke were not to be taken lightly. He
le his money the same way they did in that same hood.
one was going to tell him where he could and couldn't
Not even Spice. The next time they came in contact,
re would be gunfire.

Drew and Spice watched Black Mike run off. "You on
1e other shit," Drew stated angrily as he walked off. "I'm
it to go in here and tell them niggas to wrap shit up for a
hours since you done made the block hella hot."

"Man, that shit aint about nothing. They damn near
ta work anyway. Fuck that nigga. On some other shit,
it's popping with Tony?" Spice asked to change the
ject.

"We can talk about that later. I'm out before the police
here. You do the same. I'll handle the crib."

Spice agreed and headed to his car, while Drew went
the house to holla at Cam and Will.

---

e decided to head to the stash house to change his
hes because he had blood on him. He knew Drew would
it him there eventually. As he drove, he bobbed his head
1e sound of Rico Homie Quan's, *Some type of way*. He felt
f the rapper was speaking to him directly. In reality, he
as if he and Drew were on top of the world. They had
er had much before. The kilo's they were now touching
him feeling like a king.

Spice sang along with the music. *"My niggas been hustling' trying to make him something, ain't no telling what he'll do for the paper."* The was his favorite line in the song. As Spice bobbed his head to the lyrics, he was brought out of his thoughts by the vibration of his phone. He turned down the volume and pulled his phone from his pocket. He glanced at the screen and a smile spread across his face. On his screen, a big red ass was staring at him. His dick jumped at the thought of Ariel. She was the one who was calling him. He wasted no time answering the phone.

"Yo, what up?" he asked, doing his best to sound smooth. That ass he was just staring at, also had him hooked. He was truly a sucker for love. If he was Superman, good pussy and head would be his kryptonite.

"Hey Daddy," the soft-spoken female purred through his phone.

"Hey love. What's good witchu?" he asked, still keeping up his smooth persona.

"I'm waiting on you," she responded seductively. She knew Spice all too well and knew exactly what to say to push his buttons. The words she spoke were like music to his ears.

"Oh yeah? What you waiting for?" he asked, knowing exactly what she wanted. His grin went from ear to ear. He was like a kid in a candy store. He couldn't help but remember the last sex session they had.

"Stop playing with me Daddy. I want for you to come over here and take this pussy."

She knew Spice loved it when she talked dirty to him and she wasn't about to let up. She also knew if she played her cards right, she would continue to have him eating right out of the palm of her hands. Spice had always been generous with cash. The streets talked, and she had heard that he had stepped his game up a couple notches. That meant, bigger shopping trips for her.

Spice did his best to maintain his composure. Ariel had his dick getting harder by the minute. Just the sound of her

was enough to send him in a fit. He knew he was
osed to be meeting Drew in a few, but he already made
is mind to make a pit stop at Ariel's crib first.

How bad you want this dick?" he asked, keeping the
going. He quickly altered his route and began to head
e direction of her house.

Oooh Daddy, this pussy is dripping wet, waiting for
I want you now. My fingers ain't doing the job." She
ed and moaned with intensity to enhance the effects of
statements. "When are you coming? I miss you so
n," she added.

I'm on my way," he responded, finally admitting he was
ng to her.

Ok Daddy don't take too long," she added before
ing up.

pice called Drew. He answered on the second ring. He
dy explained to him that something had come up and
ad to go handle it. Drew already knew what that meant.
as sure it had something to do with a female. He didn't
bother to ask any questions. Spice always tried to put
front for Drew like he didn't care about any of the
ds he slept with, but Drew knew that was bologna.
could see right through him. Besides, they were nearly
of work, so they did have a little time to bullshit. The
bout Tony could wait.

44

TONY PULLED UP TO THE HOME OF HIS LONG-TIME PLUG. HE pushed the button so he could be buzzed into the newly installed entrance gate. The surveillance camera discreetly tucked in the grass next to the gate, changed positions to capture his identity. A few seconds later he was buzzed in. The gates slowly slid open and a voice came through the adjacent intercom.

"Hey Tony. Come on in," a female voice greeted him.

Tony slowly approached the house and noticed how many changes had been made. The state-of-the-art security system and $10,000 iron wrought gate had the place secured like a mini Fort Knox. Camera's from the roof to the lawn lined the property, while security staffed the front door to the home. After parking and exiting the vehicle, Tony greeted the guards.

"Come. He wait for you," one of the guards said in broken English. Tony had never seen him before. If he had, he would have known that Tony spoke fluent Spanish. Tony didn't respond. He simply nodded his head in agreement and followed the guard up the steps and into the home.

Lately, security had been unusually tight; however Tony was starting to get used to it. His plug had just moved into the new home; however, Tony had been by several times.

Each time he noticed something had been added for security purposes. The gate and intercom were new. Neither had been there a few days ago when he had stopped by for business.

When Tony entered the breathtaking home, he admired the new artwork that adorned the walls. He could tell that they were still redecorating. He knew when they were finished, it was going to be even more beautiful than their last home. As he made his way through the home the familiar scent of Spanish food greeted him.

Tony finally arrived at the back of the home where he now stood before a big, black door. Behind the door was where million-dollar deals took place. He was honored to even be privileged enough to enter. The security guard he had followed in, opened the door and allowed him in. Tony walked into the office and was instantly greeted by his plug.

"Tony!" he said jovially. He was standing behind a large, cherry-oak desk you would find in the office of a top executive or CEO. He reached his hand out to embrace Tony, whom he not only considered a loyal client, but also a friend.

"Pedro my friend! How are you old-timer?" Tony responded.

Several hours had passed and Drew was now killing time with Cam and Will at one of his other spots he sold out of. Things had died down enough where he was confident to send the duo back to open shop at the main spot. Luckily, the stunt that Spice pulled earlier didn't affect business too much. Before Drew sent off the pair, he figured he'd propose a plan to them to help them secure their future.

Drew had taken a liking to Cam and Will and almost considered them the closest thing to family after Spice. Cam and Will also had a lot of respect for Drew and Spice, but especially looked up to Drew. Knowing this, Drew knew they would be the perfect pair to carry out an important task for him.

"I need you two niggas to handle something for me," Drew said.

"Whatchu need?" Cam asked. Although there was no leader of the two, Cam was considered the more outspoken and outgoing one. Average size and brown skin, Cam had spongy hair that faded out on the sides. He was loud, and for the most part, he was well liked.

"I need y'all to snatch a nigga for me. I won't give you the details until later. Nothing too complicated. Might get ya hands a little dirty but the money will definitely make it worthwhile," Drew added, his eyes shifting from Cam to Will.

"Bet," they both replied, in unison.

Nothing more needed to be said. They had handled things for the cousins before. With Drew and Spice's newfound wealth, they knew that they were going to be getting paid handsomely. Truthfully, they would have done it on the strength of Drew simply asking; however since money was involved, all they needed was: who, what, when, and where. Nothing more needed to be said.

After promising to give them more information, Drew left and began his route to the stash house to wait for Spice, so he could update him on what he and Tony had discussed. Drew already knew Spice was probably over some freak's house tricking off. As he drove, he tried calling Spice. Just as he expected, it went right to voicemail. He was going to check him about putting pleasure before business. This was the second time today he'd called and been sent to voicemail.

Drew turned up the volume on his stereo system and Yo Gotti's raspy voice crooned through the speakers. "*I'm smoking on purple flowers.*" The lyrics forced his mind down memory lane and his thoughts drifted back to when he first met his little cousin Spice.

It was summer time, a couple days after Drew's 16th

birthday. He was posted in the hood pretending to be productive. Pretending to work and do odd jobs for people kept his grandmother off his behind. What he was really doing was small time drug dealing. Hand to hand.

Drew had been dealing since the tender age of twelve. As his full-time caretaker, his grandmother Ernestine often struggled to get by. He loved her to pieces and just wanted to help her; however, after a brief time in the game, he became addicted to the fast money. By the age of fourteen, he had quite a reputation in the streets. He never knew his dad and his mom was strung out on Heroin. She had dropped Drew off to Ernestine one day when he was eleven and never returned. She was supposed to go to a job interview that day and promised to return in a few hours. That was the last day they had ever heard from her.

Ernestine lived in the hood and she was too old to really run after Drew and monitor his behavior. She did her best, but with numerous medical problems, she couldn't keep up.

After hours on the block, Drew found himself out of work. He would run back in to his grandmother's house to retrieve more from his stash. One particular day when he entered, he walked in and noticed a boy sitting on the couch. He didn't recognize him and he appeared to only be a few years younger. Drew thought to himself that whoever he was, he'd better have a good reason being in his crib. Luckily for Spice, their grandmother appeared in the living room just as Drew had walked out. She smiled warmly when she saw him.

"Devin. Hey sweetie, you're just in time," she said, calling Drew by his government name. He hated when she did that. However, she refused to call him by his street name.

Drew looked confused. "In time for what?" he asked, glancing to Spice who was still sitting on the couch.

"To meet your cousin," she continued happily. Deep wrinkles made up her chocolate face, as she continued to smile at her two grandsons.

"He's going to be staying with us while his mother handles some things."

Drew was confused. He didn't even know that his aunt Zina had children. Zina was his mother's little sister. She too was on drugs, but she had always been a functioning addict. Unlike his mother Nina, Zina only played around with Cocaine. She worked every day and still managed to care for her son. His mother on the hand, was a stone-cold Heroin addict. She would nod off at the drop of a dime, scratch until her skin bled, and sell all ten fingers on her hand if she thought it would get her a hit.

"Oh, ok. Well that's wassup," Drew replied, seemingly uninterested. He wasn't in the mood to get to know anyone. He was trying to grab what he came for and head out. He made a mental note to watch him. He didn't feel like fucking him up for stealing. Cousin or not, he wasn't into taking losses.

"What's ya name cuzzo?" Drew asked to quickly appease his grandmother.

"Raymond. But you can call me Spice. That's what I go by in my hood."

"I'm gonna go start breakfast. Devin, show Raymond the spare room where he will be sleeping. Pull out the air-mattress from the attic until I get him a bed."

"Ok Grandma," Drew replied. "Come on," he waved, so Spice could grab his things and follow him to the upstairs of the small home.

Spice himself wasn't super excited to be staying at his grandma's house in the small city. To him, it seemed boring and incapable of offering the excitement he desperately desired. Unfortunately, he didn't have much of a choice, so he proceeded to follow Drew up the carpeted steps. He already knew his mother wasn't coming back for him. He hadn't been the most well-behaved child and he knew his mother was getting tired of dealing with him. With him gone, she would now be free to whore around and continue her coke binges.

"This where you gon sleep," Drew said, opening the door so Spice could walk into the room. It was simple: bare, with one window. There was no closet but there was a small, three-drawer dresser for him to store his belongings.

"Cool," Spice responded casually as he put down his small suitcase and book bag.

Drew closed the door behind them which surprised Spice. "Don't mind Grandma," Drew stated as he leaned against the door. "She be forgetting shit so don't pay her no mind."

"I figured that much. It's damn near dark outside and she talking bout breakfast," Spice laughed.

"Yeah. So, Raymond it is right? How old are you and what were you doing where you were at?" Drew asked out of curiosity. "Oh yeah. The only person that call me Devin is Grandma. My name is Drew and we grind out here," he added flatly.

As soon as Drew finished, Spice smiled. "I was just about to ask you where I could cop some tree." He didn't bother to answer any of the questions that had been thrown his way. They could talk about that shit later.

Drew reached in his pocket and pulled out a wrapped Philly blunt and a dime bag of some high-grade weed he had copped off a white boy he knew.

"You can smoke wit me. I'll show you where, but first let me grab something real quick."

Drew went across the hall to his room and grabbed the work he had come in for. After grabbing his pack, he headed back outside while waving for Spice to follow him.

It didn't take long for Spice to get the hang of things. The two cousins grew close very quickly, and soon were two peas in a pod. Even though Spice was two years younger, he was still street smart beyond his years. Drew also noticed that he was also violent beyond his years.

The first time Drew witnessed Spice's temper was during a drug transaction. He had started hustling with Drew to earn his own money. To get the most back off his investment, he would make his bags small. One particular addict didn't like the size and refused to buy it after carefully observing the bag's appearance. He told Spice he must be smoking too if he thought he was going to spend his money on a bullshit bag that size.

The man was barely able to get out his last word before Spice slapped him to the ground with his gun and proceeded to pistol whip him. He was only fourteen at the time. As years went on, he grew even more ruthless. Rumors spread through the city of him killing people, shooting kids over debts owed by their parents, and even torturing people in random, abandoned houses. People feared Spice while they respected Drew. The two were complete opposites but loved one another like brothers. Spice's mother Zina never came back for him as he suspected; however, she did call periodically and check on him. To her, he was too far gone and corrupt, just like her.

Drew smiled as his thoughts drifted back to reality. He pulled up to the stash house and tried calling Spice again. After a few rings, the voicemail came on. Drew shook his head in frustration. He was tired of Spice pulling the same stunts every other day. If they weren't family, he would have been cut him loose.

45

Spice thrust aggressively in and out of Ariel while she moaned and groaned in delight. He watched as her big, bright, yellow ass slammed back against his pelvic area. He quickly looked away and towards the door. Staring too long would cause him to ejaculate prematurely.

After a few more minutes of pounding in and out of her tight, slippery walls she unexpectedly moaned out, "Daddy, I'm coming!"

The revelation caused Spice to thrust harder. He felt Ariel's legs tremble and a burst of wetness flow from her center like an erupting volcano. Almost immediately after, Spice allowed himself to let go and succumb to pure ecstasy. He was glad she had finally cum. He had been holding it.

Ariel was one of the biggest freaks Spice had ever ran across. Her fuck game was long and strong, *and* she could suck the skin off a dick and spit it back on. Because of this, Spice would gladly empty his pockets for her, and run when she called for him.

"Phew," Spice panted as he collapsed into the queen size bed. He wiped the sweat from his forehead and eyes, and glanced over at his phone. It was blinking and indicating he had missed a call. After picking it up, he realized he had missed *several* calls.

"Fuck," he blurted out.

"What's wrong baby?" Ariel asked. She was also laying on the bed but had snuggled against Spice.

He didn't respond; instead, he jumped up and grabbed his clothes from the floor.

"I forgot I got some important shit to handle."

He hurried around the room, gathering his things. He kissed her and told her he would see her later. He had to go meet Drew so they could discuss copping weight off Tony. He knew his cousin would be pissed. He vowed to get more focused.

———

Drew sat in the stash house and smoked his blunt while he continued to wait on Spice. After a few more minutes of waiting, he reached down and dug his phone out his pocket to call him again. After a few rings, Spice picked up.

"Damn nigga. I've been calling you for fucking hours," Drew huffed with a little extra bass in his voice.

"My fault. I had to take care of something real quick."

"Nigga please. That wasn't real quick. Ya bluffing ass chasing pussy."

"Chill with that bullshit. I'm on my way to the spot now. I'll be there in fifteen minutes." *That* part wasn't a lie. As they spoke, he was truly pulling away from Ariel's town-house. She lived in an upscale community called River Creek, about five miles outside of the city.

"Yeah aight. Where you coming from? Ariel's house? Wit her gold-digging ass," Drew added, knowing his cousin all too well.

"Stop being nosey nigga. Just know I'm in route," he chuckled.

"Cool. Stop to the liquor store though before it close; grab some blunts and a bottle of Cîroc."

"Aight, one." Spice said before hanging up.

Drew hung up the phone and decided to call Cam to

check in. Since they were still young with grown men responsibilities, he did this often. He trusted that they would take care of things, but he could never be too sure.

After two rings, Cam answered the phone laughing. "Yo what it is?" he said.

Drew felt like he was missing something and anxiously replied, "Damn, what's good over there?"

Cam continued to laugh uncontrollably, eventually regaining his composure. "Everything Gucci. This nigga Will funny as shit."

"What happened?"

My nigga. This lil bitch just came to the trap going ham on Will."

Drew exhaled a thick cloud of smoke from his now pinky-size blunt. "Oh yeah, what happened? he asked.

"First the chick calls his phone zapping and he bangs on her. Then next thing we know, shorty coming through the front door yelling that Will burned her." Cam laughed as he explained the story.

"Fuck no!" Drew said shocked, his mouth forming an O.

"That's not the half. She went off and blast the nigga in front of everybody. Talking bout, he had a little dick, and he was out there fucking crack-head bitches raw."

"Get the fuck outta here!" Drew laughed. Now he understood what was so funny. He could only imagine how embarrassed Will had been in front of everyone.

"No bullshit. This stupid ass nigga couldn't even say shit. Had the dick look."

"Word ... that's crazy," Drew chuckled.

"Hell yeah. I had to grab the lil bitch and put her ass out to calm her down."

"Man, that bitch was lying!" Drew heard Will yell in the background of Cam's call.

"Aye, tell that dirty dick nigga to carry his ass to the clinic."

"I told his dumb ass," Cam responded, ignoring Will's attitude.

"Listen, on a more serious note. Everything else cool over there?" Drew asked.

"Yeah shit cool. We holding down the fort," he assured.

"Cool. I'm gon get up with y'all later. I'm about to handle some shit real quick."

"Aight bet. One," Cam replied before hanging up.

Drew hung up the phone. His young niggas were too much for him. He shoved his phone back in his pocket and continued to wait for Spice.

46

"So, how's everything going?" Pedro asked while leaning back in his leather chair.

"Same ol,' same ol,' Tony replied.

"So, what do I owe this pleasure for you to visit me. I know you didn't come for my wife's cooking," Pedro said jokingly.

Tony smiled in response. "The way she has it smelling, I actually need to come by more often. For breakfast, lunch and dinner." They shared a quick laugh before Tony turned serious.

"Honestly, the reason I stopped by is because I want to bring to you a business opportunity ... It would be quick and we both would profit tremendously off it in the long run."

"Okay Tony. You have my attention," Pedro responded. "Tell me more."

"So, I know a couple of guys who are making major moves on the East side. They're coming up quickly. Making major noise."

Pedro winced as if he was in deep thought. "I think I heard a little about these guys but keep going."

"Well they're trying to cop three kilos. I told them I

couldn't cover it, but I could possibly introduce them to a friend that could."

Tony prayed Pedro would be on board. Even though Tony was already making a lot of money, more money never hurt anyone. Pedro did a quick calculation in his head and was interested; however, he was skeptical of meeting new people. He needed validation.

"Do you vouch for them?" Pedro asked seriously.

In the drug world, if you vouched for someone, you became responsible for their actions. You would pay with your life if something went wrong.

"Absolutely," Tony quickly said. Consumed with greed, he didn't take the time to realistically determine if they were loyal and honest enough to do business with. He figured if anything went wrong, he would take care of them — Mexican style.

Satisfied with Tony's response, Pedro nodded. "Well, tell me how it's going to benefit me?"

Pedro had known Tony many years and even treated him like family. He trusted him. He also trusted that Tony wouldn't have come to his home to talk peanuts. Pedro wanted the details about the money involved.

"You charge them sixty instead of the normal fifty the first go around. Second transaction and anything moving forward would be fifty-five."

Pedro smiled. Basically, Tony would be getting a finder's fee and Pedro would pocket an extra $5,000 in the future for every kilo they purchased.

"How much for the first order?" Pedro asked.

"I'm cool with $15,000. Either way you're making at minimum, an extra $20,000 each time you supply them. Even more if they increase their quantity. And that my friend, is highly likely. They're very ambitious."

"How many?" Pedro asked.

"It's two of them. They're partners."

Pedro paused and stared at Tony briefly. "I like you Tony. You know that. I also admire your ambition; however, I hope you're not letting a quick profit cloud your judgement. Remember, *all money isn't good money, and everything that glitters isn't gold*." Pedro stood up from his chair abruptly.

"I'll agree to your deal. I wanna meet them though. Soon."

A giant smile crept across Tony's face. "I take full responsibility and I appreciate you doing this for me. I'm going to call them and arrange a place and time that's good for you. We all can meet then and discuss everything."

"How about this. I'm having lunch tomorrow at a friend's restaurant around 12:30, noon. Bring them there and we'll discuss everything. The restaurant is El'Mucho's. It's on Main street. When you get there call me, and I'll have one of my guys escort the three of you in to my section.

Tony nodded quickly in agreement. "Sounds good. I'll call them and let them know the good news."

He rose from his seat and extended his hand for a handshake. Pedro reciprocated and shook his hand.

"Nico. See him out please," Pedro said to his henchman who had been standing by the doorway. He was the same person who had escorted Tony in.

"You sure I can't offer you a plate?" Pedro offered.

"You know I appreciate the offer but I've gotta run. Plus, you've done enough for me already. Next time for sure," Tony responded with gratitude.

"Ok, no problem. It's always a pleasure," Pedro said as Tony walked out the door."

Tony quickly exited the massive home and got in his car. As he closed the door he felt his phone vibrate. He dug it out of his pocket. It was Black Mike.

Spice finally walked through the door of the stash house. Drew was waiting in the living room, slouched down in the couch texting. A giant cloud of weed smoke hovered over top of him. He stared at Spice as he approached. He was high, but still on point and able to take care of business.

Spice took a seat across from Drew in a faded, worn out recliner. He placed a small brown bag on the coffee table holding the Cîroc and blunts Drew had requested.

"Wassup?" Spice asked.

"Shit. Waiting on ya ass," Drew responded dryly, putting his phone down.

"My bad yo. And I see you over there babysitting that blunt. Let me hit that shit," Spice said, referring to the neglected, burning blunt in the ashtray.

Drew glanced over to the blunt he had forgotten about. He passed the tray to Spice.

"Here. Fuck it up. I'm good."

"Good looking. Who you over their boo-loving with?" Spice asked.

"You know I don't do that," he responded. "That's ya shit. That's probably what took you so long to get here," he shot.

Spice ignored him and pulled deeply from the blunt. "You know that bitch ass nigga got blood on my clothes earlier. I had to change my shit ... And damn, can I get my dick sucked if it's cool with you."

Drew sucked his teeth and frowned. "We gotta handle business nigga."

"Well, I'm here," Spice replied. "You said you wanted to holla at me about Tony. What's up."

Drew leaned over and grabbed the brown bag off the table containing the Cîroc. After pulling it out and taking a swig, he responded. "He can't cover that order."

"Damn. It's only three keys. What the fuck we gon do now?" Spice asked.

"Let me finish. He gon reach out to his man and see if he will do it for us. It's probably his connect. I'm sure he can supply us. The question is: will he? Most of them foreign motherfuckers don't like fucking with niggas. Especially niggas they don't know."

As Drew spoke his phone began to ring. He looked down and smiled. "This Tony now."

"Tony. Wassup baby. You got good news?" Drew asked as soon as he answered the phone.

"Today's your lucky day, because I do actually," Tony replied.

"Oh yea, well let's hear it."

"My guy has agreed to meet tomorrow for lunch. If all goes well, everything is everything," Tony confirmed.

Drew grinned with excitement. "That sounds good. What time?" he asked eagerly, barely unable to contain himself. This was the break they were looking for.

"Be ready around twelve, tomorrow afternoon. I'll come pick you and your friend up."

"Cool. We'll be ready. Oh, and Tony. I appreciate it. I owe you one."

"I'll hold you to it. I'll call you tomorrow," he said before hanging up.

Drew looked to Spice but didn't speak.

"What nigga? You cheesy as fuck. Let a nigga know what's up?" Spice demanded.

"Shit's bout to be popping. Tony got us in. We meet up with the nigga tomorrow afternoon."

"That's wassup," Spice responded but not as eagerly as Tony. The grind didn't excite him, neither did the money. What he could do with the money motivated him.

"What's them joints going for though?" Spice asked while reaching over to the ashtray on the coffee table. He smashed out the remaining remnants of the blunt while he waited for Drew to reply.

"That shit don't even matter right now for real. The main thing is Tony lining us up with someone that can actually cover what we're asking for. Without him, we'd soon be sitting around empty handed trying to secure a plug."

"True ... I'll celebrate though when we got the work in our hands," Spice replied. "What's up with tonight though?

You trying to fuck with Starlite's? If not, one of my lil bitches want me to chill with her tonight," he added.

Drew rolled his eyes. He had just left one of his hoes, now he was ready to go waste more time with another one. They had an important meeting tomorrow and he wanted to make sure Spice was available. He had no choice but to keep him in eyesight.

"Not really but we can slide through for a quick minute to see what's popping," Drew replied.

"Cool. I'll hit Cam and Will to see if they trying to slide out there with us," Spice said as he fished his phone from his pocket.

"Yeah. *You* paying to get them niggas in?" Drew asked. Cam and Will were clearly underage and unable to produce a ID. It was going to cost extra to get them in the building.

"Yeah I got em. Cheap ass nigga. I probably won't even have to pay," he added. "I get shit done on the strength."

"Yeah whatever Big Money," Drew replied sarcastically.

47

Tony hung up the phone with Drew and pulled in front of Ariel's townhouse. Ariel was his first cousin, but they were close like brother and sister. He looked around and saw the gold Dodge Charger he was searching for. It belonged to Black Mike. He was meeting him there.

Black Mike had called him earlier, letting him know that some shit had went down. He didn't want to say it over the phone, so Tony agreed to meet him. Tony didn't care for Black Mike and wasn't happy when Ariel had introduced them several years ago. He along with Drew and Spice, purchased work from him. Since Black Mike was in the field more, he kept him abreast on what was happening in the streets.

Truthfully, Black Mike was more of a liability than an asset. He couldn't be trusted and always gave Tony a bad vibe. Lately, some of his workers had been complaining about Black Mike stepping on their toes and selling his product any and everywhere he saw fit. This caused a problem, but because of his relationship with Tony, a lot of what he did was allowed to slide. Of course, Tony would try to address the concerns by talking to Black Mike, but for some reason, he felt that he could continue to do what he wanted without consequence.

Tony turned off his car, got out and headed up the steps into Ariel's townhouse. He knocked twice before turning the knob and realizing the door was locked. Ten seconds later, Ariel answered the door. Her facial expression was grim. Something was wrong.

Tony quickly entered. "Ariel what happened?" he asked. She didn't answer. She kept walking until she reached her bedroom in the back of her house. Following behind her, Tony stopped abruptly as soon he got to the entrance. His eyes widened, and mouth dropped open.

Black Mike was lying back on her bed. His eyes were nearly swollen shut and his head was wrapped in thick bandages. He looked like he'd been hit by a Mack truck. Tony looked over to Ariel who had sat down on the foot of the bed. He instantly grew angry.

"Ariel are you okay?" Tony asked. She appeared fine, but he could never be too sure of what had taken place.

"I'm okay Tony. He just showed up here looking like that and wouldn't tell me what happened," she responded nervously. Worry was written all over her cream-colored face.

"Is that right?" Tony replied.

"Let us talk alone please," he said to his cousin.

Ariel got up quietly and exited the room. Tony had some choice words for Black Mike. He took a few deep breaths to keep from going off. He had no idea why someone as beautiful as Ariel chose to fuck Black Mike, let alone welcome him into her home. He shouldn't have come there. She could be a target. God forbid anything happen to his cousin. He would murder Black Mike and whoever else was involved.

"What the fuck happened to you?" Tony asked, his jaws clenched.

"I got robbed and pistol whipped," he responded angrily through swollen lips.

Tony looked behind him to make sure Ariel wasn't

within earshot. Just as he suspected, she wasn't far outside the door.

"Excuse us?" Tony said to her.

"What? I wanna know what happened. He brought his ass to my house. I deserve to know," she responded.

Tony shook his head in frustration. She was right. Ariel and Black Mike had a special relationship. They were high school sweethearts. He was her first love; however, her materialistic ways turned her into a gold digger. Her many wants caused her to sleep around.

Tony and Ariel's mothers were sisters. While Tony was full Mexican, Ariel was not. Her father was Black. Her beauty attracted men from near and far; however, she was a hood-rat at heart, falling mostly for street guys and dope boys. Even though Tony brought her most of what she wanted, she still used guys like Black Mike to get everything her little heart desired.

While she loved Black Mike because of their history, she didn't want to be with him. Nevertheless, she had a soft spot for him and couldn't seem to get rid of him. This was becoming a major problem for Tony. Black Mike wasn't the most well-liked person in the city and that alone potentially put Ariel at risk. Tony was protective over his cousin. Even though she was well-aware of what went on the street, he still did his best to keep her away from it. She made that particularly hard, considering she fucked with a slew of niggas who lived a life similar to his own.

"Who did this to you?" Ariel asked, walking back into the room.

Before he could utter a word, Tony shot a stern look in Black Mike's direction. He knew he wasn't to answer that. The conversation wasn't for women.

"Who robbed you? What happened?" Ariel demanded to know.

Black Mike glared silently at Tony but didn't speak.

"Come with me outside," Tony said before walking out.

Black Mike painfully rose from where he was lying on the bed and slowly followed Tony out to his car.

"Stay here Ariel. We'll talk when I get back," he whispered to her as he walked by. He didn't want Tony to hear.

When Black Mike arrived outside, he saw Tony standing at the driver's door of his BMW. He waved for him to get in. He reluctantly walked to the car and got in.

When Drew and Spice pulled up to their trap house, Cam and Will were posted on the porch waiting for them. They anxiously hopped in the backseat. The two youngins loved riding out with Drew and Spice. They got to smoke, drink and party for free.

"Oh shit! Here come that crazy bitch Will!" Drew joked as soon as the two got in the car. Will smacked his teeth. He should have known the jokes were coming.

"I heard you was a dirty dick ass nigga," Spice continued while laughing.

"Man, that bitch lying," he whined. He'd had enough of the jokes.

"Yeah aight nigga," Drew said from the front. He didn't believe a word of what he said.

"Fuck y'all," Will said causing everyone in the car to laugh. He couldn't help but laugh with them.

The drive to Starlite's was quick. Drew was driving, and Spice had his phone hooked up to the stereo so Yo Gotti could rap through the speakers. When Drew pulled in front of the club they were shocked. The parking lot was completely empty, and it appeared closed.

"Damn, what the fuck. This shit ain't popping," Spice complained, stating the obvious.

"A blind nigga can see that," Drew replied sarcastically. "I'm going back to the trap. Pass that loud."

Spice looked puzzled. "Nigga you tripping. I gave that

shit back to you at the crib." He glanced over at Drew who didn't reply.

Butting in the conversation from the backseat, Cam yelled. "Damn! Y'all niggas all high and shit. Done forgot the loud pack."

"I didn't forget shit. This nigga did," he blurted out referring to Drew.

"Damn my nigga what's up with that?" Cam asked jokingly, tapping Drew on the shoulder.

"Chill lil nigga. Pump your brakes. We just got slide back to the spot real quick and grab it." He looked over to Spice, who was in the passenger's seat beside him. Spice huffed and sucked his teeth.

"Damn man. The fuck. We driving around in circles and shit. I could be at a freak house."

"Word, but I gotta piss anyway," Will chimed in.

"I bet ya burning ass do!" Drew yelled out, prompting everyone to laugh aloud.

Spice headed back to the house he and Drew had met at before going to the trap. They were there in no time.

"Bathroom is down the hall on the right," Drew directed Will. Cam and Will had never been to this particular house. Drew and Spice considered it their "stash-house."

"And make sure you don't drop no green shit on the floor," Spice yelled to Will as he walked off.

The trio made their way into the living room, and just like Spice had said, Drew left the zip lock bag of weed right on the couch where he had been sitting.

"What I tell you." Spice pointed to the couch.

"Fuck you nigga. Just roll that shit up," Drew said grabbing the bag and handing it to Spice. He knew he was high, so he didn't sweat the mishap.

They took a seat while Spice whipped out a Game blunt and proceeded to roll up.

"We should've gone to the store. I'm thirsty as shit," Cam complained.

"Fuck we look like? Uber nigga? We got some shit in the

fridge. It's over there," Spice pointed. He dug some weed out of the zip-lock bag and sprinkled it down the gutted cigar.

"Bet," he said while hopping up from his spot. As he headed towards the kitchen, Will came from the bathroom and took a seat in the living room with the others.

"Yo, you better not have stank my shit up," Drew said to Will. "You was back there long as shit."

"Nigga wasn't nobody shitting. I was back there talking to one of my bitches," he bragged.

"That's why ya lil young, nasty ass burning now. Too busy worried about bitches," Drew complained. "Do not follow in that nigga footsteps," he said looking over at Spice. "Money over everything. Fuck these hoes."

"Whatever," Will replied, while Spice ignored Drew.

"Ay yo, how you niggas get that safe in the fridge?" Cam asked, reappearing from the kitchen with a Styrofoam cup of soda in hand.

"None of ya business nigga. Don't be peeping around and shit," Drew said to Cam with a deadly glare.

"My bad nigga. I couldn't help but see the shit. Fuck all dat though. Wassup with that lick you was talking bout earlier?" he asked Drew.

"Word," Will cosigned by his side on the couch. "Needs that."

"What lick?" Spice asked looking around puzzled.

"We gon snatch Tony," Drew replied.

"Well damn. You keeping shit from me? When was you gon let me know?" Spice asked.

"Damn nigga fix ya face. You act like I was gon bust the move without you. The only reason I said something to these niggas was to see if they were wit it," he assured Spice. "I already knew ya thirsty ass would be wit it," he said. He tapped him playfully.

Although slightly irritated by his lack of knowledge surrounding the move, he smiled lightly.

"Nigga, who the fuck you callin thirsty? Shit, if it was up

to me we would've been got that taco eating mufucka a long time ago."

Everyone laughed simultaneously. Will pulled from the blunt that was now in rotation around the room. He passed it to Cam.

"Yo, I'm bout to call a cab and slide to this shorty house."

"Word. I'm a dip wit you and get dropped off at the trap. My phone been blowing up," Cam said, scrolling through his call log on his Samsung.

Calling it a night, Cam and Will left soon after while Drew and Spice decided to crash there for the night. They figured they could get some rest, part ways in the morning and eventually meet back up by noon. They had big business to discuss.

48

"LET'S GET SOMETHING STRAIGHT," TONY GROWLED THROUGH clenched teeth while pointing his finger in Black Mike's face. "So help me God, if you have my cousin involved in any of your bullshit, I'm going to bury you and your whole fucking family," he threatened, meaning every word he spoke.

Tony looked at Black Mike. His face was contorted in an angry scowl. Black Mike sat in the passenger seat. He knew Tony didn't care much for him, but he was shocked that he would come at him in such a disrespectful manner. He had never seen Tony so mad before. While he wanted to check Tony, he decided it was best for him to ease the tension since they still did business together.

With his hands up in the air defensively he replied, "Tony I promise I would never do no shit like that! I only did what you asked me to do."

Tony didn't respond. He started up his car and drove away from Ariel's house. Black Mike didn't say anything, but he also had no idea where Tony was headed. They sat silently for a few minutes. Finally, Tony cut his eyes over at Black Mike.

"So, what you're saying is, you got me involved in your

shit?" His fingers gripped the steering wheel tightly as he spoke.

"Fuck no! I'm just saying, I was in the hood handling business and keeping my eye on Drew and Spice's trap house when Spice ran out the house and robbed me," he explained, leaving out key details. "He took everything you gave me and beat me with the gun."

Tony continued to drive around aimlessly in the outskirts of the city. He stared straight ahead while he listened to Black Mike's story.

"So, I guess you're also saying you don't have my money or work?" he asked.

"He took everything!" Black Mike exclaimed.

Tony already knew Black was lying about getting robbed for everything. Truthfully, he didn't really care if he did or not since he always had an outlandish story to tell. It was always something: some type of excuse or some type of story as to why he was short or couldn't pay up. If it weren't for Ariel, Tony would have been discontinued his dealings with him. Frankly, he was tired of the hassle that came with dealing with Black Mike.

"Man, dem niggas think they God and can do what they want," he muttered angrily while looking through the window. His thoughts were running wild. He refused to allow what happened to him go unpunished. "I'm a kill dem niggas. You watch."

Tony knew he was full of shit as soon as he spoke the words. Everyone knew how Drew and Spice got down. The two of them alone were a force to be reckoned with. Black wasn't capable of warring with them successfully. He wasn't as ruthless, and he also lacked what they now seemed to have plenty of: money. Besides, Tony wasn't about to let him fuck up his business with the cousins. The money he was soon going to be making off the two was going to be worth more than anything that had to do with Black Mike. There was no way he was letting him come between that.

Tony abruptly pulled over to the sidewalk and put the

car in park. They were about ten minutes outside of the city in a small town called Hebron. He turned to face Black.

"This is an issue you're going to have to deal with on your own. And until you handle it, I want you to stay far away from my cousin." Tony stared silently at Black Mike with icy eyes. He wanted to be clear; he meant business.

"If I find out you've been around her and didn't do as I asked," he continued, "let's just say, it won't be in your best interest ... Now get the fuck out of my car," he said coldly.

Black could tell from the look on Tony's face that he meant everything that he had just said. He didn't reply. He lowered his head, opened the car door, and got out of Tony's car. He couldn't believe Tony was treating him like that. Here he was, all beat battered and bandaged up, and he was just going to leave him fucked up outside of the city. He had one thing on his mind as he closed the car door: revenge. Tony had just been added to the list.

As soon as Black shut the door, Tony pulled away and left Black Mike standing on the curb. He grabbed his phone the center console. Black had to be dealt with before he had a chance to jeopardize what he had in motion.

Drew jumped at the sound of his phone going off loudly. His heart slammed in his chest and he felt a little dizzy from being awaken so abruptly. He did his best to shake it off while he reached on the coffee table and grabbed his phone to answer. It was Tony.

He quickly cleared his throat and hurriedly answered the phone. "Yo T, what's up," he said, his voice still groggy.

Tony could tell from the sound of Drew's voice that he had either just gotten up or hadn't been up long. Either way, he needed him to get ready since he was getting ready to leave his house. It was 11:45 and their meeting was at twelve-thirty.

"D. What's good my friend. I hope you didn't forget

about our twelve o'clock. I'm leaving out in a few minutes. Where do you want to meet at?"

Drew sat up fully on the couch. He didn't think it was a clever idea for Tony to meet them at their stash house or anywhere near it. He looked over to Spice who was sleeping soundly, arms-length down on the couch.

"How bout we meet you at your spot. Where I met you at the yesterday. That way I can just park up right there."

"Sounds good to me, but you have to hurry because we don't want to be late. Time is money and the first impression is the best impression," he emphasized.

"Understood. We leaving out now," Drew assured him. He tapped Spice on the shoulder to wake him up. When he didn't budge he tapped him again, this time harder.

"Alright, see you in a few," Tony replied before hanging up.

The second tap caused Spice to stir. Drew hopped up off the couch. "Yo nigga! Get up and come on. We gotta go now," he called loudly.

Spice grumbled as he wiped his eyes and watched as Drew rushed off to the bathroom. He heard the water run while Drew splashed water on his face and quickly rinsed his mouth out.

"Yo nigga, get the fuck up. We gotta meet the plug at twelve-thirty," he added with urgency.

"Oh, shit," Spice said aloud, finally remembering the meeting. He jumped up from where he had been stretched out, thumbed the crust from his eyes and followed Drew out.

After they loaded up in the car, Drew hurried over to the neighborhood Tony trapped out of. He must have run every stop-light and stop-sign because he pulled up on Tony's block within ten-minutes of speaking to him. He parked his car directly behind Tony's and immediately noticed him sitting inside. They quickly locked up and jumped in with him. Drew got in the passenger seat while Spice sat in the back. They greeted him quickly before he pulled off.

"So, fellas," Tony started. "the guy we're going to meet is a very close friend and business associate of mine. I really put my neck on the line to make this meeting happen."

Drew nodded in agreement while Spice sat silently in the back.

"We understand T. And it's definitely a good look. Like I already told you, we owe you for this," Drew added.

Spice continued to sit quietly in the back. While he too was glad the meeting was taking place, he didn't like the fact Tony was throwing it in their face that he had looked out. Spice hustled because he had to. It was an easy way to make money. However, if he had it his way he would simply rob bitch ass niggas like Tony and take their shit.

Tony smiled in response to Drew as he continued to drive to their destination. "I'm just going to call him and let him know we're on our way," he said, while slowing to a stop for a red light.

He grabbed his phone from its usual location and tapped the programed number to dial out. After a few rings, Pedro answered.

"Tony, my friend. What's up?" Pedro asked brightly.

"Everything is good, Pedro. We should be pulling up in a few minutes."

The name slid over Drew's head. It sounded familiar, but he couldn't place it right away, so he dismissed it. Spice payed no attention to the conversation as he stared out the back window and made a mental note of the route they were taking. If he ever got down bad in the future, he wouldn't hesitate to pay the little spot they were headed to a visit. It could be a potential lick in the future. Especially since that's where the boss liked to be.

"Good! My guys will be standing outside waiting when you pull up," Pedro replied. Tony responded in agreement and quickly disconnected the call.

They pulled up to the restaurant soon after. Two large Spanish guys dressed in suits stood beside the door. They nodded at Tony in acknowledgment. They parked, and the three men exited and made their way to the restaurant's entrance. Tony led the way.

"That's Pedro's guys right there. They're going to escort us back to him," Tony explained in reference to the two Spanish men near the door. Drew and Spice didn't bother to respond. They just continued to follow Tony. As Tony walked, his phone vibrated. He had a text. He tapped it to read it. It simply said *done*. He smiled and shoved his phone back in his pocket.

When they got to the entrance they were escorted all the way to the rear of the establishment. The section was reserved and consisted of four large booths. Three of the booths were occupied with what appeared to be Pedro's men. Pedro sat alone in the other.

Tony, Drew and Spice approached the table that Pedro was seated at. Pedro drank a cup of black coffee while his face was covered behind a newspaper. Drew and Spice were both anxious to see who their new connect would be. They knew whoever they were about to meet was quite powerful and had the ability to put them in a position that could change their lives forever.

"Boss, they're here," one of the Spanish men that had been leading them called to Pedro.

Pedro closed the newspaper, folded it, and placed it neatly on the table. Drew's stomach instantly dropped. He knew exactly who the man before him was.

49

Despite Tony's warnings, Black Mike woke up at Ariel's townhouse with his mind on murder. It was a little past eleven in the morning and Ariel had already left out for work. Black couldn't stop thinking how Tony had disrespected him the day before. He wondered who the fuck Tony thought he was by telling him to stay away from Ariel. He decided at that moment that Tony too had to die. He was going to kill him right along with Drew and Spice.

Even though Spice had robbed him the day before, it was only for what he had on him at that time. He still had most of the work Tony had fronted him. It was safely stashed at his mother's house. He tried to call Ariel to see if she could give him a ride on her lunch break; however, she didn't answer. Since he had some time to kill, Black Mike took a quick shower and threw on the same clothes. He still felt terrible and the image he saw in the bathroom mirror confirmed that he too looked the part as well.

After dressing, he checked his phone to see if Ariel had called him back. She didn't, so he called one of his clients to see if he could get a ride. With expectation of a free high, his client quickly agreed to swing by and take Black to his mother. He rambled off his location and after five minutes, locked Ariel's door and headed out to the waiting vehicle. Once inside, he texted her and let him know he had headed out to his mother's house. As the car navigated through the primarily empty streets, Black payed no mind to the car that was following them.

"You got me right?" the agitated client asked Black for the second time since they had been in the car. He was a dope fiend and Black could tell he was in the preliminary stages of withdrawal and needed a hit. He was shaking, and a light coat of sweat lined his forehead.

"Yo, I said I got you nigga," Black responded in annoyance. "That's the spot right there," he added, pointing to his mom's two-story brick home so he wouldn't drive by.

They pulled up to the curb, and Black told the fiend to wait there. He stepped out slowly, but before he could even make it a few feet up the walkway to the front door, he heard someone call his name. He turned around and realized the voice came from someone in a vehicle that was slowly approaching him. The vehicle slowed to a stop in front of the house. The passenger waved and signaled for him to come over. Squinting to see inside of the vehicle, Black was relieved when they rolled down the window and he recognized the two males. He was surprised to see them driving.

"What's up?" Black smiled before approaching the vehicle. He put up a finger for the fiend to wait. He wanted to rap to the two youngins real quick. He figured they'd heard about the incident from yesterday and came by to check on him.

Black Mike got to the passenger's front window and opened his mouth to speak, but instead, his eyes grew as large as fifty-cent pieces. The male sitting in the passenger's seat was no longer smiling. He was now holding up a double-barrel, sawed off shot gun through the window. Black was confused and looked like a deer caught in headlights.

Before Black could utter a word, a monstrous boom erupted from the powerful weapon, blowing a bowling-ball sized hole through his chest and out of his back. The impact from the blast sent his body hurling backwards. He landed on the ground in a heap. As he lay on the ground bleeding and twitching, the fiend that had given him the ride, sped off in terror.

The male who was sitting in the passenger seat, looked around before quietly getting out of the vehicle. With the shotgun at his side, he walked over and stood over top of Black. He leveled the gun with his face. Without blinking, he unleashed another powerful shot, blowing pieces of skull and brain matter all over the ground.

He quickly hopped back in the car while Black's mother, upon hearing the shots, came running out the house. Seeing her unrecognizable son lying in front and laying in a pull off blood, was too much for her to take in. She fell to her knees. The only thing that could be heard was screaming and tires screeching as the car sped off.

Drew jumped at the sound of his phone going off loudly. His heart slammed in his chest and he felt a little dizzy from being awaken so abruptly. He did his best to shake it off while he reached on the coffee table and grabbed his phone to answer. It was Tony.

He quickly cleared his throat and hurriedly answered the phone. "Yo T, what's up," he said, his voice still groggy.

Tony could tell from the sound of Drew's voice that he had either just gotten up or hadn't been up long. Either way, he needed him to get ready since he was getting ready to leave his house. It was 11:45 and their meeting was at twelve-thirty.

"D. What's good my friend. I hope you didn't forget about our twelve o'clock. I'm leaving out in a few minutes. Where do you want to meet at?"

Drew sat up fully on the couch. He didn't think it was a clever idea for Tony to meet them at their stash house or anywhere near it. He looked over to Spice who was sleeping soundly, arms-length down on the couch.

"How bout we meet you at your spot. Where I met you at the yesterday. That way I can just park up right there."

"Sounds good to me, but you have to hurry because we don't want to be late. Time is money and the first impression is the best impression," he emphasized.

"Understood. We leaving out now," Drew assured him. He tapped Spice on the shoulder to wake him up. When he didn't budge he tapped him again, this time harder.

"Alright, see you in a few," Tony replied before hanging up.

The second tap caused Spice to stir. Drew hopped up off the couch. "Yo nigga! Get up and come on. We gotta go now," he called loudly.

Spice grumbled as he wiped his eyes and watched as Drew rushed off to the bathroom. He heard the water run while Drew splashed water on his face and quickly rinsed his mouth out.

"Yo nigga, get the fuck up. We gotta meet the plug at twelve-thirty," he added with urgency.

"Oh, shit," Spice said aloud, finally remembering the meeting. He jumped up from where he had been stretched out, thumbed the crust from his eyes and followed Drew out.

After they loaded up in the car, Drew hurried over to the neighborhood Tony trapped out of. He must have run every stop-light and stop-sign because he pulled up on Tony's block within ten-minutes of speaking to him. He parked his car directly behind Tony's and immediately noticed him sitting inside. They quickly locked up and jumped in with him. Drew got in the passenger seat while Spice sat in the back. They greeted him quickly before he pulled off.

"So, fellas," Tony started, "The guy we're going to meet is a very close friend and business associate of mine. I really put my neck on the line to make this meeting happen."

Drew nodded in agreement while Spice sat silently in the back.

"We understand T. And it's definitely a good look. Like I already told you, we owe you for this," Drew added.

Spice continued to sit quietly in the back. While he too was glad the meeting was taking place, he didn't like the fact Tony was throwing it in their face that he had looked out. Spice hustled because he had to. It was an easy way to make money; however, if he had it his way he would simply rob bitch ass niggas like Tony and take their shit.

Tony smiled in response to Drew as he continued to drive to their destination. "I'm just going to call him and let him know we're on our way," he said, while slowing to a stop for a red light.

He grabbed his phone from its usual location and tapped the programed number to dial out. After a few rings, Pedro answered.

"Tony, my friend. What's up?" Pedro asked brightly.

"Everything is good, Pedro. We should be pulling up in a few minutes."

The name slid over Drew's head. It sounded familiar, but he couldn't place it right away, so he dismissed it. Spice payed no attention to the conversation as he stared out the back window and made a mental note of the route they were taking. If he ever got down bad in the future, he wouldn't hesitate to pay the little spot they were headed to, a visit. It could be a potential lick in the future. Especially since that's where the boss liked to be.

"Good! My guys will be standing outside waiting when you pull up," Pedro replied. Tony responded in agreement and quickly disconnected the call.

They pulled up to the restaurant soon after. Two large Spanish guys dressed in suits stood beside the door. They nodded at Tony in acknowledgment. They parked and the three men exited and made their way to the restaurant's entrance. Tony led the way.

"That's Pedro's guys right there. They're going to escort

us back to him," Tony explained in reference to the two Spanish men near the door. Drew and Spice didn't bother to respond. They just continued to follow Tony. As Tony walked, his phone vibrated. He had a text. He tapped it to read it. It simply said *done*. He smiled and shoved his phone back in his pocket.

When they got to the entrance they were escorted all the way to the rear of the establishment. The section was reserved and consisted of four large booths. Three of the booths were occupied with what appeared to be Pedro's men. Pedro sat alone in the other.

Tony, Drew, and Spice approached the table that Pedro was seated at. Pedro drank a cup of black coffee while his face was covered behind a newspaper. Drew and Spice were both anxious to see who their new connect would be. They knew whoever they were about to meet, was powerful and had the ability to put them in a position that could change their lives forever.

"Boss, they're here," one of the Spanish men that had been leading them called to Pedro.

Pedro closed the newspaper, folded it, and placed it neatly on the table. Drew's stomach instantly dropped. He knew exactly who the man before him was.

50

"HEY PEDRO," TONY BEAMED, GREETING PEDRO WITH A strong handshake.

"Hey Tony," Pedro replied with a smile. He motioned for them to sit.

"These are the guys I was telling you about," Tony started as he scooted into the booth across from Pedro. Drew and Spice sat down beside him.

"Drew. Spice." Tony introduced the two men. They both extended their hand out for Pedro, who reciprocated with a firm shake.

"Pleasure," Pedro stated. "Tony's spoken very highly of the two of you," he spoke, glancing at Tony so he wouldn't forget that he had indeed vouched for the two men.

"Pleasure is ours," Drew answered with a forced smile.

He did his best not to draw suspicion from anyone. It would be the absolute worse time to be detected by Pedro and his crew. He was going to play along and play the role. Pedro clearly had no idea that he and Spice had been involved in the home invasion that killed his son. Drew planned to keep it that way.

"Anyone ordering? The food here is marvelous," Pedro added off topic. Tony, Drew and Spice all shook their head to decline.

"You seem a little quiet. Don't talk much?" Pedro asked, looking at Spice as if he were a mystery.

"Na, I'm good. Just trying to get down to business is all," Spice added staring Pedro down as if he was wasting their time.

Pedro's eyebrows immediately raised. The remark caught him off guard and seemed a bit rude. After all, he was doing them a favor by even meeting them. He truly didn't need their business.

"Excuse him," Drew spoke, cutting in, to end the immediate tension as a result of Spice's comment. "We had a rough night and we have a hectic schedule ahead of us today."

Drew looked to Spice for agreement. Clearly Spice had no idea who the man was they were sitting in front of. His eyes pleaded with Spice to cut the tough-guy act.

Pedro studied them quietly and noticed the interaction between the two. Something about them seemed familiar. He felt as if he had met the two before. In addition, Drew's voice seemed strangely familiar as well. Something just didn't sit right for him.

"You know how it is Pedro. Streets can't run themselves. They definitely are quite the busy men," Tony added with a nervous laugh. He too felt a little tension between the three men and was doing his part to ease it. He also worried about the potential free money slipping away.

"Fully understood," Pedro agreed. "Ok. So, let's get down to business," he said glancing at Spice and placing his menu down on the table.

All three men gave Pedro their full attention as he began to speak. "So, Tony has briefed me on what you two are trying to cop. Four packages?" he asked, looking from Drew to Spice for confirmation. They both nodded in unison.

"So. This is going to be the price." Pedro withdrew a pen from the front pocket of his dress shirt. He wrote down a price on the folded newspaper sitting on the table. He folded it back up and passed it over for them to take a look.

"Let me know if that's something you're comfortable with. The more we do business, the lower that number can get for you," Pedro said, eyeing Drew and Spice as they opened up the paper to look at the price.

Sixty-six per key was the price Pedro had decided on. If they agreed to that, the first order would total $264,000. Drew 's facial expression didn't change as he looked at the inflated price. He knew they could do better; however, he had no idea how long it would take to find a different plug. He also knew Pedro was the man and had the resources to supply them on a level beyond their dreams.

"We can work with that," Drew said aloud, speaking for the two of them.

Spice became immediately angry over the fact Drew had decided to speak for both of them. He believed they were being overcharged and he wasn't about to bite his tongue.

"Hold up," Spice started, surprising everyone. "Why is this number so steep?" he questioned, looking Pedro in his eyes. He looked back down at the newspaper and scoffed at the number. He pushed the paper back to Pedro. "You gotta come better than this," he argued.

Drew was mortified. He couldn't believe Spice. Here they were on their way to having a direct connect to a major supplier and he didn't even have the decency to show respect. Not to mention if somehow Pedro managed to recognize them. Tony shook his head in embarrassment from the corner of the booth. He too was at a loss for words and unprepared to do damage control from Spice's outburst.

Pedro stopped and stared at Spice icily. If looks could kill, he'd be a dead man. He didn't like the man that sat in front of him. Something about the look in Spice's eyes and his hostility sent a cold chill up Pedro's spine. Tony observed the look on Pedro's face and knew that he would have to answer for Spice's behavior later. He wanted to kill him. He never cared much for Spice, usually limiting his business interactions with him, and dealing directly with Drew. It was for reasons just like this.

"Drew," Tony started, doing his best to pull the attention away from Spice. "You agreed and then he disagreed. What's going on here? Pedro's time is very —"

"And the money we're spending is valuable to me," Spice said, abruptly cutting Tony off. And like I was saying to Pedro before you started speaking for him, we need a better number," Spice said firmly while cutting his eyes at Tony then back to Pedro. He disregarded the hard glare from Drew that was burning a hole in the side of his face.

Drew's jaws sat tightly clenched together as he wondered what had come over his cousin. He initially didn't want to bring him to the meeting, but he did because they were partners. Drew understood the drug business and knew that sometimes you had to grease a couple palms to get what you wanted. Spice however was firm on respect. He didn't like to feel like he was being played. His attitude had proven to be unsuitable for big business.

While Spice waited for a response, Tony and Drew sat at the table silently fuming. Before anyone said anything else, Pedro let out a hearty laugh to try to lighten the mood at the table.

"Okay. So, you're not satisfied with the number I presented. What's a fair price for you?" Pedro asked Spice. He gently massaged his chin while he waited for a response.

"$220,000," Spice replied without hesitation. "Fifty-five per kilo. Right now, they're going for sixty-five on the street, and that's on the arm. We're able to buy up front and as time goes on, in larger quantities," he said with certainty.

Pedro looked to Drew without responding to Spice. "Does this arrangement sound reasonable to you?" he asked, catching Drew off guard.

Drew was a little unsure how to respond. He didn't know if what Pedro was asking was a trick question. In his mind, the deal had been killed as soon as Spice opened his big mouth. For some reason, he now had a bad feeling about the remaining conversation. Even though his gut was against moving forward with any deal, his mouth still opened and responded. "Yeah that sounds fair."

"Well my friends, today is your lucky day. Since I want to start our business out on a good note, I'll give it to you for that price. Fifty-five," he stated firmly. "But only *this* time. We'll arrange a new price later. I'll have Tony contact you two with the location." Pedro looked to both Drew and Spice, making sure to address them equally. "Any questions?" Spice and Drew simultaneously shook their heads no.

"Good. I'll have Tony in touch by the end of the day," he said before rising up from the booth.

"Cool," Spice said from the middle of the booth. "Let me out this mufucka," he said to Drew who was sitting on the outside and had to move so Spice could exit.

As soon as Spice spoke the words, a chill ran down Pedro's spine. He stopped, and a wave of pain overcame him as he briefly stared into Spice's eyes. He knew he knew the two. He remembered when the masked gunmen came into the house, one of them said, *tie that bitch up. I'm bout to search this mufucka."*

He would never forget any of the words they spoke, or the way they spoke them. This particular statement he remembered because of the way he said it. Their words had been haunting him since that day. The day that his son's life had ended. He knew he was now standing face to face with Tre's two accomplices and his son's killers. Rage roared through his body and his homicidal instincts kicked in. He knew he had to wait. He had to think things through. They would pay with their lives, but not yet. He had to make a phone call. They were officially dead men walking.

Snapping out of his brief trance no one seemed to notice, Pedro looked to Drew and Spice. "Have a good day fellas. Tony, I'll call you," he said before walking out of the room, his crew trailing behind.

Drew let Spice out of the booth and breathed a sigh of relief. He was glad the meeting ended well. It could have been worse if Pedro had reacted differently to Spice's remarks. Spice truly had no idea how close he had come to fucking up a potential deal with a new connect. Drew planned to check him as soon as they were in the safe quarters of Tony's vehicle.

The three men exited from the side of the restaurant quietly and made their way to Tony's parked car. They saw Pedro be whisked away in a black town car parked in the front of the building.

51

"AYE YO, GOOD THING WE OUT OF WORK BECAUSE THE HOOD hot as shit right now!" Cam said to Will as he passed him a pinky-sized blunt he was smoking.

The two were posted up in the kitchen of their assigned trap-house waiting to hear from Drew and Spice.

"Word, we should've rocked that bitch ass nigga in front of that bitch house. At least our own hood wouldn't be hot if we did that shit over there," Will agreed.

"That nigga Tony better do right. My fucking ears still ringing from your dumbass busting that shit in the car," Cam grumbled with his face frowned up. He took his finger and dug in his ears for emphasis.

"Yeah, true. But nigga, you know that shit was perfect! Did you see the way that nigga's body flew when I hit him? Or the look on his face when he got to the window?" Will reminisced in awe.

"Yeah yeah, nigga. I seen the shit, *and heard it*," he emphasized. "But fuck all that. Whatchu think about Drew and Spice plotting on Tony?" Cam asked with a mischievous smile.

Will handed Cam back the blunt and responded nonchalantly. "Man, them niggas bluffing. That shit gon be like some Mission Impossible type shit trying to snatch that nigga. We'll make out better snatching his cousin Ariel and holding that bitch for ransom," he continued.

Personally, Will believed it was too risky and dangerous going after Tony. He not only was on a higher level street-wise, he also had a larger team of Spanish niggas ready to bust they guns.

As they were talking, Gina walked in the kitchen trying to buy a bag. Interrupting their conversation, she walked up to the two and said, "I heard you say something about an Ariel. I have a daughter named Ariel."

Caught off guard, Cam and Will frowned. They didn't know exactly how much of their conversation she had heard.

"Bitch, ain't nobody ask you bout ya kids! Matter fact, what the fuck do you want?" Will growled in annoyance. He hated to go hard on her like Spice did the fiends, but she seriously was out of order jumping in their conversation.

Gina paid no mind from the hostility coming from the two. After all, they were practically still babies to her. She was old enough to be their mother.

"I came to see if one of y'all could do something for me for $8," she said, extending her hand out with several crum-pled bills.

She was desperate for a hit and she knew she looked the part. Her lips were chapped, and her hair was matted to her head. Her once beautiful light-skinned complexion was now full of dark spots. She truly looked like death walking.

"We ain't got nothing. We waiting for some shit now," Will replied with a look of disgust painting his young face.

"Come on, please!" she begged helplessly. "I'll make it right next time."

"Gina, we got you. You just have to wait a lil while. We waiting on our folks now," Cam said hoping Gina got the message and got out their face.

Realizing that she wasn't going to get her fix from them, Gina sucked her teeth and stormed out of the kitchen.

"You would've thought that bitch would've learned her

lesson from Spice smacking the shit out her," Cam laughed while shaking his head and mashing out the now blunt roach in the kitchen sink.

"Fuck that bitch. How much you think in that safe anyway?" Will asked curiously. He knew Cam would know what he was talking about.

"Damn nigga, you stay scheming," Cam said in amazement. "Niggas do big right for us and your grimey ass plotting," he said with light disgust.

"Nigga ain't nobody plotting! Plus, fuck Spice! Drew cool. I fucks with bro the long way, but fuck Spice," he stated firmly. He smiled like he was joking, but he really meant every word.

"Man, these niggas taking dumb long," Cam said, changing the subject. He didn't want anyone accidentally walking in on *that* conversation. He walked to the window and lightly pulled down a row on the dust covered blind to peek out.

"Word, I'm bout to call these niggas now and see what's up," Will agreed impatiently. He too was growing frustrated. He dug in his pocket to call Drew.

"Yo just shoot them niggas a text. I think they had some shit to handle today. A new plug or some shit," Cam added.

"Aight, cool. I'm gon send both them niggas the same text.

Will whipped out his phone and quickly texted the two, *what's popping*. The two were growing restless and had to get back to making moves. Money stopped for no one. They either could make moves with the cousins, or without them.

"After you drop them off, come directly to my house immediately," Pedro demanded to Tony over the phone. Tony could hear the fire in his voice and figured his anger was a result of Spice's behavior at the meeting.

"Alright, I'll be right there," Tony agreed calmly as he

drove. Drew and Spice were still in the car and he didn't want them picking up on any of the conversation he was having. Pedro didn't bother to respond. He just hung up. Tony knew he was going to have a lot of choice words for him when he arrived.

He placed his phone down in the cup holder and sighed quietly. Before he could let out a full breath, his phone rang again. He grabbed it up and looked to see who was calling. It was Ariel. He ignored it and sent it to voicemail. He didn't have time to deal with her theatrics. Will had called him soon after the meeting and confirmed that they had taken care of Black Mike. He was sure the word had spread, and Ariel was calling in hysterics. He would deal with her later.

Tony re-directed his attention back to the road and focused on getting Drew and Spice out of his car. Spice had outdone himself today and made him look like a fool in front of Pedro. He wondered what the outcome would be for his poor judgement of character. He desperately wanted to address Spice's behavior and Drew's lack of control; however, he decided to wait. He was beyond angry and wanted to approach the two with a level head.

As Tony drove, Drew and Spice scrolled through their phones and were bombarded with texts about Black Mike's recent murder in their hood.

"Damn. Somebody just smashed Black Mike in front of his Mom's spot," Drew blurted out from the front passenger seat.

"Bitch ass nigga got what he deserved," Spice mumbled from the backseat with a light chuckle. He went back to texting Cam and Will, letting them know they would be pulling up soon.

Tony of course, already knew who Black Mike was and what happened; however, Drew and Spice didn't know that.

"Black Mike. He was a friend of yours?" Tony asked.

Before Drew could respond, Spice cut in from the backseat. "That bitch ass nigga ain't with us. Fuck him," he said with hostility. He did his best to contain his annoyance. Spice didn't care much for Tony.

Once again, Tony was caught off guard with Spice's blatant hostility and disrespect. He didn't know who the fuck he thought he was, but he was going to put an end to the bullshit. Tony spun around briefly, his face contorted into a grimace. Drew tried to intervene. He too was getting tired of Spice's disrespectful outburst. He was fucking up their business and they unfortunately needed Tony at the moment. Drew turned around to address his cousin.

"Yo, check this the fuck out. You been on some dumb shit all day. You so fucking stupid you don't even know what the fuck you're doing. All that tough ass shit ain't even fucking necessary!" Drew argued.

"Fuck you mean, tough shit? Nigga I'm a fucking cannon. And fuck Black Mike's fat, black ass. And the last time I checked, I just got us a great fucking deal on four birds!" he spat back, matching Drew's glare.

"See that's exactly what the fuck I'm talking about. Your dumb ass don't have a fucking clue!" Drew responded in disgust. He turned back around in his seat and realized that Spice was a lost cause. He looked to Tony who sat silently and glared forward.

"Tony. Real shit, I'm sorry for this dumb ass nigga. I know Pedro ain't gon fuck with us. So, if there is any way I can make this right and set things straight, just let me know."

Spice couldn't believe his ears. Drew was trying to play him in front of Tony's taco-eating ass. He also couldn't believe Drew was sitting there apologizing to his ass. He sounded like a straight bitch.

"Yo, my nigga. You really trying to play me in front of this nigga," he argued pointing to Tony. "You sitting here sounding like a straight up sucka, apologizing and shit. For real, fuck this nigga! And fuck that old bean burrito eating ass nigga Pedro!" Spice angrily spat just as they stopped at a red light.

The comment took the cake for Tony. He refused to let a poor, peasant nigger like Spice disrespect him anymore. It was an honor for him to even grace the presence of a man of Pedro's stature. He was past his boiling point. In one swift motion, Tony threw his car in park right at the red light and spun around to face Spice. With a vein bulging down the middle of his forehead and spit flying from his mouth, he raised his left hand and started pointing his finger at Spice, screaming.

"Listen here, you fucking monkey! You better know your fucking place and stay in it! Your bout two seconds from me burying you and your whole fucking family! You have no fucking idea who you're dealing with. You're a fucking peon! A fucking nobody! I'll make the bitch that birthed you, regret not swallowing you!" He turned back around angrily and directed his attention to Drew.

"Drew, you better fucking control your dog."

Right after Tony made that comment, everything seemed to happen in slow motion.

"I fucking knew it! I knew I knew those two from somewhere! Now it all makes sense where these two Punta's I never heard of would suddenly come up with enough money to buy four keys. They were with Antonio's son when he robbed me and took my boy away from me!" Pedro angrily yelled.

A lone tear trickled down the side of his face at the thought of his son. Memories he tried to suppress began to flash in front of his eyes. The more he thought about Christopher, the angrier he became.

Pedro quickly dismissed his emotions and focused on retribution. The more he thought about the two men, the angrier he became. He sat silently and gazed out the window of the car.

"Hurry this muthafucka up and get me home," Pedro

yelled to his bodyguard that was driving. His three men riding with him, had never seen him this intense. He was quiet but they could clearly see he was bothered by something.

"Boss is everything ok?" his driver asked.

Pedro looked away from the window and stared blankly at him. His eyes were blood shot and murderous.

"No. Everything is not alright," he replied calmly, while biting down on his lip. I want those two black muthafuckin hoods in a bag on my desk within the next twenty-four hours. And if I find out that Tony knows more than what he's telling me, I'm gonna cut his fucking heart out and shove it up his ass. In fact, I want everyone together. Everyone on my team that is strong and built for war, I want in my office within the hour," he demanded.

All three men were part of his security team and knew what to do. They would need to start making calls. His top man, who was seated by his side in the back jumped right on it and began dialing.

"And make sure you call Rico. I haven't heard from him in a week. He hasn't called me since I had someone else take care of the job he was assigned to."

"On it," his man replied from the front seat.

"Good," he responded, still clearly agitated. Still in route to his home, he used his phone to call a dear friend.

As the phone rang, his mind wandered with uncertainty. He wondered if Tony had known that Drew and Spice had taken part in Christopher's death. He wondered if Tony had been a part of the plot. All types of scenarios ran through his mind until a familiar voice greeted him on the other end. Unfortunately, it was simply the voicemail picking up. He ended the call in frustration.

"Fuck," he muttered.

Five minutes later Pedro arrived at his gated home. The ride had been short, but it still felt like hours had passed. He quickly exited the car and sped in and through to the house.

"As they come in, send them back," he said referring to the arrival of his team of men. "Try Rico again," he added.

His security team had told him that Rico wasn't picking up. Pedro decided he wouldn't waste his time calling. Rico had become unfocused lately and he didn't have time to babysit his once hungry nephew. He was supposed to be his right hand when it came to his business; however, he was nowhere in sight. Pedro made a quick decision that Rico would have to step down.

Within the hour, his men began to pour in. Soon, there were over a dozen men standing in his office. The men ranged from his Spanish henchmen to the men he supplied directly so they could supply the city. Every one of them were curious as to what the urgency was. They had never seen Pedro that upset. He was usually chipper and full of life. They knew it was something serious.

52

News traveled like lightning through the hood.

"That's fucking crazy how that nigga Tony got rocked," Cam said with disappointment.

"Word," Will replied, while swiping away a breaking news article on his smart-phone. It was all over social media as well as the news. "That nigga ain't even run us our bread. I'm pissed about that shit," he added. "Split that nigga Black Mike for nothing." Cam too was disappointed, but he wasn't about to dwell on it.

"You think Drew and Spice did it?" he asked. "The news did say it was two niggas."

"Fuck if I know. You watched the clip just like I did. It looked like the nigga Spice to me, but I didn't see a close up of his face."

"Word. What I do know, is that these niggas are taking dumb long to get here," he added. "And neither of them are answering their phones."

"Well if something happened to them, I'm hitting that safe," Will declared. He knew they had some big bills tucked away in there.

"Here you go with that shit again," Cam replied. The thoughts had also run across his mind, but Cam for the most part, was a loyal nigga; however, he was starting to think it wasn't a bad idea. If anything happened to Drew or Spice they'd be out in the cold.

"Yo, some shit just came to me!" Will said out of nowhere. He beamed brightly like a bulb had just went off in his head.

"What's up?" he questioned, curious because of the outburst.

"I bet that nigga Tony got something stashed at that bitch house."

"What bitch?" Cam asked curiously, trying to figure out what Will was getting at.

"Nigga, his cousin Ariel. If it's not there, I bet the bitch know where his shit is," he schemed.

Cam thought for a second and pondered over what Will had just said. He was right. Tony looked out for Ariel and loved her like a sister. She lived in an upscale neighborhood in a swanky townhouse, pushed the latest model Benz, *and* rocked all designers. Tony trusted her enough to have his goods around her. With Tony dead, she was the key to his stash.

"You definitely thinking my nigga. We on that asap. And soon — Before somebody else get it, *or* before her ass disappear," Cam agreed.

"We should hit that shit as soon as the sun go down. Plus, Drew and Spice missing in action, so they probably didn't bust the move for the work. I'm done sitting around."

"Word. We on it at nightfall," Cam agreed.

Cam dug his vibrating phone out of his pocket. It had been going off all day. Most of the calls went ignored since he had no work to distribute. He looked to the screen. To his surprise, it was Drew.

"Bout fucking time," he mumbled before answering.

Drew didn't give him a chance to speak. He listened as his expression turned grim. What Drew was rambling about had nothing to do with work. After the night, Cam knew that he and Will's young lives would never be the same again.

When Spice pulled up in Ariel's upscale neighborhood, it was quiet. It was still mid-day and most people were still at work. It was the perfect time to ditch the car and go unnoticed. They pulled on Ariel's street and parked in a parking spot four homes down. Drew quickly and nervously scanned the area to see if there was anyone watching. The window was shattered, so if they were seen emerging from the vehicle, it would surely cause suspicion. Drew began frantically searching through the vehicle. Spice had no idea what he was looking for.

"Yo, what the fuck are you looking for?" he asked suspiciously, ready to ditch Tony's car and head in.

Drew stopped and stared at his cousin as if he were the dumbest man on the face of the Earth. "Something to wipe my fucking fingerprints off with!" he growled. "Pop the trunk," he demanded.

He shook his head and realized just how much of a moron Spice was. He acted solely off emotion and thought nothing through. That's exactly why they were in the mess they were in.

"Damn, I forgot about that," Spice replied nonchalantly. He pushed the trunk release button as Drew instructed.

Drew hopped out and proceeded to search the trunk to wipe off their prints. Tony had some loose clothing strewn about so he grabbed the dirty t-shirt that was amongst the pile and proceeded to rub away his prints from the vehicle. Spice was watching him, so Drew took and ripped a piece from the shirt for him to use.

"Make sure you wipe down everything you touched," Drew demanded.

Spice instantly grew annoyed. He felt as if he were being chastised like a child. "Nigga I know," he replied with animosity.

"I can't fucking tell!" Drew snapped back angrily. He decided that he would ignore Spice's remarks. He'd determined his cousin was clearly an idiot; an idiot that was going to get them booked or killed.

Once they were done they headed towards Ariel's home, making sure to carry along the torn t-shirt they used. Spice didn't have a key to Ariel's place, but he knew that she kept a spare key underneath her welcome mat for emergency purposes. Once they reached the door, Spice wasted no time retrieving it. Once inside, they shut and locked the door securely behind them.

Spice's relationship with Ariel was low-key. No one would think to tie him to her, so they didn't have to worry about anyone looking for them there. They were temporarily safe. The house was quiet so Spice figured Ariel was still at work.

"Yo, you want something to drink?" Spice asked.

Drew stared at him in disbelief. He wasn't interested in a fucking beverage. He was trying to get cleaned up and get the fuck out of dodge.

"Na, I'm straight," he replied, doing his best to maintain his composure. "Spice we gotta stay focused," he reasoned. "We got some shit on our hands that could get real ugly. There's no room to slip up."

The message in Drew's statement seemed to fly over Spice's head. He walked out of the living room and into the kitchen. After grabbing a soda, he returned to the living room and stared at his cousin.

"I know you not scared of Tony's pussy ass niggas," he said. Drew shook his head at his cousin's ignorance. Spice spoke as if he didn't have a care in the world.

"First off, I ain't scared of shit!" Drew stated with fire in his eyes. "If your reckless ass wasn't so busy talking dumb and moving fast, you would've realized who the nigga Pedro was from the meeting."

"Another old, washed-up Spanish nigga with work," Spice replied sarcastically with a smirk. He cracked open his soda and took a long swig.

"Unfucking believable," Drew replied with his mouth

slightly open from shock by Spice's ignorance. "Another old, washed-up Spanish nigga huh?" Drew asked sarcastically, looking to Spice. He didn't expect a response.

"Na ... He's the same muthafucka from that move we went on with Tre. When Tre killed the little boy. Not only are we gonna soon be officially warring with Tony's big ass crew of mufucka's, but also with Pedro, who probably got a fucking hit squad looking for us now! The same way he was looking for Tre, is the same way he gon be looking for us!" Drew yelled, standing up from the couch.

Spice peered around nervously from Drew's outburst. "Yo, lower ya fucking voice," he growled. "We in an uppity ass neighborhood. Chill," he added, finally using a little common sense. He finally took a seat on a nearby couch. What Drew was saying was finally starting to sink in.

"Damn, I knew that nigga looked familiar," he responded, feeling like a fool for not recognizing their nemesis. He quickly shook off the feelings of apprehension. He knew things would soon get crazy, but in all honesty, he lived for wreck. This was his type of action and going to war was right up his alley. Win, lose, or draw, he was ready to strap up and bust his gun.

"Fuck em all," he said to Drew with an evil, icy glare. "They didn't stop making guns after they made theirs."

Drew shook his head in frustration. He knew it was pointless to go back and forth. The only thing he could do at this point was try to convince Spice that the best thing for them to do was get out of town and lay low for a while. Maybe even set up shop in another city. He thought about his grandmother. He knew she probably wouldn't want to leave. He was going to get up with Cam and Will and have them keep an eye out on her while they were gone.

"Listen Spice. We gotta get out of town," he pleaded. "If not, we're dead."

"And go where?" Spice asked. "I'm not running from none of these bitch ass niggas! That's dead."

"Well, I'm laying low nigga. Outside of this city. I suggest you do the same," Drew replied.

"You can do what you want, but I'm going to grab the money from the spot and I'm out. I'm gonna check on the spot later and maybe I'll slide out for a few days with you," Spice stated.

Drew realized that was as good as it was going to get. Time was of an essence and they had to roll. He decided he would clean up and get ready to get the hell out of dodge.

"Listen, we need to clean up and slide out to grab the bread. We can't sit in one spot too long," Drew informed him.

"Damn, we good here for another few hours. Plus, I wanted to fuck my bitch one more time before I roll," Spice laughed, doing his best to make light of the situation. "Bathroom is down the hall. You clean up, go grab the money and we meet up back here and roll," Spice agreed.

"Guess that's gonna have to work," Drew said. "Call me a cab soon as you here that water stop nigga. Ima call Cam and Will and put them on point. I'll have them meet me at the spot in about an hour."

———

"Uncle C, wassup man," Max asked. "I see where you called. Sorry I missed it. I was giving the baby a bath," he explained through the receiver of Pedro's phone.

Max was second in command after Rico. He too was considered part of the family, almost like Tony. He would be taking over their crews until he recruited someone loyal enough to do so.

Max had also been close to Rico. They practically grew up together. Max had always looked up to Pedro like an uncle and treated him like family.

"Listen. I have two problems by the names of Drew and Spice. Please tell me you know these two fucks," Pedro asked with so much fire in his voice he could have melted the phone.

Max could tell from the tone of Pedro's voice that something was up. He knew exactly who Drew and Spice were from when Rico was beefing with them. He just hoped that Pedro wasn't going to ask him to do anything he felt was beneath him, such as go to war with them personally. He used to tell Rico, he too was above the street beef. Max was a hustler. He knew how to get money and to him, beefing wasn't his forte.

"Yeah Unc, I know who they are. Is everything alright," he questioned with concern, fishing for information. He had no idea Rico had been murdered or that a war had been declared.

Pedro knew what type of guy Max was. He knew he wasn't a killer, so he wouldn't dare put him in that kind of situation. However, he knew that Max dealt with a lot of females and knew a lot of people. He figured if anyone could get information on the two cousins' whereabouts, it would be Max.

"Tell me everything you know about them."

Max never knew Pedro suspected Drew and Spice in the robbery of his home and murder of his son. Pedro never told him. He wasn't called to the meeting. Pedro felt that if he couldn't be of any assistance then it was none of his concern. Max knew a little, so he wasted no time filling Pedro in on what he did know.

"Well basically they're two, grimey stick-up kids from the East Side. They usually hustle out of a little crack house over there. I don't know the address but from what I hear lately, they've been getting some serious money. I heard it be a lot of movement, so you could probably find out from any random fiend where it is. They cannons though. They have a reputation for busting they guns. Oh, and they got some young boys over there that ride with them too. Cameron and Will. That's all I know."

Pedro nodded his head as he listened to the information

Max had given. He was quite satisfied. Killing them should be easy considering they didn't have a large team to war with.

"Ok, if you think of anything else, call me," Pedro responded.

"No doubt," Max responded.

As soon as the call ended, Pedro began making phone calls to his men to send hit squads to the East. He wanted Drew and Spice's head on a platter at any cost.

53

Spice was in a fury. No one had ever disrespected his mother. His mind went blank as tears flooded his eyes. However, they weren't your average tears of pain, sorrow, or sadness; these were tears formed by pure rage and hatred.

In a swift motion, Spice reached under his shirt and removed his compact Glock 30 off his waist and put it to the back of Tony's head. Little did Tony know, but his choice of words would cost him his life. Before Tony could take the car out of park and continue through the now green light, Spice pulled the trigger of the Glock and riddled the back of his head and front window with bullets.

Drew jumped as the gun roared, his upper body slamming against the front passenger seat in shock. Tony's body flew forward against the steering wheel as thick, hot blood leaked from his scalp. His slumped body caused the horn to blare continuously. Drew screamed out with his eyes wide, finally coming to his senses.

"Yo! Are you fucking crazy?" he shrieked at his cousin in a wave of panic.

Spice didn't bother to respond. He angrily shoved his gun back in his pants and looked at Drew as if he was overreacting.

"Fuck that nigga," he responded angrily. Spice didn't

seem to miss a beat, as he hopped from the backseat and walked around to the driver's door of the still-parked vehicle. With no remorse, he snatched Tony's lifeless body out of the car and dropped him to the ground. People who heard the gunshots either ran, or looked on from the sidewalks. Cars honked incessantly until they realized they were witnessing a murder. Once Spice looked to them with his murderous grimace, they peeled off.

"What the fuck Spice?" Drew asked, while giving Spice an ice-cold stare. The tires squealed from Spice mashing down on the gas.

"Yo, I told you. Fuck that bitch ass nigga," he yelled venomously with spit flying from his mouth. He continued to stare straight ahead. He knew his actions would probably start a war, but it was too late to go back. They had to get ghost for a little while, and he knew just the place to go.

Drew stared ahead in disbelief. He forcefully blinked multiple times to make sure he wasn't dreaming. He *prayed* he was dreaming. Drew too knew exactly what was to come from Spice killing Tony. They were going to have to go to war with Tony's entire team. That would possibly include Pedro. Spice had just started a war they weren't going to win.

A part of Drew wanted to empathize with Spice. Tony had crossed the line with his remarks, but Spice had provoked it. The disrespect he showed Tony had forced his hand.

"Listen Spice. You know I've always been a realist. This shit is, what it is. But we gotta think. Niggas on Tony's block seen us leave with him. My car is still parked on his block. We can't go back and get it, *and* we can't ride around in his shit. Cops are gonna be looking for this shit real soon. Now you done got us in this shit. Tell me, what the fuck is our next move?" Drew asked angrily.

Drew blamed himself. He had let Spice get out of hand. He knew his cousin was a loose cannon and wasn't wrapped too tight since he had met him. After he arrived to live with them and his mom decided she no longer wanted to deal with him, he had become bitter. He no longer respected life, not even his own. That's why he killed so quickly and was just as fearless when it came to dying.

Spice sat silently as he drove to his safe house. He was still in the zone. All he heard was Drew mention something about niggas on Tony's block. He didn't give a fuck about any of them. With his teeth clenched, he expressed that fact.

"Fuck them niggas. I'll smash them too!"

Spice's response further frustrated Drew. He concluded that he was going to have to take his money and possibly split from his cousin.

"Fuck that bullshit you keep saying! You're not saying anything nigga! We gotta get out of this car. It's blood everywhere. The front window is shattered. We're fucked! We're either going to jail or we're fucking dead! Think for a minute," Drew pleaded, unaware that Spice was trying to get them somewhere safe.

Spice glanced at the dashboard and realized, Drew made some valid points. The situation was certainly dire.

"Ariel doesn't live too far away. She stays outside of the city, so it'll be safe for a few. Then we move out," he reasoned.

"Aight," Drew replied. They were big time fucked.

"I want these two Drew and Spice fucks, heads on this fucking desk now! Put the word out that I have $100,000 on their heads!" Pedro angrily shouted to the men in his office while he stood behind his desk furiously.

"Those two are responsible for the death of my son. I won't rest until their dead. No product is to move. Nothing. Everything shuts down until I get confirmation that both are dead. Understood?" Pedro asked, with everyone mumbling yes simultaneously after.

Pedro was on a mission. He'd called up his hitman, but he wanted Drew and Spice's blood so bad, he couldn't wait.

Their deaths consumed him. He would pay whoever to murder the two. He'd even pay twice. He just wanted it done soon. He vowed that once he found out who was responsible for Christopher's death, he would make them pay, and that's exactly what he intended to do.

"Everyone can leave. I expect someone to call me soon with some good news," he said as everyone dispersed from his office.

He sat down slowly in his chair and reached for his phone off his desk. He was about to call Tony again. He wanted to know why the fuck he wasn't there yet. He had known Tony for years and had even considered him his friend; however, it was hard for him to tell who his real friends were these days. With that said, Pedro wouldn't hesitate to put money on his head as well if he found out he was playing foul. As Pedro punched in his memorized digits, Anna stormed through his office yelling frantically and in tears.

"Somebody killed Tony!" she screamed. "It's all over T.V!" she sobbed, her hands covering her mouth.

Pedro immediately sat forward with his eyes wide. He jumped up from behind his desk and sped into the living room to look. It was breaking news.

"Police say Antonio Rosales was murdered in cold blood by two unknown assailants. They appear to have been passengers in his vehicle. We don't have all the details, but the victim was shot multiple times and then left in the street while the suspects fled the scene. Business surveillance, as well as street surveillance capture the horrific act clearly. The two suspects are described as black males in their late twenties, early thirties, shown here. They are considered armed and dangerous. If you see them, do not approach them. Call the police immediately. They were last seen driving away from the scene in a black, new-model BMW 750. Police are working with witnesses while this investigation is underway. As soon as we have more details, you will hear it from us first. Action News 12. Stacey Ellis reporting."

"Fuck!" Pedro yelled, before storming back into his office. Anna came right behind him.

"What's going on Pedro! Tell me this instant!" she screamed. She knew a little, but not enough.

"The two men you just saw on the screen that killed Tony. They also killed Christopher. They were the ones that broke into our home. They must know we know," he replied solemnly. He grew frantic at the thought of them getting away before he had time to catch up with them.

Pedro tried to be as honest as possible with Anna, but he also did his best not to divulge too many details. There was a place for women, and this wasn't one.

"Where's Rico ,Pedro? I heard you say you couldn't reach him. I want him off the streets till this dies down! I want him hear now!" she screamed frantically.

"I'm working on it," he replied in frustration. He got up to console his wife, who had taken a seat on the plush leather couch in his office. She was holding her chest as if she were having an anxiety attack.

"Everything is going to be okay," he said to her, kneeling in front of her to hug her gently.

"I told you I didn't want this to happen," she sobbed. "You told me everything was going to —"

"Boss," one of Pedro's security men called to him.

"What is it?" Pedro grumbled looking away from Anna and towards the door where he was standing.

"We found Rico," he replied solemnly.

"Ok. Well where the fuck was he and tell him to get his ass here now."

"Boss ... He's dead. He was murdered and found beside Antonio at his daughter's home."

The words caused Pedro's knees to buckle. He fell to the ground, his chest tight. The blood curdling scream Anna let out, shook the house, and sent chills through anyone near the 10,000 square-foot home.

Pedro felt defeated. He had let down his wife. His nephew had been killed. Tears fought their way from his eyes and flooded his face. His pain could not be hidden. He sobbed loudly.

"*War*," he cried out. It was official. He had declared it.

"Send men out to lay down the blocks. Any blocks they run, any houses they frequent, any known spots. Destroy them. Don't stop until they are confirmed dead. Take down as many as necessary. Women, children ... anyone." Enough was enough.

54

ARIEL WIPED THE TEARS FROM HER EYES AND SOBBED uncontrollably as she walked out of the morgue. She had just identified Tony's body and was a nervous wreck. He was like a brother to her and she couldn't believe he was really gone. The detectives assigned to Tony's murder case wanted to ask her some questions but decided to wait due to her mental state. They also had some new evidence that could possibly be a big break in the case.

Surveillance cameras in the area near the crime scene had possibly captured the murder from a different angle. Because of this, they were now in a rush to view the video and see if they could get a better view of the suspect. They gave Ariel their business card and allowed her to leave and begin grieving.

Ariel got in her vehicle and buried her head in her hands. She didn't understand. First Black Mike, now Tony. She knew it had to be a connection. Initially, she thought that Tony was in some way responsible for the death of Black. The way Tony had acted at her house showed that he wasn't pleased with Black Mike; however, she had no idea why. Something went down and she intended to get to the bottom of it. Tony was gone and was never coming back. It felt like her heart had been ripped out of her chest.

Ariel forced herself together and began the short drive home. It felt like an eternity for her. Her mind was cluttered with thoughts of Tony, and the vision of him lying dead on the cold, steel, morgue table. She soon pulled in front of her home. She never noticed Tony's car parked down the street from her home.

The sun had started to set, and just like the darkness ready to fall outside, her life seemed to grow darker as time passed. She got out of her car and quickly made her way into the house. She just wanted to get in her bed and be alone. She shoved her key in her door and opened it. She froze as soon as she entered. The T.V was on, and she heard the shower running. She quietly tip-toed into the kitchen. Tony kept an extra gun there. She grabbed the empty blue Frosted Flakes box from the top of the refrigerator and retrieved the small caliber gun. She swiftly cocked it back just like Tony taught her. Whoever the fuck was in her house was about to pay, with their life.

"Ay yo, shit went south and got hectic! Where y'all at? Drew asked.

Cam could tell instantly that something was up. He knew it probably had something to do with Tony.

"We in the hood. Wassup?"

"I need y'all to meet me at the spot in a half hour. I'll tell you about it then. Be on point because things may get crazy," he added, while speaking as low as he could since he was in a cab. "Y'all strapped," Drew asked.

Cam was no stranger to Drew's lingo and instantly read between the lines. Something was up, and things were likely to pop off. He was ready.

"Yeah, we on deck. We'll be there."

"Good. I'm depending on you two. I'll holla at y'all then," he said before hanging up.

He shoved his phone back in his pocket and glanced out the window. All he could do was pray that the driver got him to his destination safely, so he and Spice could get the hell out of dodge.

55

"WHAT THE FUCK ARE YOU DOING IN HERE!" ARIEL SCREAMED after pulling the shower curtain back on Spice. She lowered her gun and sighed in relief.

"Yo, what the fuck!" Spice exclaimed. For a second, he had lost his breath. He wasn't expecting her home so early. She'd scared the shit out of him.

"What are you doing here without calling?" she asked. 'It's a lot of shit going on. You damn near lost your life," she admitted.

"You told me if I ever needed to get in, to use the spare key under the welcome mat," he reminded her."

"Yeah, I forgot," she shook her head, remembering that she had in fact told him those exact words. "Today's been difficult. I'm gonna go lie down okay," she added about to walk off.

"You okay?" Spice asked. He turned off the water and grabbed a thick towel hanging nearby.

"Since you asked, no I'm not. My cousin Tony was murdered today," she revealed with tears welling up in her slanted eyes.

"Spanish Tony? That drive the Beamer?" he asked abruptly. He stopped wiping his body dry with the towel and waited for Ariel to continue.

"Yeah. Our mothers were sisters. He was like my brother," she replied, wiping the tears from her eyes.

"Damn Ariel," Spice said, faking sympathy. "I didn't know that was your people. The police got any leads?" he asked curiously, going back to drying himself.

A light wave of paranoia washed over him. *Ariel and Tony were cousins.* He knew he had to hurry and leave. He wasn't safe there. There was no telling who would possibly stop by. The police. Some of Tony's friends.

"Not yet. Too early. They're still investigating," she replied solemnly. "Look I'm tired babe. I'm gonna go lay down. I just want to be alone. Lock up when you leave," she added before walking off and leaving Spice in the bathroom to himself.

Ariel walked in her room, closed her door, and climbed in her king-size bed. She didn't even bother to remove her clothes. She went to close her eyes, but her phone rang. She looked down. It was her home-girl Karen.

"Wassup?" Ariel asked when she answered the phone. She hoped Karen made it quick. She didn't feel like being bothered.

"Hey boo, I'm sorry to bother you, but they got some breaking news on channel 12 about Tony."

Ariel immediately hung up her phone and sat up quickly. She scurried to the nightstand she kept the remote on. She hurried and turned on her wall mounted flat screen to the channel Karen was talking about to see if the police had any new leads. What she heard took her breath away.

This is Stacey Ellis reporting live from Action News 12. Just a quick recap. Earlier we ran a story about the senseless murder of Antonio Rosales, who was killed in broad daylight and left in the middle of a busy intersection. Police now just released additional surveillance video of the alleged perpetrators. The video shows the suspects at a different angle that's a bit clearer. They're asking for the public's help to find the suspect who pushes the victim out of the car and drives off in his vehicle. Here's the ten second video. We're going to zoom in on the suspect.

Ariel watched the clip carefully and lost her breath when the video zoomed in on the perpetrators face. It was Spice.

Police believe there is a second perpetrator who was riding in the front seat with the victim at the time of the murder. If you know who this man is, please call the police immediately. Stacey Ellis reporting first, Action News 12.

Ariel stared at the T.V in shock. She had to call the police. She decided to get to the bottom of what happened. She quietly scooped her phone up off the bed and texted Karen to call the police to her home. She gave her no details but told her it was important to do it immediately. Ariel sat her phone back down and crawled out of bed slowly. She grabbed Tony's gun off her dresser. She had sat it there when she walked in. She walked out of her room to confront Spice. He was still there. She heard him talking on the phone in the living room.

"Spice," she called out to him as she walked into the living room.

"Wassup?" he asked as he spun around to see what she wanted. He immediately dropped his phone to the floor when he saw Ariel with a gun aimed at him a second time.

"Yo. What the fuck are you doing?" Spice asked while he nervously eyed the gun that Ariel had pointed at him.

"What's going on? What happened to my cousin motherfucker?" she cried, her knuckles white from her tight grip on the gun's handle.

"What are you talking about?" Spice stammered.

"I saw the surveillance video Spice. So, don't fucking lie to me! It's all over the news!" she yelled hysterically.

Spice knew he was fucked. Things had happened so quickly when he shot Tony that he never even thought about the store cameras on the busy block. He had fucked up. Drew was right. They needed to get out of town, but first he had to figure out how he would get out of the house alive.

"Ariel ... Let me explain. But first I need you to put the gun down," he said while speaking slowly and steadily, doing his best to calm Ariel. Her chest was heaving, and her emotions would soon be clouding her judgement. He had to do something and do something quick.

"I don't want you to explain shit," she spat. "I saw you on the video with my own fucking eyes. You killed my cousin! And now you're going to pay. You're not going anywhere until the police get here," she told him, her gun still planted on him to keep him there. If Karen had called them when she instructed her to do so, Ariel figured they should be arriving any minute.

"You called the cops Ariel?" Spice asked in amazement. You wanna see me locked the fuck away and you don't even know what happened."

"That's right," she admitted. "And I hope you rot in that bitch. I hope you suffer just like I'm suffering," she cried. She used her free hand to wipe the tears on her face.

Seizing the opportunity, Spice smacked the gun to the floor with all his might. It flew into the corner. Caught off guard, Ariel screamed out and tried to run into her room to safety. Before she could escape, Spice pulled his own pistol from his waistband, aimed at the back of her head, and fired. She hit the wall with a thud and slid to the floor.

"Now go be with ya cousin," he muttered, before scooping up Tony's keys from the kitchen table and fleeing from the house before the cops arrived.

Drew threw some crinkled bills to the front of the cab to cover his fare and hopped out quickly. He ran up the steps of the trap house and entered, locking the door behind him.

"Yo Cam! Will!" he called out.

"We in the kitchen," Cam replied.

Drew walked into the kitchen but stopped when he saw his safe on the table.

"What the fuck?" he asked. He looked to Cam and Will in disbelief.

"You come for this right?" Will asked with a grin. Cam already had his gun pointed at Drew's chest.

"What the fuck you two niggas doing?" he asked in shock. He didn't understand what was going on.

"You won't be needing this where you're going," Will continued. "You see. We saw Spice on the news. Everybody saw him," Will chuckled. "And everybody knows you were with him in that car. The police are looking for you and so is Tony's team. But the biggest problem for you is that you and Spice have money on ya head. $100,000. Somebody wants you dead. Badly," he emphasized. Will didn't bother to continue. Drew already knew what time it was.

"I'm sorry bruh," Cam stammered. "Shit ain't looking up for y'all. You might as well end this shit. Spice started a war y'all ain't gon win. Might as well let us eat."

Drew couldn't believe his ears. He clenched his teeth in anger. Rage took over him and he lunged at Cam. As soon as he moved Will put two in his chest, sending him crashing to the floor.

"Come on. Let's skate," Will said while Drew lay on the ground struggling to breath. They each took a side of the heavy safe and ran out of the house.

Karma was a bitch and *she* had caught up with Drew. He didn't try to fight. He used his hand to hold his wound until he slipped into darkness.

Spice parked Tony's car in front of the stash house. He knew Drew was waiting on him. He hoped he had a plan because he sure didn't. They couldn't drive Tony's car out of town. They had to figure out a way to get ghost soon.

"Drew!" Spice yelled after entering. He peered around nervously. Something wasn't right. The door had been ajar, and it was quiet. He walked through the living room and into the kitchen. He saw Drew lying on the floor. His chest was covered in blood. He knew he was dead. His eyes were wide, and he was still.

"What the fuck," Spice cried out. "No, No—"

Spice didn't have a chance to utter another word. He was silenced by a bullet to the brain.

Smoke had been waiting at the house for him. He arrived to see two teenagers flee from the home. It was like déjà vu. Only the tables had turned. His work was done. He pulled out his phone and called Pedro. He answered on the second ring.

"Done," he stated.

"Thank you," Pedro said with tears immediately forming in his eyes from overwhelming emotions. He could now truly finally rest.

EPILOGUE

Tiffany's eyes fluttered. The hospital monitors around her beeped lightly, indicating they were functioning properly and monitoring her closely. She looked up at the bleak, white ceiling and forced her eyes back closed. She just wanted to stay in the dark. There was nothing left for her other than the darkness. She could feel the tears sting her eyelids before they forced their way from the corners of her eyes. Thoughts of her father swirled her thoughts. She let out an agonizing moan. She didn't care who heard.

"Why don't you just let me die!" she screamed weakly. She didn't want to go on, but they wanted her to. The nurses, doctors and the rest of the staff. She kicked and squirmed wildly but to no avail. Her hands were restrained at her sides, limiting her movement.

She had been at the Little Creek Mental Hospital for several months and nothing had changed. She wanted out; she needed out. Since her father, lover, and brother had been simultaneously slain, she had been inconsolable. She had been diagnosed with an extreme case of Post-Traumatic Stress Disorder, refusing to eat and doing nothing but screaming until her lips were chapped and voice was hoarse.

"Just let me die!" she yelled once more, drawing the attention of an older, black nurse who worked on her unit.

Janice, the nurse peeked into the room and her heart immediately went out to Tiffany. She worked there five days a week and had to witness this each day.

"Shh-Shhhh, sweetie. There, there, it's okay," she said to Tiffany, stroking her head. Janice had heard the story about her family being murdered along with her fiancé. She knew why she wanted to die; she had no one. Tiffany continued to moan and cry, this time softly. She was weak. She had lost a massive amount of weight and every day was a struggle.

"It's gone be okay," Janice assured her. "You have to fight. You have to overcome this. You've got to do it for them. They wouldn't want you like this."

Something about the way Nurse Janice said it caused something to go off in Tiffany. *They wouldn't want her like this.* She'd always been strong.

Janice stroked Tiffany's head one last time and said, "You're gone overcome this Ms. Anderson. You're gone overcome this and you're gone be stronger than ever. If not for you, do it for them," she said while tapping the diamond ring on Tiffany's ring finger.

Tiffany opened her eyes and glanced to her left hand where the ring was. Her nurse was right. She was going to overcome this. And when she did, she vowed vengeance. Not just for her, but for *them*, and everything they took, that should have been.

BOOKS BY MESSIAH RAYE

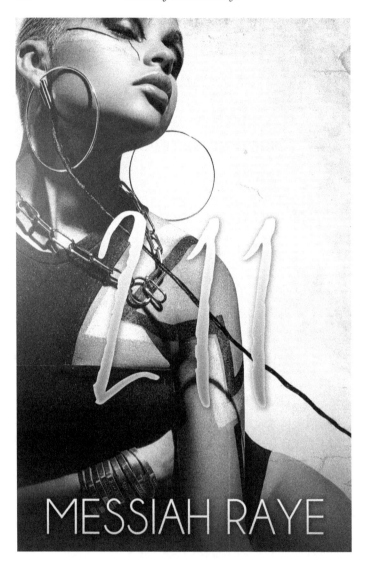

BOOKS BY SHONTAIYE

DH

THROUGH
THE
HOOD RAT
a Eyes

SHONTAIYE

WRONG TURN

SHONTAIYE

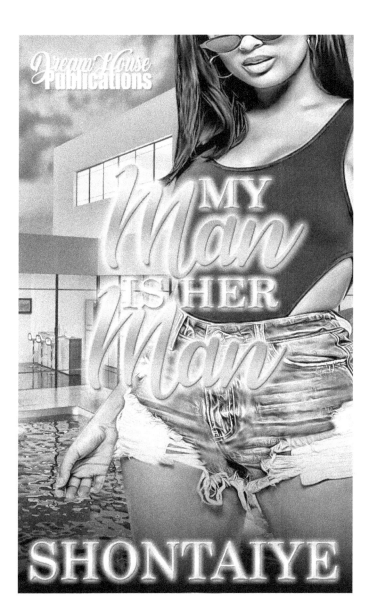

Dream House Publications

MY Man IS HER Man

SHONTAIYE

GO TO DREAMHOUSEPUB.COM FOR ALL
TITLES

CPSIA information can be obtained
at www.ICGtesting.com
Printed in the USA
LVHW032057100220
646421LV00015B/1394